> *"I'm not pretending to care about you because I'm concerned about you. I'm concerned because I care."*

Arden wanted to believe him but was afraid to trust him, afraid to trust her own feelings for Shaun. There were still things she didn't want Shaun to know. Things she might never be ready to tell him.

"Did you think I wouldn't find out that the fire in your apartment was deliberately set? Did you think I wouldn't connect this arson to the last letter you received?"

"I'm sorry. I didn't—I don't—" She remembered his reaction after the fire: his fear and concern, and the way he'd made love to her, slowly and tenderly, until she felt as if she were really cherished. "I'm not used to having people worry about me."

"Then you'll have to get used to it," Shaun said. "Because I'm not going away."

Dear Reader,

Our exciting month of May begins with another of bestselling author and reader favorite Fiona Brand's Australian Alpha heroes. In *Gabriel West: Still the One*, we learn that former agent Gabriel West and his ex-wife have spent their years apart wishing they were back together again. And their wish is about to come true, but only because Tyler needs protection from whoever is trying to kill her—and Gabriel is just the man for the job.

Marie Ferrarella's crossline continuity, THE MOM SQUAD, continues, and this month it's Intimate Moments' turn. In *The Baby Mission*, a pregnant special agent and her partner develop an interest in each other that extends beyond police matters. Kylie Brant goes on with THE TREMAINE TRADITION with *Entrapment*, in which wickedly handsome Sam Tremaine needs the heroine to use the less-than-savory parts of her past to help him capture an international criminal. Marilyn Tracy offers another story set on her Rancho Milagro, or Ranch of Miracles, with *At Close Range*, featuring a man scarred—inside and out—and the lovely rancher who can help heal him. And in Vickie Taylor's *The Last Honorable Man*, a mother-to-be seeks protection from the man she'd been taught to view as the enemy—and finds a brand-new life for herself and her child in the process. In addition, Brenda Harlan makes her debut with *McIver's Mission*, in which a beautiful attorney who's spent her life protecting families now finds that *she* is in danger—and the handsome man who's designated himself as her guardian poses the greatest threat of all.

Enjoy! And be sure to come back next month for more of the best romantic reading around, right here in Intimate Moments.

Leslie J. Wainger
Executive Senior Editor

Please address questions and book requests to:
Silhouette Reader Service
U.S.: 3010 Walden Ave., P.O. Box 1325, Buffalo, NY 14269
Canadian: P.O. Box 609, Fort Erie, Ont. L2A 5X3

McIver's
Mission
BRENDA HARLEN

Silhouette

INTIMATE MOMENTS™

Published by Silhouette Books

America's Publisher of Contemporary Romance

SILHOUETTE BOOKS

ISBN 0-373-27294-4

McIVER'S MISSION

This edition published by arrangement with Harlequin Books S.A.

® and TM are trademarks of Harlequin Books S.A., used under license.
Trademarks indicated with ® are registered in the United States Patent
and Trademark Office, the Canadian Trade Marks Office and in other
countries.

Visit Silhouette at www.eHarlequin.com

Printed in U.S.A.

Books by Brenda Harlen

Silhouette Intimate Moments

McIver's Mission #1224

BRENDA HARLEN

grew up in a small town, surrounded by books and imaginary friends. Although she always dreamed of being a writer, she chose to follow a more traditional career path first. After two years of practicing as an attorney (including an appearance in front of the Supreme Court of Canada), she gave up the "real" job to be a mom and to try her hand at writing books. Three years, five manuscripts and another baby later, she sold her first book—an RWA Golden Heart Winner—to Silhouette.

Brenda lives in southern Ontario with her real-life husband/hero, two heroes-in-training and two neurotic dogs. She is still surrounded by books ("too many books," according to her children) and imaginary friends, but she also enjoys communicating with "real" people. Readers can contact Brenda by e-mail at brendaharlen@yahoo.com or by snail mail c/o Silhouette Books, 233 Broadway, New York, NY 10279.

This book is for Neill,
my husband and my hero,
for always believing.

And for Connor and Ryan,
heroes-in-training,
for giving me a reason to follow my dreams.

With thanks to:
Sheryl Davis, Sharon May and Kate Weichelt,
for their critiquing expertise
and priceless friendship;

Tom Torrance,
for teaching me more about writing romance
than I thought a man ever could;

and Susan Litman,
for loving this story enough to buy it.

Chapter 1

Laid to rest.

The words taunted Arden Doherty with the illusion of comfort, the suggestion of peace. There had been little peace in the lives of Denise and Brian Hemingway, even less in the way their lives had been taken from them. Abruptly. Tragically. Unnecessarily.

Arden turned away from the gathering. Her absence wouldn't be noticed by the small crowd of mourners who'd come to say goodbye. She wasn't family; she hadn't been a friend. There was no reason to stay any longer, nothing she could do now.

Still, she glanced back one more time, not sure why she felt compelled to take that final look. She knew she'd never forget the image of those two glossy wood coffins, side by side—one less than four feet in length—gleaming in the late-September sun.

Just as she'd never forget that she was responsible for them being there.

Arden walked briskly, as if she might outdistance her

thoughts, her grief, her guilt. She paused outside the cemetery gates to put on her sunglasses. The dark lenses cut the bright glare of the afternoon sun and masked the tears that burned behind her eyes. She desperately tried to switch mental gears, to think of something, anything but the mother and son who would soon be buried.

She turned into Woodfield Park, her steps slowing as the top of the courthouse came into view: thick stone walls; gleaming, multifaceted windows; towering white pillars. More impressive to Arden than the architecture of the building was what went on inside. The law was a complicated piece of machinery that churned tirelessly, if not always successfully.

The building was a visible symbol of the unending fight for truth and justice. Arden had dedicated her life to that same fight, and her own office was just down the street, where she could look out her window and see the peaked roof of the courthouse. Sometimes that glimpse was all she needed to remember why she'd become a family law attorney: to fight for the women and children who couldn't fight for themselves.

Today, she wasn't feeling very inspired, and she wasn't ready to go back to the office. Not yet. She needed a few minutes by herself to grieve, to acknowledge the helplessness that now seemed so overwhelming. She found a vacant bench nestled in the shelter of towering oak trees and settled against the wooden slats, confident that she was hidden from the pedestrian traffic on the path by the massive stone fountain. Here, if not solace, she could at least have solitude.

She tilted her head to look up at the sky, staring at the cloudless expanse that, even through the shade of her sunglasses, was so gloriously blue it almost hurt her eyes. The trees had started to change color, flaunting shades of gold and russet and red. Birds chattered somewhere overhead, although it wouldn't be long before most of them headed south to escape the cold Pennsylvania winter.

It was a beautiful day. Or it would have been if she could have forgotten, for even half a minute, about the scene she'd walked away from in the cemetery. And the part she'd played in putting the mother and son there.

She felt a tear spill onto her cheek, swiped at it impatiently. She'd learned a long time ago that tears were futile, crying a sign of weakness. But right now she couldn't help feeling helpless, ineffectual.

"Arden?"

She stiffened at the sound of the familiar voice. The last thing she wanted right now was company. Especially Shaun McIver's company. She ignored him, hoped he'd keep walking.

Of course, he didn't. Anyone else would have respected her need for privacy, but not Shaun. Arden had met him eight years earlier when her cousin had married Shaun's brother the first time. After a five-year separation Nikki and Colin had recently remarried, and Arden had danced with Shaun at the wedding.

It had been an obligatory dance between the maid of honor and best man, but it had opened the door to feelings Arden had buried long ago, introduced her to desires she preferred to ignore. Uncomfortable with the emotions he stirred inside her, Arden had resolved to stay away from him. But Shaun was a lawyer, too, which meant that she had occasion to cross paths with him both personally and professionally.

"Please, go away." Her tone wasn't as firm as she'd wanted, the words not quite steady.

He ignored her request and lowered himself onto the bench beside her. No doubt Shaun believed he had the right—maybe even an obligation—to intrude on her pain.

Arden braced for the questions, prepared to deflect any attempts at idle conversation. But he didn't say anything at all. He just slipped his arm across her shoulders and drew her close to the warm strength of his body.

The quiet compassion, the wordless understanding, unraveled her. She felt another tear slip out, track slowly down her cheek. Then another. Arden pulled off her sunglasses, brushed away the moisture with her fingertips. She drew in a deep breath, fought for control of her emotions. She tried to pull back, to pull herself together, but Shaun didn't release her.

"Just let it go," he said.

And she did. She wasn't strong enough to hold back the tears any longer, and they slid down her cheeks. Tears of regret, despair, guilt. Helpless to stop the flow, she turned her face into the soft fabric of his shirt and sobbed quietly.

Shaun rubbed his palm over her back, soothing her as a mother would soothe a child—as Denise Hemingway might have once soothed four-year-old Brian. Arden's tears flowed faster, and still Shaun continued to hold her. She didn't know how long he sat with her, how long she cried. Eventually her sobs subsided into hiccups, her tears dried. Still, her throat was raw, her eyes burned, her gut ached with the anguish and futility of loss.

She felt something soft pressed into her hand and focused her bleary eyes on it.

A handkerchief?

It almost made her smile. She didn't think anyone carried them anymore. She should have known that Shaun would. She pulled away from him and unfolded the pressed square of white linen to wipe her eyes, blow her nose.

"Do you want to talk about it?" he asked.

Arden shook her head. "No."

Maybe he thought she owed him some kind of explanation after such an outburst, but she hadn't asked him to intrude on her grief. She wasn't used to leaning on anyone other than herself. That she'd needed someone, and that he'd been there for her, both surprised and irritated her. And she was just waiting for him to pry, to demand, so she'd have a reason to be annoyed.

But he didn't pry. He didn't demand. Instead he tipped her chin up and looked at her with genuine concern and compassion in the depths of his dark green eyes. "Are you going to be okay?"

She drew a deep breath. "I'm fine."

"Okay."

Shaun glanced at his watch, and she hoped he had somewhere else he needed to be. She didn't like to seem ungrateful, but she'd cried all the tears she had in her, and now she just wanted a few minutes to herself to gather her thoughts. Then she would head back to the office and bury herself in any one of a dozen cases that needed her immediate attention.

"Do you want to grab some dinner?" he asked.

Arden frowned. "With you?"

One side of his mouth curved in a wry smile, and she felt a jolt of something deep inside her. Something she didn't understand and wasn't prepared to acknowledge.

"Yes, with me," he said.

"I don't think so." She was baffled by the invitation and wondered if all that crying had somehow short-circuited her brain.

"Why not?" he asked in the same casual tone.

Her frown deepened. Why was he pursuing this? She couldn't ever remember him seeking out her company. "Because I have to get back to the office."

"You're not going to get any work done tonight."

"Despite the outburst," she said, irritated by his confident assertion, "I didn't have a complete mental breakdown."

"You need to get your mind off what's bothering you."

"And having dinner with you is going to do that?" she asked skeptically.

"It might."

"Look, I appreciate the offer. And I appreciate the shoulder. But I don't have time—"

"Dinner with me," Shaun interrupted without raising his voice, "or I'll call Nikki."

Arden lifted one eyebrow, silently communicating her displeasure that he'd drag her cousin into this. "Why would you call Nikki?"

"Because I'm concerned about you. You're upset about something, and I don't think you should be alone right now."

"I have things I need to do."

He pulled a cell phone out of his jacket pocket and held his thumb poised over the keypad. "She's on speed dial."

Arden sighed. The last thing she wanted was her cousin to be worrying about and fussing over her. "I want Mexican."

"Mexican it is." He dropped the phone back in his pocket.

Shaun sat across from Arden at a scarred wooden table, studying her as she studied the menu, wondering how they'd ended up here together. His invitation had been as much a shock to himself as it had been to her. But he couldn't leave her alone when she was obviously distraught about something.

Her nickname around the courthouse was "ice princess," and everything he knew about her confirmed that she'd earned that designation. Not that he'd ever referred to her as such. Not out loud, anyway. Although it seemed to him more of a compliment than an insult—a tribute to her ability to remain detached and professional as she represented her clients.

There'd been nothing cool or detached about the woman who'd cried in his arms. She'd curled into him, her body soft and fragrant and completely feminine. She'd been vulnerable, almost fragile, her sobs wrenched from somewhere deep inside. As he'd held her, the outpouring of grief had squeezed his own heart.

He frowned, disturbed by this thought. He didn't want to have warm, tender feelings toward Arden. He didn't want to have *any* feelings for Arden. He respected her as a professional acquaintance, he appreciated her as a woman, but he had no personal interest. Besides, she was practically family.

Okay, so she wasn't related to him in a way that would make any sexual interest illegal or immoral. But the connection was close enough that he'd have to be a complete idiot to risk a romantic interlude. If it ended badly, it would be awkward for both of them on family occasions.

Besides, he had his own reputation as a love-'em-and-leave-'em kind of guy. It was as inappropriate as he now knew Arden's to be, but it didn't bother him. The reputation was an effective deterrent to all the marriage-minded women who might otherwise set their sights in his direction. He hadn't had a serious relationship since Jenna had ended their engagement six years earlier, and he wasn't in the market for one now.

The appearance of the waiter brought his attention back to the present. Arden still had her nose buried in the menu, although he could tell by the distant look in her deep brown eyes that her thoughts were elsewhere. He reached across the table to pluck the menu out of her hand and return it to the waiter.

"Why don't we start with the deluxe beef nachos, followed by chicken fajitas?" he suggested.

"That's fine," she agreed.

The waiter scribbled down the order.

"And a couple of Corona," Shaun added.

The waiter returned almost immediately with two bottles topped with wedges of lime. Shaun picked up his beer and tapped it against hers.

"To better tomorrows," he said.

She forced a smile, but the sadness continued to lurk in her eyes. "I don't think I thanked you."

"I got the impression you would've preferred to be left alone."

"I would have," she admitted. "I don't like to fall apart. I like it even less when there are witnesses."

"There's no shame in needing someone to lean on every once in a while."

She tipped the bottle to her lips and sipped. "When was the last time you soaked someone's shirt with your tears?"

He sat back, considering. "I can't remember."

"Yeah," she said dryly. "That's what I thought."

"Sometimes it's harder to let go than it is to hold it in," he told her, knowing that it was true for Arden.

What had happened to her that she felt compelled to bury her feelings so deep? Why was she always so determined to be strong and independent? And why was he so affected by the hint of vulnerability in the depths of those beautiful eyes?

He reached across the table and covered her hand with his own. She jolted, and the furrow on her brow deepened. He found he enjoyed seeing the cool and controlled Arden Doherty flustered. And he found it quite interesting that his touch—even something as casual as his hand on hers— seemed to fluster her.

She tugged her hand away, but not before he noticed the way her pulse had skipped, then raced. It made him wonder how she might react if he ever *really* touched her. And it forced him to admit that he *wanted* to really touch her.

He shook off the thought, took a mental step in retreat. Offering to share a meal with a woman wasn't analogous to feeling an attraction. He did *not* want to touch Arden. He wasn't looking for any kind of involvement.

And if being here with her had him contemplating something more than dinner, it was just that he'd obviously been too long without a woman in his life. Besides, contemplating was steps away from acting, and he had no intention of making any kind of move on Arden Doherty.

Still, he was relieved when the waiter returned with a heaping platter of nachos.

Arden's stomach grumbled; Shaun grinned.

"I missed lunch today," she admitted, as she dipped a nacho chip laden with spicy beef, cheese, and jalapeños into the dish of sour cream. "I was tied up in court all morning and then…I had…somewhere else I had to go."

Her evasive comment intrigued him. "Somewhere else" was obviously where she'd been before he'd found her in the park. It shouldn't matter to him; he shouldn't care where she'd been or what had upset her.

He decided to redirect the conversation. "I can't believe we've never had dinner together before."

"We've had dinner together plenty of times."

"With Nikki and Colin," he agreed. "Never just the two of us."

"Why would we?"

He shrugged. "We're colleagues, of sorts. We're family, almost. It just seems strange that we've never shared a meal."

"We wouldn't be doing so now if you hadn't blackmailed me," Arden reminded him.

He grinned. "I must admit, it's a novel approach for me with a woman."

Her lips twitched in a reluctant smile, and Shaun's breath caught. He'd always known she was beautiful. Almost too beautiful. It was an observation, he assured himself, not an attraction. Yet, he couldn't discount the immediate physical response of his body when those sensual lips curved, parted slightly. He wanted to touch his mouth to hers, just once, to know if she tasted as sweet as the promise of those lips.

"There's no need to waste your charm on me," Arden said.

"Why do you think it would be wasted?"

"We both know I'm only here with you because you thought I'd fall apart again if you left me alone."

"I was concerned about you. I *am* concerned," he admitted.

"Don't be."

It was her tone as much as the words that informed him the ice princess was back. Or so she wanted him to believe. But why? What had happened to make her so distrustful, so wary?

He shook off the thought. Whatever it was, it was *her* problem. She'd said as much herself. He didn't need to worry about Arden Doherty, and he didn't need any complications in his own life right now.

As she shared dinner and conversation with Shaun, Arden found herself beginning to relax. She'd wanted to be annoyed with him for having forced the situation. She didn't like being coerced into anything. But she was also grateful. She had planned to go back to work, but she knew that by six o'clock the office would be empty. There would be no one with whom to share meaningless conversation, nothing to distract her from thinking about Denise and Brian, wondering if there was something more she could have done, something that might have changed the way things had turned out.

She'd thought she wanted to be alone, but what she really wanted—what she needed—was a diversion.

Shaun McIver was one hell of a diversion.

He was certainly a pleasure to look at: more than six feet of well-honed male with sun-kissed golden highlights in his dark blond hair. His face was angular, with slashing cheekbones and a slight dimple in his square chin. But it was his eyes that got to her. They were a dark mossy green with amber flecks that could take her breath away if she let them.

Which she didn't. He might be a beautiful specimen of masculinity, but she wasn't interested. Not in Shaun McIver, not in any other man. She'd learned a long time ago that opening herself up to love meant opening herself up to

heartache. Her mother, her stepfather, her almost-fiancé—
everyone who'd ever claimed to love her had hurt her. She
wouldn't make the same mistake again.

Still, she had no moral objection to sharing a meal with
Shaun, especially when the food was Mexican and she was
starving.

By the time they left the restaurant after dinner, the temperature outside had dropped several degrees. Arden shivered, and Shaun slipped an arm over her shoulders. She
shivered again, but this time it wasn't from the chill in the
air.

Arden frowned. She didn't understand her reaction to
him. Surely she didn't have any romantic feelings for
Shaun—that was too ridiculous to consider. Maybe it had
just been too long since she'd been with a man. Too long
since she'd even *wanted* to be. In the past several years, she
hadn't met anyone who understood the importance of her
career. Even the lawyers she'd dated thought her commitment bordered on obsession. And there were times, even
she had to admit, when it did. When it had to. Because there
were times when she was the last hope for the abused
women and children who came to her for help.

Shaun turned automatically in the direction of Arden's
apartment building. She'd forgotten that he knew where she
lived, that he'd been drafted by Nikki to help Arden move
several months earlier.

"You don't have to walk me home," she protested.

"What would Nikki say if I didn't see you safely to your
door?"

Arden shrugged but didn't bother to respond as they
headed down the street. They walked in companionable silence, listening to the muted sounds of the evening. Fairweather was hardly a booming metropolis at the best of
times, and by eight o'clock on a Friday evening, this part
of the downtown core was pretty much asleep. A few streets
over, people would be filtering in to the bars and dance

clubs, but here everything was quiet. Her apartment, just a few blocks ahead, would be quieter still.

"I really should have gone back to the office," Arden said, wondering if she should do so now.

"It's Friday night," Shaun reminded her. "If it's that important, it will be there tomorrow."

She nodded. He was right, but she couldn't help thinking that work might help keep her mind occupied, help her push the events of the day aside—at least for a while. Shaun's company had provided a reprieve, as he'd promised, but she knew that the haunting memories would come back as soon as he was gone.

She turned up the walk to the front door of her building, his arm dropping from her shoulders as she reached in her pocket for the key. "I can find my way from here."

"Is that a not-so-polite way of saying good-night?"

"I thought it was polite," she said.

He smiled, and her heart stuttered. She told herself the reaction was a result of her exhaustion and not indicative of any attraction. She almost believed it.

"It would be more polite to invite me inside for a cup of tea," he said.

"I don't have any tea."

"Coffee, then."

She didn't really want to be alone, but she didn't understand why he wanted to spend any more time with her. "Fine. Would you like to come up for a cup of coffee?"

His smile widened; her pulse accelerated. "That would be great."

The old, converted home that housed her apartment didn't have the luxury of elevators, so she led the way through the small lobby to the stairs. On the second-floor landing, they passed Greta Dempsey, one of Arden's neighbors, with Rocky, Greta's toy poodle. The flamboyant Greta was dressed for an evening in front of the television in a fuchsia satin robe with lime-green slippers on her feet and curlers in her hair. Rocky had fuchsia bows on both of his ears. After exchanging greetings, Mrs. Dempsey looked Shaun up and down, then grinned at Arden and indicated her approval with a thumbs-up.

Wishing Mrs. Dempsey a good evening, Arden hurried up the last flight of stairs to her third-floor apartment, grateful that the dim lighting in the hallway wouldn't reveal the flush that infused her cheeks.

She unlocked the door of her apartment and stepped inside, her hand halting in mid-air by the light switch as her gaze landed on the envelope on the hardwood floor.

And the knot in her belly that had only started to loosen, tightened again.

Chapter 2

Shaun hadn't missed the sudden hitch in Arden's breathing as she fumbled for the lights. Concerned, he stepped into the apartment and closed the door behind him. Her eyes were wide and focused on the floor. Following her gaze, he bent to pick up the envelope. There was no postage, no address, no return address. Nothing but her name printed in red ink. Nothing at all to explain the prickling sensation at the back of his neck or his sudden and instinctive desire to protect her.

"Do you always get mail delivered to your door?" he asked casually, offering her the envelope.

Arden blinked, then took the letter from him. "Not—" she cleared her throat "—not usually."

She walked into the kitchen, tossed the piece of mail onto the counter as if it was of no importance. But he'd seen the fear in her eyes, the erratic throbbing of the pulse at the base of her jaw as she'd taken the envelope from his hand. It was as if she already knew what was in the letter.

"Aren't you going to open it?" he asked.

Arden tried to smile, but her lips trembled rather than curved. "It's probably just from…my landlord. There's a…a new tenant in the building. Downstairs. He's been complaining…about noise." She shifted her gaze, cleared her throat. "He—the landlord—has been delivering warning notices…to keep the new guy happy."

Shaun knew she was lying, and he couldn't help being concerned. Arden didn't rattle easily. She was self-assured, strong, independent. And right now she was terrified.

He bit back a sigh, wondering what the hell was going on in her life, wishing he could just walk away, and knowing he wouldn't. He reached out and gently laid a hand on her shoulder, surprised when she jumped as if he'd pulled a gun on her. He dropped his hand. "Are you okay?"

"Sure. Fine." She stepped away from him. "Why wouldn't I be?"

"The letter—from your landlord." He caught a flicker in the depths of her dark eyes. "He isn't harassing you about this noise complaint, is he?"

"No." She shook her head. "Gary's a good guy."

He wanted to press, but she had already taken the carafe from the coffeemaker and crossed to the sink to fill it with water. Instead he leaned back against the counter and watched her, and he almost forgot the multitude of unanswered questions niggling at the back of his mind.

She was a pleasure to watch: tall and slender, with subtle curves in all the right places. She emptied the water into the reservoir, then replaced the carafe, and he felt his mouth go dry as she reached for the buttons that ran down the front of her jacket. She was wearing a blouse underneath, but still, watching her unfasten those buttons, slide her arms out of the sleeves, seemed so…intimate. She tossed the jacket over the back of a chair and turned to the refrigerator.

Shaun swallowed and tried not to notice the way the silky fabric of her blouse molded to the curve of her breasts. Then she opened the fridge and bent at the knees, her black skirt stretching enticingly over the smooth curve of her shapely buttocks as she reached for the tin of coffee.

He tore his gaze away.

What was wrong with him? This was Arden. She was practically family.

She was also a woman. An incredibly attractive woman. Although he'd never been blind to her attributes, the attraction had never before hit him in the same way. It had been a while since he'd felt more than the most basic stirring of desire, and this sudden and fierce attraction concerned him.

Why had he even suggested coming up to her apartment? Why couldn't he have taken her less-than-subtle hint that she wanted to be alone?

Because it was Friday night and *he* didn't want to be alone.

He also didn't want to be hanging out at a smoky bar with the usual crowd, trying to seem duly enthralled with Sarah Jones, a court clerk he'd dated a few times last year. He was tired of the bar scene, weary of the dating game. Which was why he'd practically leaped at the opportunity to have dinner with Arden. He felt comfortable with her. And because he wasn't trying to get her into his bed, he didn't have to impress her. He didn't have to pretend.

But if he really wasn't interested in Arden, why was he finding it so difficult to tear his eyes from her? Why was he unable to stop imagining the subtle curves hidden beneath her tidy little suit?

In the interests of self-preservation, he moved away from her, stepping out of the kitchen to survey the modest apartment.

The living room walls were off-white in color and completely bare. No artwork or photos marred the pristine surface. The furniture was deep blue: a plush sofa and two matching chairs that were covered in some suedelike fabric. In front of the sofa was a dark wood coffee table polished to a high gloss. A matching entertainment unit sat against the opposite wall, containing a small television, a VCR and a portable stereo.

There was a short bookcase beside the front door with two framed photos on top of it. Shaun stepped closer. One frame held Nikki and Colin's wedding picture, the other, their daughter, Carly's, most recent school photo. There were no other mementos or knickknacks around the room. No magazines tossed on the coffee table, no decorative cushions on the sofa, no fancy lamps or little glass dishes. There were no plants or flowers, no signs of life. In fact, there was nothing in the room—save those two photos— that wasn't useful or necessary.

Even the books on the shelves, arranged in alphabetical order, were legal texts. The room was very much a reflection of its tenant, he realized. Practical, efficient, ruthlessly organized. A beautiful façade, offering no hint of anything inside. The realization frustrated him, as did his sudden curiosity about a woman he'd known for so long. Except that he didn't really know her at all.

He glanced in the direction of the dining room. At least, he assumed it was the dining room. It was hard to tell as the room was bare of furniture except for the packing boxes stacked four and five high against the back wall.

Beyond the dining room was a short hallway, probably leading to Arden's bedroom. He turned away. The last thing he needed to think about was where she slept. What she slept in.

He moved back to the kitchen.

There were no dirty dishes in the sink, no crumbs on the countertop. Just the coffeemaker, currently bubbling away, and a microwave. Curious, he peeked over her shoulder as she opened the refrigerator again. She put the can of coffee inside and pulled out a carton of milk. Other than those two items, there were half a dozen containers of yogurt, a couple of cans of diet cola and a half-empty bottle of white wine.

That was it. He frowned. No wonder her kitchen was spotless—she didn't eat here.

As she closed the door again, he noticed the flutter of a small newspaper clipping that had been taped to the outside. It was the obituary of Denise Hemingway, age twenty-nine, and her four year-old son, Brian. He remembered reading about them in the paper, how they'd both been killed by Eric Hemingway—Denise's husband, Brian's father—before he'd turned the gun on himself.

It was hard to miss the story. Things like that might be commonplace in bigger cities, but in small-town Fairweather, Pennsylvania, domestic slayings were a rare occurrence and, consequently, front-page news. The victim, he realized, must have been Arden's client.

He scanned further, noted that the funeral was…today.

Finally the pieces clicked into place and confirmed his earlier suspicions about Arden. She wasn't cool or detached. She was a woman who cared about her clients, and cared deeply. Not only had she taken the time to go to the funeral, she'd shed deep, grief-filled tears for the mother and son who had lost their lives so tragically.

"How do you take your coffee?" Arden asked.

"Black."

She filled the two mugs and handed one to him, then added a splash of milk to the other.

"Denise Hemingway," he said, and saw her back stiffen.

She set the milk carton down before turning to face him.

"What about her?" Her eyes were stark, almost empty, her voice the same. But he knew now that it was a mask, that her emotions ran deep.

"She was your client?" he prompted.

Arden nodded.

"That's where you were earlier today," he guessed.

She nodded again. "Yes."

She didn't ask for his compassion, but he felt compelled to offer it. He set his mug on the counter and moved toward her, breaching the few-foot gap that separated them to take her in his arms. She resisted at first, her back straight, her shoulders stiff. But he continued to hold her, running his hand down her back, his fingers roaming over the silky fabric of her blouse.

Would her skin be as soft? He chastised himself for the wayward thought. He was supposed to be offering her comfort, not speculating about the feel of her naked skin beneath his hands.

She didn't cry again, but she finally let out a long, shuddering breath and relaxed against him.

"She came to me for help," Arden said, sounding completely dejected. "She was counting on me, and I let her down."

"You did everything you could for her," he said, knowing it was true, and knowing she would find no comfort in that fact.

Arden pulled out of Shaun's arms. She didn't want to talk about Denise and Brian, she didn't even want to think about them right now. When Shaun went home, when she went to bed, she'd think about them then. She wouldn't be able to stop. Nor would she be able to stop the nightmares that plagued her sleep.

"Why don't we take our coffee into the living room?" she suggested.

"Okay," Shaun agreed.

She was grateful that he didn't ask any more questions or try to appease her with useless words or platitudes. Nothing anyone could say or do could make up for what had happened.

She moved over to the sofa and curled up in her usual spot at one end, then wished she'd chosen a chair when he sat down beside her. She wasn't sure why she was so unnerved by his presence today. She'd spent a fair amount of time in his company over the past few years. When Arden had been living with her cousin, Nikki, and Nikki's daughter, Carly, Shaun had visited often to spend time with his former sister-in-law and his niece. Maybe that was the difference. It was just the two of them tonight, and being alone with him felt strange to Arden.

"This is great coffee," Shaun said.

Arden was grateful for the change of topic. "It's Jamaican. I don't share it with everyone, but I figure you earned it. Putting up with me this afternoon, buying me dinner."

"It was my pleasure."

She managed a smile. "I doubt it, but thanks."

"That's what friends are for," he said easily.

She propped her feet up on the coffee table, crossing them at the ankles as she settled back against the cushions. "I don't need anyone to take care of me, McIver."

"Did I suggest you did?"

"No, but I think your sudden offer of friendship was inspired by the fact that I cried on your shoulder. Believe me, it was a one-time thing."

"That's too bad," he said. "I thought it was a pretty good excuse to hold you in my arms."

"I wouldn't think you needed any kind of excuse to hold a woman. Aren't they lining up for the privilege?"

Shaun grinned. "I wasn't talking about *any* woman. I was talking about you. You fit in my arms, Doherty."

She rolled her eyes.

"I noticed it before, when we danced at Colin and Nikki's wedding."

Arden didn't want to be reminded of the dance they'd shared. Of the way their bodies had melded together, like two pieces of a puzzle. It had made her wonder if they would mesh so perfectly if they were horizontal.

"Anything you want to share?" Shaun sounded amused.

"No," she snapped, conscious of the flush in her cheeks.

"I've never seen you blush, Doherty. It's…endearing."

"I don't blush."

"Yeah." He stroked a finger down the curve of her cheek, and her breath caught in her throat. "You do."

She pulled back, stood up. "Do you want more coffee?"

His smile was lazy, satisfied. "Sure."

Arden retreated to the kitchen, chastising her overactive hormones. All he'd done was touch her, and her skin had burned. She took several deep breaths before returning to the living room with the pot of coffee. She refilled his mug, conscious of his gaze following her even though she avoided looking at him. She wasn't sure she understood what was going on here, what the undercurrents were about. She was probably experiencing some kind of emotional meltdown—a normal reaction after the kind of day she'd had.

Somewhat reassured, she returned to her seat on the sofa.

"What's in all the boxes?" Shaun asked, gesturing to the stack against the dining room wall.

"Books."

"What kind of books?"

"Textbooks, case law."

"Why aren't they unpacked?"

"I don't have any shelves."

He looked around, visually confirming her statement. "I could build some for you."

She frowned. "Why?"

"I like to work with my hands," he said.

The innocent comment brought to mind erotic images of things she'd like him to do with those hands, and building shelves wasn't in the top ten. "I'm sure you have better things to do with your time," she said, sounding just a little breathless.

"Not really. And it would give us a chance to get to know each other better."

"Why?" she asked again.

"Why not? We're friends, aren't we?"

"I guess so," she agreed, not completely convinced.

"I built the shelves in Nikki's den," he told her. "In case you have doubts about my abilities."

No, Arden had no such doubts. "Fine, you can build shelves for me if you want to."

"Great. I'll come by tomorrow to take some measurements. Think about what kind of wood you'd like."

As if she would know the difference between maple and mahogany. She smiled. "All right."

"You have a beautiful smile, Doherty."

Arden tried to shift away from him, but her hip was already against the arm of the sofa. "Thank you."

"Why does that make you uncomfortable?" he asked.

She didn't bother to deny it. She'd always felt that too much importance was placed on appearance, and she knew she hadn't done anything to earn her looks. The flawless skin, the silky hair, the dark, almond-shaped eyes were a result of genetic makeup. She looked like her mother, and she'd never been particularly proud of that fact. Every time she looked in the mirror she was reminded of the woman who'd given birth to her, and who had abandoned her. "Looks are superficial," she said. "They shouldn't matter."

He seemed to consider her statement, then nodded. "You also have a beautiful heart."

His words caused an unfamiliar warmth to expand inside her. Uncomfortable with the feeling, she set her mug on the coffee table. "It's getting late, Shaun."

"You're trying to get rid of me again."

"Yes."

"That's not a promising start to a friendship," he said.

"I would think a friend would appreciate honesty," she countered.

He sipped from his cup. "I'm not finished with my coffee."

"Too bad. I have a busy day tomorrow and I need to go to bed."

''Now that brings to mind all kinds of interesting possibilities,'' he said.

A reluctant smile tugged at her lips. ''Go home, McIver.''

''All right,'' he agreed, and drained the last of his coffee.

Arden followed Shaun to the door. She should have been relieved that he was leaving, but now that his departure was imminent, she wasn't so eager to see him go. She'd enjoyed the verbal sparring, the chance to think about things other than the hellish day she'd had, and she didn't want to be alone with the memories and regrets that plagued her.

As if sensing the direction of her thoughts, Shaun paused with his hand on the doorknob. ''Are you sure you're okay?''

''I'm fine.'' Or she would be, anyway. If there was one thing she'd learned over the years, it was how to take care of herself.

Still he hesitated. ''You know you can call me if you need anything. Anytime.''

It was a nice thought, but she couldn't—wouldn't—take him up on it. ''Go home, Shaun.''

He smiled, and her traitorous pulse skipped a beat before she ordered it to behave. She wasn't going to get all giddy and weak-kneed just because Shaun McIver smiled at her. But she couldn't help the way her breath caught in her throat when her eyes met his, watched them darken.

Something crackled in the air between them. Something powerful and unexpected and just a little scary, and if her brain hadn't seemed to shut down, she might have stepped away. Instead, she stood rooted, mesmerized.

He leaned toward her, and if Arden didn't know better she might have thought he was going to kiss her. But she did know better, and she knew—

Chapter 3

Whatever it was Arden thought she knew slipped from her mind as Shaun's lips touched hers.

She watched his eyelids lower, felt her own flutter, then close. In darkness her other senses were heightened, the impact of the kiss magnified. The touch of his lips sent tingles down her spine; the musky, male scent of him clouded her brain; and she lost herself in his kiss.

His lips were warm and firm as they moved over hers with a mastery that was either pure God-given talent or the result of much practice. A mastery that didn't so much coax as demand a response. She responded, and demanded in turn.

The sensations that stirred inside her were as unwelcome as they were unfamiliar. She'd been kissed by more than a few men in her thirty-one years, but she'd never been kissed like this. The heat building inside her was like an inferno: burning, raging, devouring. Desire wasn't a new emotion, but the intensity of this desire baffled her even as her mouth moved against his. Had any of her brain cells been functioning, she might have pulled back. She might have recognized this as insanity and withdrawn from it. But that first touch of his lips on hers had abolished all rational thought, leaving only edgy, achy need.

When his tongue slipped between her parted lips and stroked the ultrasensitive ridges on the roof of her mouth, she almost moaned. He tasted of salsa and coffee and man: spicy and potent and hot.

She vaguely registered the pressure of his hand on her back, drawing her slowly but inexorably closer to the hard length of his body. She didn't, couldn't, resist. Her arms wound around his neck, her breasts crushed against the solidity of his chest. His heart beat against hers, as fast and heavy as her own.

His hands slid lower, cupped her buttocks, positioned her more firmly against him. She could feel the evidence of his arousal, and the answering, aching heat between her thighs. She wanted him. Oh, how she wanted him. It was irrational, insane, but it was real. She wasn't the type of woman to indulge in meaningless sex. She didn't have casual affairs. She'd never been tempted.

But she was now, and she was dangerously close to giving over to her impulses and dragging Shaun to the floor with her.

It was Shaun who drew back, easing his lips from hers with obvious reluctance. His hands moved up to her hips, held her steady. She might have pulled away, if she'd been sure her legs would support her.

"That was…um…" She swept her tongue along her bottom lip nervously. "Unexpected."

"Yeah," he agreed, the husky tone of his voice making her wonder if he'd been as affected by the kiss as she'd been. "And probably not wise."

Although she could think of a dozen reasons why she knew it wasn't smart to kiss him the way she just had, she wasn't sure she appreciated his commentary on the matter. "*You* kissed *me*," she reminded him.

He grinned. "You kissed back pretty good."

Arden felt color flood into her cheeks. "You were leaving," she reminded him, managing to pull out of his arms.

"Yeah, I guess I was."

But still he hesitated, and it took more willpower than she'd known she possessed not to ask him to stay.

"Good night, Arden."

Then he was gone.

It was the sound of the door latch clicking into place that mobilized her, and Arden moved to engage the dead bolt. Then she leaned back against the locked door, her knees as limp as overcooked spaghetti, her lips still tingling.

Arden awoke Saturday morning feeling rested, and she realized that the previous night was the first since Denise and Brian were killed that she'd slept deeply, peacefully, without the nightmares that had recently plagued her.

She sat up in bed, frowning as hints of a dream nudged at her subconscious.

Not a nightmare; a dream.

A dream about a man.

A kiss.

She touched her fingertips to her lips. She could still feel him there. Taste him.

Shaun.

She covered her face with her hands.

The last thing she needed was to be fantasizing about her cousin's husband's brother. Despite the events of the previous evening, Shaun McIver was the last man in Fairweather she would consider getting involved with.

Not that he'd offered her anything more than dinner, she reminded herself. She wouldn't put too much stock in the fact that he'd flirted with her. To men like Shaun, flirting was as natural as breathing, and he'd only paid attention to her because she'd cried on his shoulder.

What had come over her? She *never* lost control like that. Not since she was ten years old and Aunt Tess had brought her to Fairweather. Maybe the tears had been building up for too long. She knew she could represent her clients better if she viewed their cases objectively, and for the most part, she managed to project an image of detached professionalism. But it wasn't in her nature to shut off her emotions, and she'd never managed to distance herself from others' problems.

In the six years since she'd been out of law school, hundreds of clients had passed through the doors of her law office. Those who could afford to paid an outrageous hourly fee for her passion and expertise and thus subsidized those who could only manage a reduced rate. Some paid nothing at all. She didn't like to turn away a client; she wouldn't turn away someone who needed her.

Denise Hemingway had needed her. Arden had first met Denise at the women's shelter six months earlier. It wasn't the first time Denise had gone to the shelter, but it was the first time she'd shown a willingness to discuss leaving her husband. Still, it had taken four more months—and several more beatings—before she'd done so. Only after her husband knocked their four-year-old son down a flight of stairs had Denise realized it was crucial to get out. Not just for her own sake, but for her child's.

Arden had got Denise a restraining order against Eric Hemingway and a judgment for interim custody and child support. Denise and Brian had both gone into counseling, Denise was actively seeking employment, and Brian had just started school. Arden had believed that things could only get better for them.

She'd been wrong.

She'd never forget Denise and Brian, but she knew she had to put the tragedy behind her and move on. She had to believe that she could still help other women, or there would be no reason for her to get out of bed in the morning.

Arden spent a few hours at the women's shelter, answering questions and dispensing legal advice. If one woman listened, if one woman managed to break the pattern of abuse, she knew the time was well spent. Just as she also knew that most women would return to their homes, their partners, the abuse. Even more never found the resolve to leave at all. And those were the ones whose lives, and those of their children, were in danger.

She sighed, again remembering Denise and Brian. Their deaths had proven that leaving isn't always enough, and that a restraining order is no match for a gun.

Arden also knew that it was next to impossible to protect someone from an unknown threat. On her way home from the shelter, she stopped at the police station, anyway.

She sat in a hard plastic chair across from Lieutenant Creighton's desk and studied him. Early thirties, she guessed, with hair so dark it was almost black, eyes a clear and startling blue. Today his jaw was unshaven and his eyes showed signs of fatigue. Still, he was a good-looking man, and she wondered why he failed to make her heart race and her blood heat the way Shaun McIver could do with a simple smile.

"Ms. Doherty. Good morning."

"I got another letter," she told him, carefully lifting the envelope by the corner so as not to destroy any fingerprints that might be on it.

"Today?" he asked, already starting to scrawl notes on the legal pad on his desk.

"Last night," she admitted.

He looked up at her and frowned. "I gave you my pager number. Why wasn't I contacted right away?"

"I didn't think the delivery of another letter was an emergency." It was the third one she'd received, after all.

"You haven't opened it."

"I didn't want to contaminate it," she explained. And she wasn't sure she wanted to know what it said. "This one—" she swallowed "—was delivered to my apartment."

His head came up, his eyes sharp, concerned. "With the rest of your mail?"

"No. It wasn't in the mail slot. It was under my door."

"You should have called me," Creighton said, pulling on a plastic glove before picking up the envelope.

Arden nodded again. She couldn't admit that she'd forgotten the letter—and everything else—when Shaun had kissed her.

Creighton sliced open the flap and withdrew the single sheet of paper inside. When he unfolded it, she could see that the words on it were in the same careful block print and the same red ink as her name on the outside of the envelope.

"YOU WILL PAY FOR WHAT YOU'VE DONE."

She wrapped her arms around her waist and leaned back in her chair, as if she could ward off the threat by distancing herself from the letter.

"We'll send the letter and the envelope to the lab to check for prints."

Arden nodded, but she knew better than to expect that they would find anything. The only prints on the other letters had been her own. "Oh, um, a friend of mine picked the envelope up off the floor," she told him. "His prints will be on it."

"Who?" Creighton asked.

"Shaun McIver," she said, unaccountably embarrassed.

"Colin McIver's brother?" Creighton asked. "The lawyer?"

Arden nodded.

"I played peewee hockey with Colin," he told her. "Even then we knew he was going to be a superstar."

"Colin's married to my cousin," Arden told him, wondering why she felt the compulsion to share this information. Maybe to somehow explain Shaun's presence at her apartment Friday night. Not that it was anyone's business but her own.

"Small world," Creighton said.

Smaller town, Arden thought wryly.

"As a member of the local bar association, his prints will be on file. That will make it easy to isolate any unknowns."

"There weren't any prints on the other letters."

Creighton nodded. "There probably won't be on this one, either, but we have to go through the motions. Sometimes these guys get sloppy."

Arden didn't think so. Every step this guy took had been planned with care and deliberation. He wouldn't slip up.

Lieutenant Creighton pulled copies of the other two letters out of the file. Arden glanced away as he laid them side-by-side on the top of his desk. The bold lettering was ominous and compelling, drawing her gaze reluctantly back to the pages.

"YOU SHOULD HAVE KNOWN I WOULD FIND YOU."

"YOU HAD NO RIGHT TO INTERFERE."

The first note had been delivered to her office. She'd found it within the stack of regular mail, although the envelope bore no postage or address, just her name scrawled in the same bold lettering. That had been almost two months ago. The second had also been delivered to her office, about three weeks later. But it was this last letter, delivered to her home, that increased her feelings of trepidation. Somehow she knew this wasn't a prank, an empty threat. The letters were a warning of something to come. But she didn't know what or why.

"You're sure you have no idea who might have sent these letters?"

She shook her head. "If I did, I'd tell you."

"This one—" Creighton pointed to the first letter "—suggests that you're acquainted with your pen pal."

Arden wrapped her arms tighter around herself and pushed away the painful memories that nudged from the back of her mind. More than twenty years had passed since Aunt Tess had brought her to Fairweather; there was no reason for Gavin to look for her now. Mentioning her stepfather's name, reliving the humiliation and the pain, would only hurt her again. She refused to give him that kind of power. "If I thought I knew who was doing this, I'd tell you."

"An ex-boyfriend?" Creighton prompted.

Arden's thoughts drifted from Gavin to Brad. But the way their relationship had ended was unlikely to suggest that he was obsessed about her. "No."

"A beautiful woman like yourself must have admirers."

She frowned.

He held up his hands. "I didn't mean any offense," he said. "It's just an objective observation."

"I'm sure it's not an ex-boyfriend."

"A rejected suitor, perhaps?"

Arden rolled her eyes; Creighton shrugged.

"You know as well as I do that almost one-third of all violent crimes against women are perpetrated by their partners or former partners."

"I know," Arden agreed. "And I know this isn't a boyfriend, an ex-boyfriend or a wanna-be boyfriend." That was all she was going to say without admitting outright that she hadn't had a date in the past two years.

"Okay," Creighton relented. "Then we're back to considering that the threats must be related to one of your cases."

"That seems like the most reasonable explanation," she admitted. "But I've gone through all of my files, concentrating on new clients in the few weeks preceding the arrival of the first letter, and nothing strikes me as out of the ordinary."

"I'd like a list of those clients," Creighton said.

Arden hesitated. "I can't breach confidentiality."

"I don't need any details," Creighton said. "Just names."

She hesitated, hating that her fear outweighed her sense of professional obligation. "All right."

When Arden returned home after her meeting with Lieutenant Creighton, Shaun was seated on a bench in front of her building, his long, denim-clad legs stretched out in front of him. Her heart gave a little sigh. No man should look so good.

One of his wide-palmed hands idly stroked Rocky's back as he chatted with Greta Dempsey. The dog's tongue was hanging out of his mouth, his eyes closed. Arden couldn't blame him. It was all too easy to remember the feel of those hands on her back, stroking, seducing, and she'd been pretty close to drooling herself.

She shook off the memory and stepped closer, heard the musical tinkle of Greta's laughter. The older woman's eyes sparkled and her cheeks were flushed, confirming to Arden that her own reaction wasn't unique. Women—young and old and in between—adored him.

Shaun's lips curved in response to something Greta said, and all Arden could think about was how it felt to have those lips on hers. How much she wanted to feel them again.

Greta spotted her first and waved her over. "Arden, I was hoping to catch up with you. I have a plate of warm oatmeal-raisin cookies with your name on them."

Arden stepped toward them. "I'm going to have to buy a new wardrobe if you keep baking me cookies."

Greta dismissed the comment with a careless wave of her hand. "A few extra pounds won't do you any harm. A man wants a woman with soft curves he can cuddle up to." She turned to Shaun and winked. "Isn't that right?"

Shaun grinned. "I won't argue with that."

Greta nodded, satisfied. "Well, then. Come on upstairs to

get the cookies. You can take them to Arden's apartment to have with your tea.''

"I haven't invited Mr. McIver up for tea and cookies," Arden said dryly.

"If you're a smart woman, you will," Greta said then gave a gentle tug to Rocky's leash. "Come along, sweetie. We don't want to miss *Jeopardy*."

"I'm sorry," Arden apologized to Shaun after Greta and Rocky had disappeared inside the building. "She's a wonderful lady who just can't seem to mind her own business."

"She cares about you," Shaun said simply.

"She's obsessed with finding a nice young man for me to settle down with."

"I got that impression."

Arden cringed. "What did she say to you?"

"It wasn't what she said so much as how she said it. Greta Dempsey could teach the members of the Fairweather P.D. a thing or two about interrogation," he said.

"I am so sorry. She doesn't seem to understand that I'm not looking to settle down."

"You don't want a husband and two-point-two kids and a house with a white picket fence?"

She lifted an eyebrow. "Is it my turn to be interrogated?"

He flashed her that quick, sexy smile. "I'm curious about you, Doherty."

"Why?"

"I'm not sure," he admitted. "But when I figure it out, I'll let you know."

"Are you going to tell me why you're here?"

He held up a tape measure. "To take measurements. For your shelves."

"Oh."

"You forgot?"

"Actually, I thought you'd forget."

"Why?"

"Because I didn't think you really wanted to build shelves for me."

"I wouldn't have offered if I didn't want to," he told her.

"Then I guess I'll have to invite you in to take measurements."

"Am I going to get tea and cookies, too?"

"Cookies," Arden told him. "I still don't have any tea."

"Coffee would be okay," he suggested. "Maybe some of that Jamaican stuff."

Arden laughed. "Now I know the real reason for your visit."

"Just an added bonus," he assured her.

She opened the front door of the building and led the way up the stairs. Mrs. Dempsey was just coming out of her apartment with a plate heaped with cookies as Arden turned down the hall. She could smell the mouth-watering scents of nutmeg and cinnamon.

She wanted to ask Mrs. Dempsey if she'd seen anyone she didn't recognize in the building the previous afternoon, but she couldn't do so in front of Shaun. If she did, he'd know she'd been lying about the envelope coming from her landlord. And she had no intention of discussing the letters with him.

Greta passed off the plate of cookies to Arden and smiled. "Smart girl," she said in a stage whisper.

"Thank you, Mrs. Dempsey," Arden said. Then, to clarify, "For the cookies."

Greta winked at them both. "Enjoy."

Arden shook her head as she juggled the plate of cookies and her briefcase, trying to reach the keys in her pocket, but she was smiling. Shaun took the cookies, inhaled deeply, and a low hum of pleasure sounded in his throat. The sensual sound caused Arden's insides to quiver.

She stepped away from him quickly, into the apartment, and set her briefcase down. "Mrs. Dempsey makes fabulous cookies."

"And oatmeal-raisin are your favorite," Shaun said.

"How do you know?"

"She told me." He followed her into the kitchen.

Arden didn't want to speculate about what else her neighbor might have told him. "That doesn't mean she has to give me three dozen."

"She thinks you're too skinny," Shaun reminded her, helping himself to a cookie.

"If she wants cuddly, she should get a teddy bear."

He laughed. "She worries about you. She doesn't have any children of her own to fuss over."

Arden measured coffee grinds into the filter. "How long were you talking to her?"

"I didn't clock the conversation," he said dryly.

"Approximately?" she prompted.

"Half an hour." He grinned. "It was…informative."

"I'll bet."

He bit into the cookie, finished it off in two bites and reached for another. "These are fabulous."

"I'll send some home with you," she promised.

"Thanks. Mrs. Fields can't compare to Mrs. Dempsey."

Arden smiled and took a cookie for herself. "I'll be sure to tell her you said so." She pulled a couple of mugs out of the cupboard and filled them with fresh-brewed coffee. Then she carried both cups to the table, setting one in front of Shaun.

"I didn't only stop by to take measurements," he told her.

Arden sipped her coffee, waiting for further explanation.

"I wanted to make sure you were okay—after yesterday."

After her breakdown in the park? Or after his kiss? Her answer would be the same in either case, but she chose to accept the first interpretation. Just because she was obsessing over that kiss, she wasn't going to delude herself into thinking that he was. Shaun McIver probably went around kissing women all the time; she just happened to be the only one in the vicinity last night. What bothered her more than the way he'd kissed her was the way she'd kissed him back. Her response to him had been disproportionate and out of character.

"I'm fine," she told him.

He nodded. "Good. You look good." His gaze skimmed over her and he smiled. "A little on the skinny side, but good."

"You might want to think about whose cookies you're eating and whose coffee you're drinking before you start throwing the insults around."

"I apologize," he said with mock solemnity.

Arden pushed the cookie plate a little closer to him.

"I was a little concerned when you weren't here this morning," Shaun told her.

Arden frowned. She wasn't comfortable with other people worrying about her. "I told you I was okay."

He nodded. "Mrs. Dempsey guessed that you were at the women's shelter. She said that you spend a few hours there a couple of days a month."

"That's true."

"Visiting clients?"

"Sometimes. Sometimes just to talk to the women about their legal options."

"Can you bill for that?"

"Not everything is about billing," she said testily.

"It was just a question," he said. "There's no need to get defensive."

She sipped her coffee, considered another cookie.

"I think it's admirable that you're willing to share your time and expertise. Not many lawyers do pro bono work anymore."

"It's surprising, and depressing, how many clients I get from the shelter."

"It's probably reassuring, though, for those clients to

meet you in an informal setting. Most people don't like having to see a lawyer at the best of times. I imagine it would be a lot worse for a woman who's been abused, having to face someone she's never met and share the horrors of her life—particularly if the lawyer is a man.''

His insight surprised her. Most people didn't want to hear about the work she did, didn't understand her commitment. Still, his sudden interest confused her.

"I'm sure you don't want to talk about my career, or my crusade, as some call it.''

"Everything about you interests me, Doherty.''

She tilted her head. "Are you hitting on me, McIver?''

"If you have to ask, I'm doing something wrong.''

She laughed softly. "Don't bother. I don't date lawyers.''

In fact, she hadn't dated at all in a long time. But even if she was looking to date someone, even if she was willing to bend the rule, it wouldn't be for Shaun McIver. Shaun was everything she didn't want in a man.

"Neither do I,'' he admitted, contradicting his earlier statement.

"Your fiancée was a lawyer, wasn't she?''

"Yes,'' he said shortly.

She nodded. "I could give you a speech about how you shouldn't let one bad experience disillusion you against a whole profession—but I'm not sure it's true. Life is a hard lesson, and we should learn what we can from it.''

"You sound like you're speaking from experience,'' he said, his dark green eyes intent on her.

She wasn't happy that the conversation had taken such a personal turn. She didn't mind talking about his life and his past, but she had no interest in rehashing her own sordid history. "No one lives thirty-one years without having some experience,'' she said lightly.

Shaun finished his coffee and pushed away from the table. To Arden's surprise, he came back with the coffeepot in one hand and the carton of milk in the other. He refilled both of their mugs, then added a splash of milk to her cup.

She stared at her coffee, then at Shaun's back. It was only the second time he'd been in her kitchen, and yet he moved around as if he was comfortable there, as if he belonged there.

"So tell me about this wealth of experience you've acquired in your thirty-one years," Shaun suggested, when he was again seated beside her.

She gestured around the spartan apartment. "As you can see, it's not the only wealth I've acquired."

He grinned. "Smart, sexy and a sense of humor."

"Can you turn off the charm, or does it always flow that easily?"

"Maybe you bring out the best in me."

"Is that your best?" she challenged.

"Not even close."

Her lips curved in a reluctant smile.

"If you won't succumb to my endless charm, how about desperation?"

"Do I look desperate?"

"Not you, me."

She cupped her mug in her palms and raised an eyebrow. "What do you want, McIver?"

Before he could respond to her question, the kitchen window exploded in a shower of glass and Arden was on the floor.

Chapter 4

Shaun didn't have time to think or plan. It was pure instinct that had him leaping from his chair, knocking Arden from hers and rolling with her to the floor as glass sprinkled down around them.

"Ow. Dammit." She rubbed the back of her head, her eyes wide with confusion. "What are you doing?"

He felt her shift beneath him. The subtle movement made him all too aware of each and every curve of the body pinned beneath his, causing his to respond in a very predictable fashion. "Stay down."

"I can't go anywhere with you sprawled on top of me."

He felt his lips curve, marveled at the fact that she could make him smile at a time like this. "Don't move," he said, slowly levering his body off hers.

Glass crunched beneath his feet as he crouched beside the window and cautiously peered out. People were starting to converge on the sidewalk below, questions and explanations exchanged through a mixture of agitated voices and frantic hand gestures. In the distance he heard the low wail of a police siren.

He returned to Arden, offered a hand to help her to her feet. "Are you okay?"

"I think so. What happened?"

"Somebody took a shot through your window."

"A shot?" She sounded more puzzled than concerned.

"With a gun," he clarified, and watched as her cheeks drained of all color. "What did you think that sound was?"

"I thought it was a car backfiring."

"This is reality, not the movies."

"This is Fairweather, not Philadelphia," she countered. "Why would someone be shooting through my window?"

"I'm sure that's a question the police will be asking you," Shaun said as the sirens grew closer.

She lifted a hand to push her hair away from her face, and her fingers trembled. She dropped her hand quickly and tucked it into the front pocket of her pants.

"It's okay to be scared," he said softly. "And to admit it."

Arden just shrugged. "I should call my landlord about getting that window fixed."

He bit back the oath of frustration. Why wouldn't she open up to him? Why couldn't she trust him? He decided to try another tack. "Do you want to come home with me until the glass is replaced?"

"That's one I haven't heard before."

He grinned. "I've had the pleasure of you writhing beneath me once already, but I thought the next time we might try someplace a little more comfortable than your glass-strewn floor."

"Is body slamming your usual method for getting a woman horizontal?"

"No," he admitted. "I don't usually have to resort to blackmail to get a date, either. You seem to inspire me to new heights, Doherty."

"Should I be impressed?"

"I might have saved your life."

"And given me a concussion in the process," she grumbled.

"Doubtful, considering how hard your head is." But he combed his fingers through the silky strands of her hair and encountered a small lump at the back of her head. He touched his lips to it gently. "Maybe I do need to work on my knight-in-shining-armor routine."

She managed a smile. "I guess you did pretty good."

He let his hand linger at the back of her neck, considered kissing her again. Her eyes were wide, wary, but she didn't pull away. His gaze dropped to her lips—soft and pink and tempting. Before he could decide whether or not to follow his impulse and cover her lips with his own, a loud knock sounded.

Arden jolted, and the opportunity was lost.

"Fairweather P.D.," a voice called from the other side of the door. "Is anyone in there?"

Arden moved away from him quickly, her hand not quite steady as she wrapped it around the knob.

An interesting and complicated woman, Shaun mused. She seemed more unnerved by the heightened awareness between them than by the knowledge that she'd been shot at. Her demeanor with the police officer confirmed his suspicions. Arden answered the questions smoothly, her voice never wavering. It was only because he was watching her so closely that he saw the flicker of unease in her eyes, noted the way she clasped and unclasped her fingers.

Almost an hour passed before the officer was gone and the broken window boarded up and they were alone again.

"Do you feel any better?" Shaun asked.

Arden rubbed her hands down her arms and shrugged. "It's hardly reassuring to know that something like this can happen in this town. And in broad daylight."

"The police figure it was just a bunch of kids joy-riding in a stolen vehicle."

"The police don't know—" her outburst ended abruptly.

Shaun's eyes narrowed. "What don't they know?"

She shrugged. "They can't know anything for sure. Not until they find whoever was in that car."

It was a valid response, but he somehow knew it wasn't what she'd originally intended to say. "Do you know something that the police don't?"

"Of course not," she denied, but she didn't look at him.

"Is there any reason for you to think that you might have been the shooter's target?"

She shook her head. "As the police said, mine weren't the only windows blown out."

He nodded slowly, but he wasn't convinced.

"I'm going to get some Tylenol," she said. "My head is still pounding."

Shaun nodded again, wondering how his life had become so complicated since yesterday afternoon. The answer was obvious: Arden. Since he'd encountered her in the park less than twenty-four hours earlier, he'd experienced a wider range of emotions than at any time in the past twenty-four months. Empathy, compassion, attraction, desire. He'd held her while she cried, he'd laughed with her, argued with her and dodged bullets with her. It made him wonder what other surprises might be in store if he spent more time in her company. One thing he knew for sure: he wouldn't be bored.

"I was about to tell you that I needed a date," he said when she returned. "Before we were so rudely interrupted by gunfire."

"*You* need a date?" Her voice was filled with skepticism.

He nodded. "For the Criminal Lawyers' Association Annual Ball."

"Are you asking for a recommendation?"

"No. I want you to go with me."

She raised an eyebrow, and he wondered if she had any idea how sexy she looked, how his blood heated when he thought about that kiss—and about kissing her again. It didn't matter that she wasn't his type, that he wasn't in the market for a romance right now.

He was concerned about her. He knew there was something going on in her life, something that worried her, and he figured if he spent some time with Arden, it might encourage her to confide in him. And if they engaged in a little flirting or shared a few kisses along the way, well, there was no harm in that.

"I don't date lawyers," she reminded him.

He'd heard her the first time, but her insistence only made him all the more determined to break through her barriers. Because he was concerned about her, he reminded himself again.

"It wouldn't really be a date," he said.

"I'm not agreeing to be your pretend date," she said, sounding miffed. "And I don't believe you're so desperate you'd need to take me. The ball isn't until sometime in December. I'm sure you'll be able to find a date before then."

"I want a date who won't have any expectations."

"How do you know I won't?" she challenged.

"Because you've already stated—twice—that you don't date lawyers, and you're about as interested as I am in a romantic relationship."

"That's not a very flattering invitation."

"I could try flattery," he admitted. "But you'd see right through me."

"I might have appreciated the effort, though."

Shaun grinned. "I thought you'd appreciate a more honest approach."

"The answer's still no."

"I haven't finished outlining the terms of the proposed contract."

"Contract?" Her lips twitched in the beginnings of a smile. "And what kind of consideration would I get for entering into this contract?"

She sounded so sexy when she was in lawyer mode; the combination of that smoky voice and cool attitude went straight to his loins. "Other than the pleasure of my company?"

"Other than that," she agreed dryly.

Now he smiled. "Tickets to the opening night performance of *Rosencrantz and Guildenstern are Dead* next month." He'd learned, again courtesy of Greta Dempsey, that Arden loved the theater. It was a happy coincidence that he had season tickets to the Fairweather Players' Theater.

Arden's eyes narrowed. "That's an interesting offer."

She was practically salivating, but he wasn't above sweetening the deal. "Box seats."

"Damn," she swore under her breath, but she was smiling. "I really don't want to go to the ball. All those lawyers, talking shop." He didn't think her shudder was feigned.

"But you really want to see that play," he guessed.

"How did you know?"

He didn't think it necessary to tip his hand just yet. He had a feeling that Mrs. Dempsey might be an invaluable ally, but not if Arden knew he was tapping her for information. "Is it a deal?"

"I'll check my calendar." She came back into the kitchen with her appointment book in hand. "When is the ball?"

"Saturday, December fourth."

She flipped through the book. "I have appointments that day."

"In the evening?"

"Well…no," she admitted.

"Then pencil me in," he told her.

She did so, but with obvious reluctance. Her calendar, he could tell even from a distance, was quite full.

"Is it hard dealing with marital disputes day after day?" he asked.

"No harder than dealing with career criminals, I imagine."

Shaun grinned at the jibe. "Did you ever consider anything but family law?"

"No."

"Why not?"

She shrugged. "I just felt that it was the one field in which I could make a difference for people."

He hesitated, certain she wouldn't appreciate his prying. Still, he felt compelled to ask, "But at what cost to yourself?"

"What do you mean?"

"You were a wreck yesterday, Arden." His words were gentle but firm.

"Yesterday was the first time I buried a client. I think I was entitled to a few tears."

"Nobody's suggesting otherwise," he agreed.

She folded her arms over her chest, a clearly defensive stance. He decided to back off—at least a little.

"Do you believe that happily-ever-afters can happen?" he asked.

"I like to think so," she admitted. "But it's hard to imagine, when I spend so much time dealing with the aftermath of relationships that fall apart."

"What about Colin and Nikki?"

"I think they're the exception rather than the rule."

"Maybe," he allowed.

"And they had their share of heartache first," she reminded him.

"Some would call it paying their dues." And they had both paid dearly when Colin walked out on the wife he hadn't known was carrying his child. He hadn't trusted that Nikki loved him enough to move halfway across the country with him. When Colin had finally come home, Nikki hadn't trusted that he loved her enough to stay. But somehow they'd worked through the barriers of the past and were now blissfully happy together—Colin and Nikki and their daughter, Carly.

"I don't ever want to fall in love if that's the price I have to pay," Arden said.

"You've never been in love?"

She shook her head. "No."

He sat back and studied her. It was hard to believe that a woman who was thirty-one years of age had never been in love. Then again, he *had* been in love, and he couldn't think of a whole hell of a lot to recommend it.

Still, he wanted a partner with whom to share his life. Someone with similar goals and values. And he wanted to have children. Not that he was in any particular rush to get married and start a family, but someday.

So he'd approached the problem like any other legal dilemma: with reason and research. He'd even made a list of the attributes he wanted in a wife: nurturing personality, good with kids. He would prefer to find a woman who'd be willing to stay at home to raise their children. His practice was successful enough that they wouldn't need a second income, but he was willing to be flexible. His wife could work, so long as her choice of career wasn't too demanding.

His sister-in-law had laughed when he'd explained his criteria to her. Nikki had accused him of trying to pencil love into his Daytimer like a court appearance, of wanting a woman who would be his subordinate rather than an equal partner. Shaun couldn't deny there was probably some truth in that. After all, it had worked for his parents. And his experience with Jenna had shown him how easily conflicting ambitions could destroy a relationship.

He wasn't looking for love. He didn't want passion. No, thanks. He'd tried that before, and although fun while it lasted, it hadn't lasted long. He wasn't prepared to go through that heartache again.

Still, he couldn't deny that he was attracted to Arden. Which made him wonder why he'd ever suggested this friendship thing. It would be a lot easier to get her out of his mind—and out of his fantasies—if he wasn't spending time with her.

But, no, he had to propose that they be friends. Yeah, like *that* was likely. And they had a date scheduled for the annual ball in December. Not a date—a contract. An exchange of service for consideration.

He frowned. He'd never had to bribe a woman to go out with him before. He might try to convince himself he was sticking close to Arden to look out for her, but the truth was that he just wanted to be with her.

Shaun didn't like to admit how often his thoughts wandered to Arden throughout the following week. How many times he picked up the phone, tempted to call her. Just to see how she was doing. He told himself it was because he was concerned about her, but he knew it was more than that.

He was attracted to her. He wanted her. And he had no idea what to do about it.

She'd made it clear she wasn't interested. She wasn't looking for a relationship, and she didn't want to get involved with him. He'd have to be a complete idiot not to get the hint. He wasn't an idiot.

He also wasn't able to turn down a challenge.

Arden challenged him. It wasn't a macho thing. It wasn't that he wanted to get her into bed just to prove to himself that he could. He did want her in bed—after all, he was a healthy, fully functioning man—but it was more than that.

He liked that they had so much in common, and that they argued. Arden wasn't afraid to disagree, to stand up for what she believed in. She had strength and conviction and heart. And the memory of the kiss they'd shared continued to linger in his mind and haunt his dreams.

Of course, she was a lawyer, and that was a pretty big stumbling block as far as he was concerned. He wouldn't get involved with another lawyer—he'd made that mistake once already. He'd met Jenna while they were both attending law school at Harvard, and the attraction between them had sparked from the first. She was everything he'd ever thought he wanted in a woman: beautiful, sophisticated, intelligent, ambitious. He'd thought theirs was a love of the happily-ever-after variety; he hadn't anticipated that her ambition would override all else.

He didn't blame Jenna for walking out on him. She'd always been honest about what she wanted, and she'd made no secret of the fact that she did not want to stay in "Small Town Pennsylvania," as she'd dubbed his hometown. It was Shaun who'd made the mistake of assuming she could be happy there, that her love for him would override her plans for her career.

He'd been wrong.

When she'd received an offer from a high-profile criminal defense firm in Boston, she hadn't even hesitated. She had asked him to go back to Boston with her, but just as she'd known she'd never be happy in Fairweather, Shaun knew he'd never be happy anywhere else.

Maybe he hadn't loved her as much as he thought he had. If she'd really been "the one," he would have gone. And if she'd really loved him, she would have stayed.

He'd reached two conclusions as a result of his experience with Jenna. One, similar goals and expectations were more important to the success of a relationship than either sex or love. Two, he would not get involved with another lawyer. The next time he fell in love it would be with a woman who could love him back, who would be willing to put their relationship above all else.

Which proved that he shouldn't even be thinking about Arden Doherty. By her own admission, Arden was committed to her career; her clients were the focus of her life.

Then again, just because she was the wrong woman from a relationship perspective didn't mean that they couldn't be friends. Except that he'd never found himself so preoccupied by thoughts of a "friend" before.

When the phone on his desk buzzed, Shaun picked up the receiver, grateful for the interruption. "Yes?"

"There's a Ms. Doherty here to see you," his receptionist informed him.

He felt his lips curve. "Send her in, Claire."

"She doesn't have an appointment," Claire said pointedly.

"That's okay," he said. "She's a friend."

"All right." But the receptionist didn't sound pleased by this overt breach of office policy.

Shaun didn't care. Arden was here.

He cleared his throat, banished the grin from his face and grabbed one of the files that was stacked on the corner of his desk. He flipped it open, pretending to be hard at work.

When he heard the knock and saw Arden peek around the door, the smile that returned to his lips was completely natural. He'd carried a mental picture of her in his mind all week, but it didn't compare to the reality of her. There was something about Arden that reached him on a basic level and stirred his most primal urges.

Today she was wearing a dark-green skirt and jacket with a cream colored blouse. Her hair was twisted into some kind of fancy knot at the back of her neck, but a few strands had escaped to frame the clear creamy skin of her face. "Arden." He stood up from behind his desk. "This is a surprise."

"Next time I'll make an appointment."

His smile widened. He liked to think that Arden would have reason to come by his office again—as any friend might. "Claire takes her job seriously," he apologized.

"Well, obviously you're busy—"

"Not too busy," he interrupted to assure her. "Have a seat."

She hesitated, then moved over to one of the chairs facing his desk. She perched herself on the edge of the seat, the green skirt riding up on her thighs, exposing a few more inches of creamy flesh.

"Nice office," she said, surveying the spacious surroundings.

He managed to tear his gaze away from her legs before she caught him staring. "I like it."

She glanced at him, and their eyes locked for a long moment. Shaun would have sworn the air crackled with the awareness between them. Then she looked away and the moment passed, or maybe he'd just imagined it.

"I was heading back to my office after court," she said, "and I thought I should stop by to return this." She took his handkerchief out of her pocket, passed it across the desk to him.

He'd forgotten that she had it. He tucked it into his own pocket. "Aren't you going to be at Carly's birthday party tomorrow?"

Arden nodded. "Yes. I thought about waiting to return it, but I wasn't sure if I'd have a chance to speak to you alone. Not that I want to be alone with you. I mean—"

She broke off, drew in a deep breath. He fought against the grin that tugged at his lips. Damn, but she was cute when she was flustered.

"I only meant that I didn't want Nikki to know that I had your handkerchief, because then she'd have a ton of questions. She worries about me," Arden admitted reluctantly.

"It's natural to worry about those you love." He tilted his head, studying her. "Why does that bother you?"

She shrugged. "Because it's unnecessary."

One day, he promised himself, he would get to the bottom of this stubborn independence of hers. He'd find out what had happened to make her so unwilling to rely on others, so reluctant to accept help when it was offered. For now it was enough that she was here.

"I saw you and Warren Blake having coffee at the courthouse Monday." He wasn't sure what compelled him to blurt out the statement. He hadn't realized that the sight of Arden with the assistant district attorney had bothered him, but apparently it had, more than he wanted to admit.

"And?" she prompted, sounding baffled.

He shrugged. "I thought you didn't date lawyers."

"Is that a not-so-subtle way of asking about my relationship with Warren?"

He didn't give a damn about being subtle, and he didn't like the way the man's name had rolled off her tongue. "Do you have a relationship with Blake?"

"Do you have a problem with the new ADA?" she countered.

"He's arrogant and self-righteous and unreasonable."

She raised an eyebrow. "Did he refuse to grant bail to one of your clients?"

He had, but "That's not the point."

She smiled.

"He was hanging all over you."

"Not that it's any of your business," Arden told him. "But we were having a professional discussion over coffee."

Her explanation failed to appease him. A professional discussion. "Since when do you represent criminal defendants?"

"I do a lot of work with young offenders," she told him.

"Oh." He'd forgotten that. Still, he didn't like the way Blake had been looking at her. Not that he could blame the man for finding Arden attractive, but he sensed it was something more than that. He had no grounds for his suspicions, though, so he kept them to himself.

"Any more questions?" Arden asked.

"Not right now."

"Good." She stood up. "I have to get back to the office."

But Shaun was reluctant to let her go. "I haven't forgotten about your bookshelves," he told her. "I just haven't had a chance to get the wood."

"I'm not in a hurry."

"Oh. Okay. I'll call you, then, when I'm ready to get started."

"Sure," she agreed. Then, "I'll see you at Colin and Nikki's tomorrow?"

He nodded, already looking forward to it.

It was amazing, Arden thought as she stepped out of the path of an oncoming child, how vocal a group of six-year-olds could be. And it wasn't a particularly large group, either. She tried to count the heads as they rushed past, but they changed direction in midstream, circled around and disappeared up the stairs again.

"How many kids are here?" she asked Nikki.

"Six," her cousin answered. "Including Carly."

"I never would have thought that six kids could make so much noise."

Nikki shrugged. "You get used to it."

"How long is this party supposed to last?"

"Until three o'clock."

Arden glanced at her watch. It was a little past one. The party had started at noon, with hot dogs and potato chips for lunch. Then Carly had opened her presents, and now the kids were playing some kind of game that apparently required running around the house at full speed and full volume. Arden concentrated on helping Nikki pick up the scattered remnants of wrapping paper and ribbon, refusing to think about the fact that Shaun had yet to make an appearance.

"How's your new associate working out?" Nikki asked.

"Good. It took her a while to get her bearings, but she's settling in well."

"So what's bothering you?"

"Nothing."

Nikki sent her a pointed look; Arden sighed.

"I'm not sure."

"Must be a man," Nikki said, smiling.

"No. Well, sort of."

"He's sort of a man?"

Arden laughed. He was *definitely* a man. "He sort of bothers me."

"It's about time."

"What do you mean?"

"You always close yourself off from people, never letting anyone get too close. If he bothers you, it means he's getting to you."

Arden frowned. It frustrated her to realize that she still carried the emotional scars from a man who'd been gone from her life for so long, and that her inherent distrust was so apparent. "Do you think I'm cold?"

"No," Nikki responded immediately. "You're the warmest, most giving and caring person I know, but you don't often let other people see it."

Arden stuffed a wad of wrapping paper into the bag in Nikki's hand.

"Does he see it?" Nikki asked.

"He thinks he does."

Nikki grinned. "I like him already."

"You would," Arden muttered.

"Speaking of men," Nikki mused, as she scooped a huge purple bow from the floor. "I wonder what happened to Shaun. When I talked to him last week, he said he was going to be here."

"He told me the same thing yesterday," Arden said, not thinking about the implications of her statement until the words were out of her mouth.

Nikki turned to look at her. "You saw Shaun yesterday?"

"Um…yeah." *Hell.*

"I keep forgetting that you guys must run into one another all the time at the courthouse."

Arden decided not to correct her cousin's misapprehension. There was no reason to invite speculation, and the chime of the doorbell forestalled any further discussion of the matter.

That will be Shaun, Arden thought.

"I'll get it," Colin said, coming through the dining room from the kitchen. He stopped on his way to brush a soft kiss on Nikki's lips. The tenderness of the gesture almost made Arden sigh.

She had expressed more than a few reservations when Colin had come back into town, after a five-year absence, claiming to still love Nikki. But he'd stuck, and if appearances were any indication, they were very much in love. Nikki and Colin had been remarried for four months now, and it warmed Arden's heart to see how happy they were together, and if she was a little envious—well, it was just a little.

"Isn't the honeymoon period supposed to be over by now?" she teased.

Colin ended the lingering kiss to respond to the door. Nikki, bless her, actually blushed. "I wouldn't have thought it was possible," she admitted. "But I love him more every day."

"They say that's the way it's supposed to be."

"You don't have to sound so skeptical," her cousin chided.

Arden shrugged. "I don't see a lot of cases of love at its finest. But it's great to see you so happy."

"I want you to be happy, too."

"I'm not unhappy," Arden said.

"No," Nikki agreed. "But you're not really happy, either."

Arden shrugged again but was saved from answering by Colin's return, accompanied now by his brother.

Shaun's eyes met hers, held for a moment. "Hello, Arden."

"Hi," she responded, lamenting the sudden acceleration of her pulse. She'd always been aware of his innate maleness and sensuality, but there was something different now. Since the night he'd kissed her, she sensed a corresponding awareness from Shaun that had never existed before.

Shaun crossed the room to kiss Nikki's cheek. "Sorry I'm late," he apologized, setting a large, brightly wrapped box on the table.

"You missed lunch," Nikki told him.

"Hot dogs, wasn't it?" The face he made suggested that his tardiness might not have been accidental.

"There are a few left, if you want one," she said.

"No. Thanks." Then, "I didn't miss cake, though, did I?"

Nikki chuckled. "No, you didn't miss cake."

He grinned. "Then I'd say I'm right on time."

She shook her head and handed the bag of garbage to Colin.

"Where is the birthday girl?" Shaun asked.

"Upstairs trashing her new toys." It was Arden who responded to his question, since Nikki and Colin had their heads together again and were whispering intently as if they were alone in the room. "Do you want me to get her?"

"No. I'll go up to see her in a minute." He nodded his head in the direction of his brother and sister-in-law. "What's up with them?"

"Love," Arden said, sounding disgusted.

Shaun laughed.

"If you guys are going to make snide comments, we're not going to share the news," Colin said.

"What news?" Shaun asked.

Arden glanced from Nikki, who was practically bursting with excitement, to Colin, whose expression matched.

"We're going to have another baby," Nikki said.

Arden swallowed around the tightness in her throat and stepped over to hug her cousin. "Congratulations." Then she turned and hugged Colin, too.

"Wow." Shaun sounded like he was in shock, but he was smiling. He slapped his brother on the back and lifted Nikki off the ground in a heartfelt embrace.

"When?" Arden asked.

"March," Nikki said.

"Have you told Carly?"

She nodded.

"Is she excited?"

This time it was Colin who nodded. "And adamant that the baby's going to be a girl."

"This is such wonderful news," Arden said. And it was. So she wasn't sure why her eyes stung, why she felt an emptiness inside herself. She was happy for her cousin. Thrilled. Nikki and Colin deserved all the happiness in the world; they'd certainly earned it.

It was the sound of hundreds of pounding feet—or six pairs of six-year-old feet—on the stairs that banished her melancholy. Then Carly swooped into the room, followed by her entourage.

"Can we have cake now, Mommy?"

"Is everyone ready for cake?" Nikki asked.

"Yes," the children chorused in response.

"Then find your places at the table," Nikki advised.

She carried the cake in from the kitchen, candles lit. The children sang loudly and off-key, and Carly managed to extinguish all of the candles with a single breath and very little spit.

"I'll take this back to the kitchen to dish it up," Arden said.

"I'll give you a hand," Shaun offered.

Arden sliced through the cake, sliding the pieces onto paper plates decorated with Cosmic Cat, Carly's favorite cartoon character. She glanced at Shaun as she removed the lid from the tub of chocolate ice cream. "I thought you were going to help."

"I really just wanted to talk to you," he admitted.

"About?"

"I lied to you the other day," he told her.

Arden frowned as she dipped the scoop into the ice cream. "When?"

"When I said I wanted us to be friends."

"You don't want to be friends?" It shouldn't have bothered her. After all, it had been *his* suggestion in the first place.

"I don't want to put a label on our relationship that might limit the scope of it."

Arden busied herself scooping ice cream. She wasn't sure what point he was trying to make, and he sure was taking his time getting to it. "Sometimes you sound just like a lawyer."

He smiled, unoffended. "I like you," he told her. "And I respect you. And because I like and respect you, I figure I should be honest with you."

"Then just say whatever it is you're trying to say," she told him.

"I want to have sex with you."

Chapter 5

The scoop slipped in Arden's hand, and a half-formed ball of ice cream flew out of the tub and smacked against the front of the cupboard. It slid down slowly, leaving a sticky wet trail on the wooden door before dropping onto the countertop.

Arden could feel Shaun's presence behind her. He was obviously waiting for some kind of response, but she was too stunned to know what to say to him. Okay, maybe she should have been prepared. His physical response when he'd kissed her indicated that there was some interest, but she didn't know how to deal with his sudden pronouncement.

She stared at the trail of ice cream on the cabinet. That, at least, was something she could deal with. She turned to the sink and rinsed out the dishcloth, wiped the cupboard door and the melting scoop on the counter, then resumed serving up ice cream onto the cake plates.

"This is a little…abrupt," she said, without even a glance at Shaun.

"Is it?"

His voice was low and husky, his breath warm on her ear. He was close, too close—his masculine scent clouding her senses. She couldn't even breathe when he was standing so near, how the hell was she supposed to think? She stepped to the side and slowly turned to face him.

"Not more than a week ago you didn't seem to be aware that I was female, and now you expect me to jump into bed with you?"

"I was always aware that you were female," he said, and grinned. "But you always seemed unapproachable."

"I haven't changed in the past week," she told him.

"No," he agreed. "But my perceptions have. That day in the park, when I held you in my arms, I realized how soft and warm, how completely feminine, you are."

She glared at him, not appreciating this reminder of her moment of weakness. "Is that what turns you on, McIver? A woman crying on your shoulder?"

He grinned again. "Are you really interested in what turns me on?"

"No."

"And I don't *expect* anything from you," he continued. "Although I wouldn't object if you wanted to jump into bed with me."

"I don't," she snapped.

"Don't be so quick to dismiss the possibility."

"This whole conversation is ridiculous."

"Can you honestly tell me that you haven't thought about that kiss? That you haven't wondered what might have happened that night if I hadn't pulled back?"

"Nothing would have happened." She believed that. She had to believe it. She wasn't the type of woman who let passion overrule common sense—and having sex with Shaun McIver would definitely violate all common sense. She turned away from him and resumed scooping ice cream.

Shaun shrugged. "Maybe not. Still, that kiss changed things."

"I'm not going to sleep with you."

"Never say never," he chided.

"I'm sure I should be flattered that you've suddenly taken an interest in me, but I don't have time for games and I don't want things to be awkward between us on family holidays. Like now," she said pointedly.

"We're both adults," Shaun reminded her. "I'm sure we could handle whatever might happen."

"Nothing's going to happen," she said again.

Shaun loaded up an armful of plates and disappeared into the dining room.

"Maybe we should just agree to disagree on that matter," he said when he returned.

Arden sighed. "I'm not playing hard to get, Shaun. I'm just not interested in any kind of relationship right now."

"There's only one problem."

"What's that?" Arden asked warily.

"I can't be in the same room with you without thinking about that kiss. Without wanting to kiss you again."

She swallowed around her suddenly dry throat. She'd thought they should talk about that kiss, had even considered bringing it up herself. But she'd decided that it would be too awkward, that talking about something he'd probably forgotten would make it seem too important. Apparently he hadn't forgotten it, either.

"Look, McIver, I'm sure…" Her words trailed off as Shaun stepped closer. She moistened her lips with the tip of her tongue, took an instinctive step back, needing to re-establish the physical distance between them. Suddenly she wasn't sure of anything, except that his statement echoed her own thoughts and desires.

"It surprises me," he said, continuing to move forward, "that a woman so cool and poised is unnerved by a simple sexual attraction."

"I'm not unnerved," she denied. "I just don't want to be having this conversation."

"At all?" he asked. "Or with me?"

"Both," she admitted.

"Why?"

"Because I want us to be friends. I don't have time for anything more complicated than that right now."

He shrugged. "Okay, then. We'll be friends."

She started to exhale a slow sigh of relief.

"For now," he added, then grinned.

Shaun was mildly disappointed when Arden turned down Nikki's invitation to stay for dinner. She claimed to have some work to do at the office; it was more likely that she wanted some time away from him. His revelation had surprised her, and maybe that had been his intention.

It had surprised him, too. Not the fact that he wanted to have sex with her—he'd come to that conclusion about three seconds into that sizzling kiss they'd shared in her apartment—but the bold statement of his desire. He usually exhibited a little more finesse with women, and a lot more patience. But there was something about Arden that undermined his resolve, that made him want her even though he didn't *want* to want her.

His only consolation was that he knew Arden was affected by him, too. When he'd told her he wanted her, she'd been shaken. And interested. It wasn't ego that made him think so, it was the awareness that had flared in her eyes, the fluttering of her pulse, the quickening of her breath.

He didn't mind too much that she'd taken off—he knew she'd be thinking about him. As he'd be thinking about her.

They had lasagna for dinner—one of Nikki's specialties and a favorite of Carly's. After the dishes had been cleared away, Nikki had shooed her husband and brother-in-law out to the porch while she got the birthday girl ready for bed.

Shaun was still puzzling about Arden when Colin went back into the house to get them a couple of beers. He'd meant what he said when he told Arden he didn't date lawyers. As a rule he didn't. And yet, he'd concocted an elaborate ploy to get her to agree to be his date for the Law Ball. It wasn't as if he couldn't get a date if he wanted to. But since Jenna, he'd been careful to date women who wanted the same thing he did from a relationship: no strings, no complications.

Arden Doherty had complication written all over her. They were too many facets to her character, too many layers. And yet, she was the only woman he wanted.

The screen door creaked, announcing Colin's return. Shaun accepted the beer his brother offered, looking forward to some conversation to get his mind off of the situation with Arden. So he didn't know what compelled him to ask, "Do you think it's possible to be just friends with a woman?"

"No way." Colin's response was immediate, adamant.

"Why not?"

His brother rolled his eyes. "Because sex complicates things."

Shaun frowned. "What if they're not having sex?" He did believe it was possible for a man and a woman to be friends, but he couldn't see it for him and Arden. Not after that kiss.

"Even if they're not doing it, they want to. Or one of them does, anyway." Colin twisted the cap off his bottle of beer, took a long swallow. "Who are you not having sex with?"

"The list is endless," Shaun replied dryly.

"Come on," Colin prompted. "Who is it you're not having sex with because of delusions of friendship?"

"No one."

"Someone I know?"

"No one," Shaun said again.

"Whose idea was this friendship thing—yours or hers?"

Shaun gave up trying to convince his brother it was no one. "Mine."

"What was her response?"

"She was skeptical."

"Do you want to have sex with her?"

Shaun sighed. "Yeah."

Colin grinned.

"But it would be a monumental mistake."

"Why?"

Because she's Nikki's cousin. It was the response that sprang to mind, but it wasn't something Shaun could tell his brother.

Maybe the emotions that had suddenly surfaced were the result of some kind of empathy or compassion. That was the most logical explanation. After all, these feelings had only begun to stir when he'd comforted her through an emotional trauma.

Like hell, he thought. He was a man, pure and simple, and seeing how nicely Arden filled out those tidy little suits she habitually wore, watching her sexy lips curve into a soft smile, seeing the lingering hint of sadness in her eyes, the sparkle of quick joy when she laughed, reminded him of that fact. And that he'd been sleeping alone for far too long now.

An attraction to any other woman he might have pushed away. But Arden was practically family, and that made him wary. If he decided to pursue this, and he wanted to, he'd have to watch his step. Either one of them ending up hurt wasn't an option, not when they were destined to cross paths in the future.

"Why would it be a mistake to have sex with her?" Colin repeated the question.

"She's…complicated," Shaun responded at last.

"Complicated." Colin grinned again. "Unlike the two-dimensional women you've dated since Jenna?"

"They weren't all two-dimensional," he felt compelled to protest.

"All except my wife," Colin said dryly.

"Nikki is one of a kind."

"So is Arden."

Shaun nearly dropped his beer. "Arden?"

"It *is* Arden, isn't it?" Colin pressed.

"What's Arden?" Shaun asked cautiously.

"The woman you're not having sex with."

"No," Shaun said quickly. Too quickly.

Colin took a long swallow from his own bottle. "You *are* having sex with Arden?"

"Of course not."

"Then what's going on?"

"Nothing." It wasn't really a lie; it just wasn't the whole truth.

"It didn't look like nothing when the two of you were cozied up in the kitchen."

"I was helping her with the cake."

"Yeah, that's what it looked like." Colin's voice dripped with sarcasm. "I'm surprised the ice cream didn't melt with all the heat you two were generating."

"I don't know what you're talking about."

"Fine. We can play it that way," Colin said. "But if you break her heart, I'll have to hurt you."

"You're *my* brother," Shaun said, unaccountably irked.

Colin nodded. "And Arden is the closest thing Nikki has to a sister. They grew up together. And maybe I feel I owe Arden for the years she was there for Nikki and Carly when I wasn't."

"I was there, too," Shaun reminded him.

"But Arden is Nikki's best friend as well as her cousin, which means there's a lot more at stake here than your getting laid."

"It's not just about sex," Shaun said. Although he hadn't given up hope that sex might be a fringe benefit of his developing relationship with Arden, he was genuinely concerned about her and whatever had put that haunted look in her eyes the night they'd had dinner together. He knew that it hadn't just been about Denise and Brian, and he was determined to get to the root of her fear. And to find out if there was any connection between her wariness and her windows being shot out. "Besides, there's nothing going on between me and Arden."

Colin's cocky grin faded. "I know it's none of my business—"

"Then back off."

"She's been through a lot, Shaun. More even than I know."

Shaun had suspected as much. He sensed there were scars that ran deep. He wanted to know why. He wanted her to open up to him. And he wanted her.

"I can't give you any assurances about what might or might not happen," Shaun said. "But I care about her." More than he was ready to admit, even to himself.

Colin nodded. "I guess that's good enough for now."

"What's good enough for now?" Nikki asked, stepping out onto the porch and into the cool early-October evening.

Shaun flashed his brother a warning look. The last thing he needed was for Nikki to mention to Arden that he'd been talking to Colin about her. Arden would be furious. Not that he could really blame her. She'd made it clear that she didn't want Nikki worrying about her, and he knew Nikki would worry if she thought there was something going on between her cousin and her brother-in-law.

"Shaun's promised to help me clear out the spare bedroom upstairs so we can turn it into a nursery for the baby," Colin told her.

Shaun didn't know whether to be impressed by his brother's quick response or ticked that he'd managed to turn the situation to his own advantage. But he managed a smile for his sister-in-law.

"That's so sweet," she said, lowering herself onto the swing beside her husband.

"That's me," Shaun said dryly. "A sweet guy."

Colin laughed. "Of all the adjectives I could think of to describe you, *sweet* would not be one of them."

"This from the man who wants me to clean his house."

"And paint," Colin added.

Shaun just glared at him.

After Carly's birthday party, Arden resolved that the best way to deal with Shaun was to avoid him. She usually faced a problem head-on, but she had no idea how to handle Shaun. He'd said that he couldn't be in the same room with her without thinking about the kiss they'd shared, so she decided not to be in the same room with him. It seemed like a simple solution. The problem was, it didn't stop *her* from thinking about that kiss.

But she figured the more time that passed, the easier it would get. All she had to do in the interim was avoid Shaun.

Unfortunately she had less than forty-eight hours to test her strategy before she crossed paths with him again.

It was just before ten o'clock Monday morning and she was at the courthouse filing documents for an upcoming hearing when she saw him. He was standing outside Courtroom Four talking to Warren Blake. Whatever they were discussing, their conversation seemed heated, almost antagonistic.

She should have taken her documents and made her escape, but she couldn't help lingering a moment to observe the two men. She knew Shaun didn't like Warren, which wasn't surprising since they were destined to be on opposite sides of the courtroom all the time.

"Is it the assistant district attorney who has you looking all dreamy-eyed, or the other guy?"

The question startled Arden out of her reverie. She turned to Marcy Crawford, the young associate she'd hired only two months earlier.

"I'm not dreamy-eyed," Arden denied, stuffing the papers she'd been holding into her briefcase.

Marcy just grinned. "It must be the other guy. He's coming this way."

Arden glanced up, saw that Marcy was right. "Damn," she muttered under her breath.

"Waiting for me?" Shaun asked when he'd joined them.

Arden flushed, embarrassed that she'd been caught loitering in the courthouse, wondering if he'd seen her watching him. "Actually, I was waiting for Warren."

Shaun scowled. "You're kidding."

Arden laughed. "Yeah, I am."

Shaun turned to Marcy and gave her one of his trademark killer smiles. "Shaun McIver," he said, offering his hand.

Marcy looked pretty dreamy-eyed herself as she smiled back at him. "Marcy Crawford, and I'm very pleased to meet you."

"Marcy's my new associate," Arden said, annoyed with Shaun's flirtatious manner and Marcy's predictable reaction. It shouldn't matter to her; she shouldn't care. In fact, if she was smart—and she liked to think she was—she'd be trying to set Shaun up with Marcy. It might get him off *her* back. The idea held little appeal. Suddenly she wasn't so sure she wanted him off her back.

"Do you ladies have time for coffee?" Shaun asked.

"I wish I did," Marcy told him. "But I've got a pretrial in ten minutes."

"Arden?" Shaun asked, turning to her. "I wanted to talk to you about something, if you've got a minute."

No. All she had to do was say that one simple word and she could go back to her office and back to her plan of avoidance. But her brain and her mouth were obviously having some kind of communication problem, because when she opened her mouth to respond, she said, "Sure."

"I don't think they have Jamaican Blue Mountain," Shaun said as they made their way down the stairs to the café.

"As long as it has caffeine." She assured herself that she

had agreed to this meeting only because he said they needed to discuss something, even though she had no idea what that "something" was.

They took their coffee—or rather, Arden took her coffee and Shaun took his tea—to a small table on the perimeter of the café where lush, overgrown foliage spilling out of clay pots gave the misplaced illusion of a tropical rainforest.

"How is the new lawyer working out?" Shaun asked when they were seated.

Arden wasn't sure if she detected some personal interest in the question or if he was just making conversation. "Fine," she said.

Shaun's lips curved, and Arden felt her insides melt. At least she knew she wasn't the only woman to react this way. Marcy had practically dissolved at his feet when he'd aimed that smile at her.

"Good. It will be easier for you to get away for a weekend if you have someone to hold down the fort."

"I don't have any reason to get away for a weekend," she told him.

He smiled again. "I'm working on it."

"Is this part of your elaborate ruse to get me into bed with you?"

"Sometimes simplicity is best," he said. "And I won't need a ruse. When we make love, it's going to be because you want it as much as I do."

Despite the arrogance of his words, she couldn't help the heat that flooded through her. She did want him, and God help her if he ever figured that out.

"Some women might find that kind of arrogant machismo appealing," Arden said. "I don't."

"We'll see."

"You said you wanted to talk about something."

"Not really."

Arden set her cup down, narrowed her eyes.

"That was just an excuse to spend some time with you," he admitted.

"I don't have time for games."

"You have to learn to make time for the fun things in life."

"I have fun," she said defensively.

"That's why you left Carly's birthday party early to go to the office."

She picked up her coffee and sipped. She had gone into the office, only because she'd needed something to occupy her mind. Work had always succeeded before, but Saturday night, after he'd stood in Nikki's kitchen and matter-of-factly told her he wanted to have sex with her, nothing had banished the echo of those words from her mind. Or the corresponding twinges of excitement and apprehension that coursed through her system.

"I had work to do," she told him.

"Speaking of work," he said, "I picked up the wood for your bookshelves. If you're going to be home tonight, I could come around and get started."

Arden frowned into her mug. "I do appreciate the offer, but I'm not sure this is such a good idea."

"Why not?"

"Because."

"Oh." He nodded in apparent understanding. "I get it."

"Get what?"

"You're afraid to be alone with me."

"Of course not," she denied.

"You're worried that if we spend time together it might weaken your resolve not to get involved with me."

"I don't weaken that easily," she said.

He grinned. "Then why don't you want me to build your shelves?"

"I just think you must have better things to do with your time."

"Not at all."

"Fine." Arden pushed her empty cup aside and stood up. "I should be home by six-thirty. Come over and build the damn shelves if you're that intent on doing so."

Chapter 6

Because he was intent on building her shelves, and because it gave him a valid excuse to spend time with her, Shaun was at Arden's apartment promptly at six-thirty that night. Just as she was arriving home from the office.

Arden frowned at the armful of wood he carried into her apartment. "If you took all the measurements you needed, why can't you just build the shelves at your place and bring them over here when you're done?"

"Because," he explained as he set the mahogany boards on the living room floor, "then I wouldn't have the pleasure of your company."

"I don't plan on keeping you company," she said. "I have reading to catch up on."

"Then I'll just enjoy being in the same room with you."

"I'll be in my bedroom."

"I can bring my tools into the bedroom," he suggested hopefully.

Arden shook her head, but she was smiling. "Forget it, McIver."

He shrugged. "It was worth a try."

"Try forgetting I'm here," she said.

Then she turned and disappeared down the hall to what must have been her bedroom, because he heard the soft click of a door latching shut a few seconds later. Undaunted, he set to work.

Arden didn't surface again until almost two hours had passed. When she did so, she'd changed into a pair of faded navy leggings and an oversize flannel shirt with the sleeves rolled back. Her hair was down and tousled sexily. Shaun felt the tug of lust deep inside, pushed it aside and pretended to concentrate on sanding the edge of a piece of wood he'd just trimmed. She came out of the kitchen a few minutes later with a cup of yogurt and a spoon in hand.

He wanted to comment on what he assumed was her dinner, but he didn't. "Is the noise bothering you?" he asked instead.

"No," she said. "I seem to be able to tune everything else out when I'm working."

"Too bad not everyone can do the same."

She seemed confused by his statement, but made no comment as she stirred the yogurt.

"Did you sort out that problem with your landlord?"

Her brow furrowed. "What problem?"

"The noise complaint. Your downstairs neighbor," he reminded her, watching closely for her reaction.

She popped a spoonful of yogurt in her mouth, then swept her tongue along the fullness of her bottom lip to remove any lingering traces. Shaun nearly groaned aloud, remembering how wonderful her mouth had tasted, wishing it was his tongue stroking those luscious lips. If she was trying to distract him from his topic of inquiry, she was doing a hell of a job.

"Oh. Yeah. Everything's, um, taken care of."

"That's good. I was a little worried that the sawing and hammering might bother him."

"It might make more sense for you to make the shelves at home."

He grinned. "It would."

Arden sighed. "Well, I've got some, um, research to do. I'm going to head over to the…library for a while."

"Now?"

She frowned. "Yes, now. Why?"

"You shouldn't be going out on your own at this time of night."

She glanced at her watch. "It's not even nine o'clock."

"It's dark outside."

"It was almost dark when I came home," she said.

Now it was Shaun's turn to frown. "You're going to leave me here?"

"I didn't realize you were afraid to be left alone."

"Very funny."

"Do you have any other objections?"

"What if I need to leave before you get back?" He really didn't want her going out on her own. He wasn't sure why the idea bothered him so much, why he felt so protective of her.

"I won't be too long," she said. "But if you need to go before I get back, just leave."

"I'm not going to leave your apartment unlocked and unattended."

"It's a secure building, Shaun."

"That didn't stop someone from shooting out your windows."

"The police are convinced that was just a childish prank."

"It was a real gun," he reminded her. "I won't go out and leave your apartment unlocked."

Arden sighed and went into the kitchen. "Here," she said, thrusting a key into his hand. "It's a spare."

He studied the key for a moment, grinned. "I've had

women give me keys to their apartments before,'' he said. ''But never with such enthusiasm.''

Arden glared at him. ''It's so you can get *out,* not come in.''

He felt his grin widen as he pocketed the key. ''It works both ways.''

She picked up the briefcase she'd dropped at the door. ''If you're not here when I get back, thanks for the work you're doing.''

''Anytime,'' he said.

Arden spent a couple hours at the library. She didn't have anything pressing that required immediate research, but she'd needed an excuse to get out of her apartment. To get away from Shaun. It wasn't just that his presence unnerved her, although it did, it was the way he looked at her—as if he saw so much more than she wanted to reveal.

She'd nearly blown it when he'd asked about her downstairs neighbor. She'd forgotten about the story she'd concocted to explain that letter. She sighed and pushed her hair away from her face. She didn't know whether to be grateful or annoyed that Shaun's presence made her so easily forget the problem that seemed to be at the forefront of her mind at any other time. So she'd fled, reverting to her plan of avoidance. She wasn't proud of her behavior, but Shaun McIver threatened every aspect of her well-ordered life and she wasn't willing to risk everything for a temporary fling.

She could only hope that Shaun would be gone by the time she returned to her apartment.

He wasn't.

And he came back the following night, and again the night after that.

Arden let him keep the spare key, preferring to stay late at the office or run errands after work. Anything to avoid spending time with Shaun.

Thursday night when Arden arrived home, she was

greeted by the sharp odor of wood stain. "You're finished?" she asked, trying not to sound too hopeful.

Shaun grinned at her as he wiped his hands on a rag. "For now."

"Oh."

"They'll need a second coat and then a protective sealant," he told her.

"They look good," she said. And they did. It made her wonder if there was anything Shaun McIver couldn't do well. She severed the thought before it could go any further.

"I should be able to finish up this weekend, then you'll be able to unpack."

"You haven't given me the receipts," she reminded him. He'd refused to accept payment for the labor, but Arden had insisted that she'd buy the materials. After all, they were her bookcases.

"Haven't I?"

"No."

Shaun shrugged. "Don't worry about it."

"I can't let you pay for my shelves."

"How about a trade?" he suggested.

She narrowed her eyes. "What kind of trade?"

"Dinner."

"Would you like me to order it for you?" she asked dryly.

He grinned. "I'd like you to share it with me."

"Oh."

"Have you already eaten?"

"No," she admitted.

"Neither have I."

"I guess the least I could do is buy you dinner."

"You could smile and pretend to enjoy it, too."

She did smile at that. "I'm sorry. I must seem incredibly ungrateful, and I do appreciate all the work you've done. Where did you want to go?"

"DiMarco's," he said. "We have reservations for eight o'clock."

"Reservations?"

He nodded as he piled his paint cans and tools in the corner. "That will give me just enough time to grab a quick shower before we have to go."

"You planned this," she said accusingly.

"You can't get a table at DiMarco's without reservations," he said, as if that explained everything.

"I'm not going to fall in with your plans, McIver."

He shrugged, suggesting that her agreement or lack thereof didn't matter to him. "I've been living on fast food all week. I'm hungry and I want a decent meal. I thought you might, too."

Arden sighed. She hated that he was always so reasonable, and she *was* hungry. "Fine. There are towels in the cupboard in the bathroom. You've got twenty minutes for a shower."

"I'll be ready in ten," he promised, then he sauntered down the hall to the bathroom.

Arden shook her head as she watched him go. She didn't understand why he was so intent on spending time with her. Did he think she was going to fall into bed with him just because it was what he wanted?

Probably, she admitted to herself. She didn't imagine there were many women who were immune to his charms. She knew that she wasn't.

He was out of the bathroom in the ten minutes he'd promised, his hair damp from the shower. He looked good. Too good.

"Ready?" he asked.

She thought he was referring to dinner, but the sparkle in his eyes made her wonder. "What's going on here, McIver?"

He didn't hedge or pretend not to understand, for which

she was grateful. ''I think we need to take some time to figure that out.''

She shook her head. ''You know we're completely wrong for each other.''

''I used to think so. Now, I'm not so sure.''

He leaned toward her, and her breath caught in her throat. This time she knew he was going to kiss her, but she wasn't any more prepared for it. He touched his mouth to hers once, softly, fleetingly. Then again, lingering this time. She resisted, for about two seconds, then her lips softened, responded.

She could smell her soap on his skin, but the scent enhanced rather than detracted from his masculinity. His hands were on her hips, as if to hold her in place, but it was his kiss that immobilized her. She couldn't think or move or speak; she could only feel. Her lips parted on a sigh, her tongue met his.

''You make me wish I'd asked for more than dinner,'' he said huskily when he'd ended the kiss.

She took a deep breath, tried to ignore the yearnings of her own body. ''I don't want to get involved,'' she said after a long moment, refusing to meet his eyes. ''I can't.''

''Too late.''

''It's not too late.'' She was vehement, almost desperate.

''You know it is,'' he insisted. ''That's why you look so panicked every time I touch you.'' He reached out and cupped her cheek gently in his hand, and she pulled back instinctively. ''Why is that? What are you afraid of?''

''Nothing. I'm not afraid.'' She glanced away. ''I'm just not interested.''

''Liar.''

She sighed. ''I'm not good at relationships.''

He smiled. ''We'll start with dinner.''

Shaun was feeling just a little cocky as the hostess led them to a quieter, more secluded area at the back of the restaurant—as per his request. Despite Arden's assertion that she wasn't going to fall in with his plans, she had, in fact, done just that.

The table was small, the chairs positioned at right angles rather than across from each other. Tall plants and pots of greenery allowed for a certain amount of privacy; the single rose on the table and the flickering candle inside the hurricane shade provided a hint of romance.

And that's what this night was about: romance.

He'd given up trying to figure out what it was about Arden Doherty that he found so intriguing, so compelling. He knew the reasons didn't matter so much as the result. He wanted Arden, and he would do whatever needed to be done to have her.

Romance, he'd decided logically, was the first step. Yes, Arden was a practical person, an independent career-minded woman. But he had yet to meet a woman who was immune to romance.

So when Arden sat down, eyeing the flower and candle warily, he wondered if she might be the first. "Don't you think this is overkill?"

"What do you mean?" Shaun asked innocently.

"I'm not going to get involved with you, Shaun. Flowers and candlelight aren't going to change my mind."

"Wine?" he asked, accepting the list the hostess proffered.

"That might improve your chances from 'when hell freezes over' to 'not in this lifetime.'"

He chuckled, wondering at the perversity of his nature that allowed him to be charmed by a woman so determined to be contrary. "Red or white?"

Arden shook her head, but she was smiling. "Your choice."

He scanned the menu, ordered a bottle of pinot noir that he knew to be of a particularly good vintage. The wine came, they ordered dinner, then they chatted casually while they sampled the wine and waited for their pasta. Shaun deliberately kept the conversation light, sensing Arden's tension and hoping to relax her.

By the time their meals were delivered, she was smiling more easily and had even laughed at a couple of his lame jokes.

"Does this improve upon the 'not in this lifetime' to 'maybe tomorrow'?" Shaun asked hopefully, offering her the basket of garlic bread.

Arden shook her head again. He wasn't sure if it was a refusal of the bread or a response to his question.

"I don't do casual sex, Shaun."

"Sex should never be casual," he agreed. "It's an activity that should be entered into only after careful thought and deliberation, with serious attention given to the enjoyment of both parties."

Arden twirled her fork in her pasta. "Careful thought and deliberation?"

"I've given this careful thought and deliberation," he assured her. "With serious attention to the various ways in which I might ensure your enjoyment."

"Isn't it true that the average man thinks about sex once every seven seconds?"

"When I'm with you, it's more like every three or four seconds."

"And is that your definition of 'careful thought'?" She lifted an eyebrow, clearly unimpressed.

Shaun grinned. "I could share some of my thoughts with you, Doherty. If you're interested."

"I'll pass, thanks."

Shaun chuckled at her dry tone. He was tempted to pursue the conversation—to share some of his more erotic fantasies and gauge her reaction. But he'd vowed to give her some time and space, and he knew that further discussion of his desires would compromise his ability to keep that promise.

Instead he ordered dessert. Arden insisted she couldn't

eat another bite, but Shaun indulged himself by feeding her spoonfuls of the double-fudge brownie sundae, anyway. Her eyes closed and she murmured her throaty pleasure as she savored the first bite, and he couldn't help but wonder whether her sexual appetites would be as easily sated. He definitely wanted to find out. Would she writhe in ecstasy, scream in gratification?

He tried to redirect his thoughts, but knew he was lost when her tongue swept along her bottom lip, licking away the remnants of hot fudge. He wanted desperately to kiss her—to taste the sweetness of the chocolate, and the sweeter bliss that was Arden.

Throughout the drive across town, he reminded himself that there were parameters to this relationship. Arden was still insisting that she wanted to be friends, and although Shaun didn't doubt that he could change her mind, he'd vowed to take things slowly. He just hadn't anticipated that it would be so difficult to do so.

He found a parking space on the street outside her building and walked her up to her apartment. He could feel the tension building inside her, mounting with each step. He could almost hear her ongoing mental debate about whether or not to invite him inside. Whether she did or didn't wouldn't matter. He'd already decided that the evening would end at her door. She was expecting him to push, so he'd decided to pull back a little.

She turned at the door, her key in hand.

"It's late," she said, her breathy tone in contrast to the dismissive statement.

"Yes, it is," he agreed. "Good night, Arden."

He turned away. And he smiled as he walked down the stairs because he knew she was staring after him, stunned.

She'd expected him to kiss her. She'd *wanted* him to kiss her. He'd seen the desire in her eyes that mirrored his own. But he'd decided to stop being so predictable, to give her a dose of the unexpected. And though his body was craving full contact, his mind was satisfied with the strategic retreat. He knew he was in for another sleepless night, but he was willing to bet that Arden would be tossing and turning as well.

Arden had to be in court Friday morning, for which she was grateful. After her dinner with Shaun the previous evening, she'd tossed and turned all night. She tried not to think about him, tried not to speculate as to what was going on between them, but it was an exercise in futility. When she finally did sleep, she dreamed about him.

She wasn't comfortable with the array of emotions he evoked in her, not the least of which was desire. It wasn't as if she'd never been attracted to a man before. She'd had boyfriends, lovers, but she'd never felt the depth or strength of passion that she felt when she was with Shaun. Not even with Brad.

She didn't want a relationship. She didn't have time for complications. But she couldn't stop thinking about Shaun.

She was tired and a little dejected when she returned to the office after her morning in court. She loved her work—it gave her a sense of accomplishment and a feeling of satisfaction to know that she was doing something important to help people.

She didn't feel as if she'd helped anyone today. Against Arden's advice, her client had insisted on withdrawing her application for a protection order and reconciling with her estranged husband. The client's decision had almost broken Arden's heart, partly because she was afraid for her client, mostly because of the client's eight-year-old daughter. The little girl had stood silently by her mother's side, her wide blue eyes filled with a mixture of fear and helplessness and resignation. Arden knew those emotions only too well, and she could do nothing to help her.

It was days like this that she wished she'd chosen a profession that was less emotionally demanding. But she took a deep breath, straightened her shoulders and prepared to enter the chaos of her office.

She wasn't prepared for the flowers.

They were sitting in the center of her desk—a huge bouquet of yellow gerbera daisies. She reached up and brushed a fingertip gently over the velvety soft petals, then buried her nose in the flowers, inhaling their subtle fragrance. She picked up the card that was tucked amid the blooms.

"Just wanted to let you know I was thinking about you, Shaun."

She felt her heart sigh and chastised herself for the reaction. She'd told him that flowers and candlelight wouldn't change her mind about becoming involved with him, and yet here she was, mooning over a bunch of yellow blossoms. Her only consolation was that he couldn't see her, wouldn't know the effect the gesture had on her.

She pushed the vase to the corner of her desk, where she'd be able to see them throughout the day and think of him. She'd been so sure she had Shaun McIver pegged, but he was turning out to be a lot more complex than she'd expected. A lot more complex than she wanted.

She'd told him, time and time again, that she didn't want a relationship. Every time she did, he nodded in apparent agreement, then did something—like send her beautiful gerberas for absolutely no reason—that made her want to reconsider. Maybe it wouldn't be so bad to be in a relationship, she thought briefly, if it was with someone like Shaun.

She shook her head. Getting involved with Shaun was a bad idea. Tempting, but still bad. Besides, she was no longer even certain that Shaun wanted to get involved with her. The kiss he'd laid on her before dinner had practically buckled her knees, but at the end of the evening, when he'd walked her up to her apartment, he'd simply wished her good-night and turned away. He hadn't even *attempted* to kiss her again. And she'd wanted him to kiss her, dammit.

She shook her head, shook off the frustration. Knowing

Shaun, he was sending her these mixed signals on purpose, deliberately trying to keep her off balance. Maybe hoping she'd topple right into his bed. She wouldn't—couldn't—let that happen.

But her heart gave another little sigh as she ran her fingers over the words he'd inscribed on the florist's card. Then she tucked it away in the top drawer of her desk, out of sight of prying eyes.

"Nice flowers."

Arden jolted, then quickly slammed the drawer shut as her cousin walked through the door.

"Hi, Nic."

"Hello." Nikki paused to sniff at the blooms, smiled. "These are gorgeous."

Arden nodded.

"There's no card," Nikki said, disappointed. "Who are they from?"

"Maybe I bought them myself—to brighten up the office."

Nikki tilted her head, as if considering. "It's not something you would think of. You keep your office stocked with pens and paper and toys for the kids, but flowers are purely decorative. I don't think I've ever seen flowers in here before."

Probably because no one had ever sent her flowers before. "Well, now you have."

"So who sent them?"

"A friend."

Nikki smiled again. "We should all have friends like that."

"Did you need some legal advice?" Arden asked pointedly. She never minded when Nikki stopped by her office, but she didn't want to answer any questions that led back to Shaun.

"No. I need a favor."

"What's that?"

"A baby-sitter for tonight, if you don't already have plans."

"When do I ever have plans?" Arden asked.

"When do you ever have flowers on your desk?" Nikki countered.

"I told you—they're from a friend."

Nikki shrugged. "And maybe you have plans with this...friend...tonight."

"I don't," was all Arden said.

Shaun sat at his desk, staring at the telephone as if he could will it to ring. He'd debated an inordinate amount of time about whether or not to send the flowers. With any other woman, he would have just followed his gut. With Arden he was always second-guessing his own instincts.

Once he'd made the decision to send flowers, he'd debated even longer about what kind. Roses were too common; orchids too flashy; carnations too plain. He considered a mixed bouquet—a combination of the ordinary and the extraordinary. When he'd seen the gerberas, the decision had been made. They reminded him of Arden: bright and beautiful and unpretentious.

It had seemed like the right idea at the time. Now that he knew it was too late to rescind his order, he wasn't so sure. And it annoyed him that he was so preoccupied with her response to the gesture.

This wasn't at all what he wanted from their... relationship, he decided, for lack of a better term. He wanted a casual distraction, something simple and easy. Instead he was all tied up in knots trying to anticipate her reaction to a gesture as simple as a delivery of flowers.

She wasn't his type, he reminded himself. She was too stubborn and independent. He wanted a woman he could take care of; someone who needed him. And yet, it was Arden who occupied his every waking thought. Arden who haunted his dreams.

She must have received the flowers by now. Would she call to acknowledge the gift? Did she like them? He groaned under his breath. For all he knew, Arden could be allergic to flowers and she couldn't dial the phone because she was wheezing and covered in hives. He shook his head, exasperated with his own wild imaginings. He didn't have time for daydreams; he had work to do.

But when Claire buzzed through to say that Arden was on the line, he leaped for the phone.

He forgot all his annoyance and paranoia when he heard the low, sexy voice that never failed to punch him in the gut. He knew she had no idea how unconsciously seductive that voice was. Arden could talk about legal precedents or coffee or laundry in that voice, and all he could think about was sex. Not sex in general; sex with Arden.

He shifted uncomfortably in his chair and forced himself to concentrate on the words she was speaking.

"They're beautiful," she said.

"I'm glad you like them," he told her. "I wasn't sure if you had a favorite flower. Or if you were allergic to flowers. And I was walking by the florist, and it was an impulse and—" He broke off, horrified to realize that he was babbling.

"Thank you," she said softly.

He swallowed, grateful that she couldn't see how embarrassed he was. "You're welcome."

There was a short pause, then she said, "Well, I should get back to work. I just wanted to say thanks."

"You're welcome," he said again.

"Goodbye, Shaun."

"Arden, wait." He cleared his throat. "I, uh…I have a couple of tickets to *Shirley Valentine* at the Fairweather Players' Theater tonight, if you're interested."

There was a slight pause before she replied. "I'd love to see it, but I already have plans."

"Oh." He tapped his pen against the blotter on his desk,

annoyed that her refusal bothered him so much. It was, after all, a Friday night, and very short notice. He should have guessed that she'd have plans. "A date?"

She laughed softly. He loved her laugh, the subtle sensuality of it. "Not exactly."

He waited, but no further explanation was forthcoming. "What are your plans?" he asked, irritated that he'd had to pry, irritated that it even mattered to him.

"I'm baby-sitting."

"Oh." He considered. "Carly?"

"Yes. Colin's taking Nikki out to dinner."

"Maybe some other time, then," he said, already formulating a contingency plan.

Chapter 7

"Do you want butter?" Arden asked, raising her voice to be heard over the steady popping of the hot-air popper.

Carly nodded enthusiastically. "Lots and lots."

Arden took a stick of butter out of the fridge and sliced off the end. She put the chunk in a glass bowl and set it in the microwave.

"All done," Carly announced.

Only then did Arden realize the popping had stopped and the plastic bowl was overflowing with hot popcorn. She couldn't help but feel a slight twinge of guilt for her distraction. She loved spending time with Carly. She'd lived with her for the first five years of Carly's life, until Nikki and Colin remarried, and she missed the little girl a lot. But tonight, her thoughts were with Shaun.

She wondered if he'd found someone else to take to the play, and she tried not to imagine who might be sitting beside him in the darkened theater. Sarah Jones, the criminal court clerk, who he'd dated a few times last year? Or Libby Walker, the new corporate attorney he'd recently hired?

She shook off the speculation. It shouldn't matter. It *didn't* matter. After all, it wasn't as if she and Shaun were dating. They were just friends, and that's the way she wanted it. Still, there was at least a small part of her that wished she could have been with him tonight.

She poured the butter over the top of the popcorn. Lots and lots of it, as Carly had requested.

"Let's go watch your movie," she said, helping the child off the counter where she'd sat to watch the popcorn pop.

"Okay." Carly skipped eagerly ahead.

Arden had just stepped into the living room when she heard a knock. She set the bowl of popcorn on the table and went to see who was at the front door.

It was Shaun.

Her heart expanded in her chest, making it difficult to breathe. Somehow she managed to unlock and open the door. "I thought you were supposed to be at a play to-night."

"I gave the tickets away." He didn't wait for an invitation but stepped past her and into the house.

"Uncle Shaun." Carly launched herself off the couch and into Shaun's arms.

Shaun scooped her into the air. "Mmm. You smell like baby powder and popcorn."

Arden sighed wistfully as she watched them together. He was so natural with her, so comfortable. She knew he would be a great father. It was just one more reason she and Shaun were completely wrong for one another.

"Auntie Arden and me were just gonna watch a movie," Carly said.

"The Little Mermaid?" Shaun guessed.

"Uh-huh." Carly nodded emphatically.

"Haven't you worn out that tape yet?"

"She got it on DVD for her birthday," Arden told him.

Shaun rolled his eyes. "Who gave her that?"

Arden grinned. "I did."

"Do you wanna watch it with us?" Carly asked.

"Are you going to share your popcorn?"

"Uh-huh."

"In that case, I'd love to watch it."

Arden pressed a button on the remote to start the movie. "I'm going to get Carly some juice," she said to him. "Do you want something to drink?"

"Sure." He followed her into the kitchen.

Out of sight of the child in the living room, he spun Arden around to face him and covered her lips with his own. She didn't have time to think, to protest. Her mind simply blanked and her body melted into his. She couldn't breathe, but breathing no longer seemed important. Nothing mattered but kissing him back. He deepened the kiss gradually, until her blood was humming, her body was aching and her heart was trembling on the brink of something that terrified her. She pulled away, overwhelmed by the need churning inside her.

"We're supposed to be friends," she said.

He brushed his thumb over her lips, swollen from the pressure of his kiss. "Friendship is a good foundation," he agreed.

She didn't ask for what. She wasn't prepared to debate their relationship again, not when her mind was still swimming from the effects of his kiss. Instead she stepped away, took a minute to steady herself. His signals confused her: one minute he seemed to accept the guidelines she'd set for their relationship, and the next he was kissing her mindless.

It was no wonder her own reactions baffled her. Never had she felt so out of control. Never had she been so willing to relinquish control.

What would happen if she gave in to the impulse and made love with Shaun? She was almost afraid to find out.

She shook off the thought, the temptation. Whether or not she might, at some later date, explore the possibility, it wouldn't be tonight. Not in Nikki and Colin's house with a six-year-old child in the next room.

She went to the refrigerator and pulled out a jug of fruit punch, poured some into a plastic cup for Carly.

"Why did you give your theater tickets away?" she asked.

"Because I wanted to be with you."

Her heart did a slow, cautious roll inside her chest. "I think we've been spending too much time together."

"We're friends," he said, turning her words to his own advantage. "Friends are supposed to spend time together."

"Friends don't kiss like that," she said, almost accusingly.

"Is there something wrong with the way I kiss?"

"You know darned well that isn't what I meant."

He stepped closer. "What did you mean?"

"We need boundaries. If we're going to be friends, you can't kiss me anymore."

"Screw the friendship thing," Shaun growled, dipping his head to nibble down the column of her throat.

"Shaun." She wasn't sure if it was a plea for him to stop or to continue.

"You want me, Arden. As much as I want you."

She couldn't deny it. She didn't dare admit it. "What if Nikki and Colin come home and find you here?"

"They'll assume, correctly, that I stopped by for a visit."

"I don't want them to suspect that there's anything going on between us."

"Why would they?" Shaun countered.

"No more kissing," she said emphatically.

He grinned. "Whatever you say."

Her eyes narrowed, but she passed him a can of cola without further comment.

Carly was yawning hugely by the time the movie ended, and she gave no protest when Arden told her to go upstairs and brush her teeth. She didn't even ask for a story, but kissed both Arden and Shaun good-night and snuggled into her bed, asleep before they'd left the room.

Back in the living room with Shaun, Arden reminded herself that they weren't really alone. But she felt unaccustomedly awkward and self-conscious all of a sudden. He tugged on her hand and pulled her onto the couch beside him. She didn't resist; she didn't want to.

"I can't believe Nikki and Colin are going to have another baby," he said.

"I'm just glad that Colin's going to be around for this one," Arden told him, relieved by his introduction of a neutral topic of conversation. "I don't think I could coach Nikki through another sixteen hours of labor."

"That bad?"

"I often wonder why women willingly put themselves through that kind of pain and torture."

"You don't want to have kids of your own?"

"Not without heavy sedation first."

"Wimp."

She nodded. "Yep."

"Seriously, though. Do you want to have children?"

"Maybe. Someday." She shrugged, as if she'd never given the matter much thought. "How about you?"

"Do I want kids?"

She nodded.

"Yeah, I do. I always said I'd love to have a dozen, but I think it's probably too late for that. I tend to be a traditionalist about certain things, and I'd like to have a wife before the children come along."

"So why are you still single?"

He shrugged. "After my engagement fell apart, it was a long time before I showed any real interest in a woman. And I found myself looking—consciously or not—for someone who was the complete opposite of Jenna."

"Nikki?" Arden guessed.

"How did you know?"

"I lived with her," she reminded him.

"She saw right through me."

"What do you mean?"

"I managed to convince myself that I was in love with Nikki. But she knew it wasn't true. I wanted to love someone like Nikki because she was so different from Jenna."

"So…um…what happened?"

He must have heard the tension in her voice, because the corners of his lips curved. "She kissed me."

Arden frowned.

"She planted a real kiss on me." He paused, sighed dreamily, covered his chuckle with a cough when her eyes narrowed. "But it did nothing—for either of us."

"I'm not sure I get the point."

"There was no chemistry. Nothing."

"There's more to life than chemistry."

"Sure," Shaun agreed. "But without chemistry, there's nothing to build on." He brushed his fingertips over the back of her hand, and the sparks practically danced. She pulled her hand away, tucked it in her lap. "We have chemistry, Arden. And I believe we could build something really special together."

"You're assuming we're going to build something."

"We are."

"Don't I have any say in this?"

"I don't think either one of us does. The attraction between us is stronger than either one of us is to resist it."

"Then maybe we shouldn't spend any more time together."

He laughed. "I'd never have pegged you for the type of woman who'd run away scared."

"I'm not going anywhere," she denied.

"Tell me why you don't believe in love."

She hesitated for a minute, considering how much she wanted to say. "People use love as an excuse to justify hurting each other."

"Who hurt you, Arden?"

She swallowed, already regretting what she'd revealed. "No one."

"Then why have you never fallen in love?"

"I don't want to fall in love," she told him.

"It's not a matter of choice or preference."

"Then what is it?"

He shrugged. "Maybe it's as simple as finding the right person at the right time."

"Do you really believe there's a 'right' person for everyone?"

"I like to think so."

"Maybe you're more optimistic than I am." She smiled. "Or maybe just more naive."

Shaun laughed. "You might be right. But I do think you could be the one for me."

"I'm not a good bet," she warned him.

"I've never believed in playing it safe."

"There's a lot of stuff going on in my life right now."

"Tell me about it," he suggested.

Arden sighed. "I've got at least a dozen cases coming up for pretrial or trial in the next few months. And while I'm trying to prepare for those, I'm also trying to find a temporary—and competent—replacement for my receptionist, who'll be going on maternity leave early in the new year. In a moment of sheer insanity, I committed to serving on the board of directors of Community Legal Services for the next three years. I also have a wonderful but nosy neighbor who keeps prompting me for updates on my new relationship, which is nothing more than friendship, except that the man in question doesn't seem to accept that. And, to top it all off, some nutcase has been sending me threatening letters."

It was the last part, tacked on almost as an afterthought, that had Shaun's blood running cold. "Are you kidding?"

Arden didn't ask which part of her explanation he was referring to. "No."

"Jesus, Arden. Have you told anyone about this?"

"Of course. I've given the letters to the police. They're investigating."

"How many letters?"

She frowned. "Why does it matter how many letters?"

"That night—the first night I went to your apartment, the letter under the door."

She stiffened. "I told you, that was a letter from my landlord."

"You lied to me."

"I did no—"

"You lied to me," he said again. "I could tell you were scared about something that night, that there was something you weren't telling me."

She remained stubbornly silent, not acknowledging the truth, but no longer denying it, either.

"And the next day," he continued, "the gunshots…"

"The police don't think there's a connection."

"But he does know where you live."

She shrugged. "Apparently so."

"You're not listed. Your number's not in the book. How did he find you?"

Arden sighed. "I've already been interrogated."

"I'm sorry, I didn't meant to…" His words trailed off as the full impact of the situation sank in. Despite the copious amount of popcorn he'd consumed, his stomach felt hollow. He couldn't imagine anyone wanting to harm Arden—she was so beautiful and warm and generous—but clearly someone did. He'd been with her when those bullets had come through her window.

He'd believed, because he'd wanted to believe, that it was a random act. Her revelation about the letters forced him to reconsider, and, faced with the very real possibility that her life could be in danger, Shaun knew he would do whatever he could to protect her. Whether she wanted his protection or not.

"Dammit, Arden. You can't just drop a bomb like that and expect me to accept it with no questions asked."

"I don't want to talk about it anymore," she said. "I only told you because I want you to understand why I need some space right now."

She wanted him to give her space? While some wacko was threatening her? No way!

"You think I'm going to back off because some nut's writing you letters?"

"I hope so."

"Well, I'm not. I care about you, Arden. And I'm not going to walk away when your life might be in danger."

"I don't think the threats are real."

"How do you know?"

"It's not the first time I've been threatened."

"It's not?"

She shrugged. "Nothing has ever come of it."

"That's not very reassuring."

"Like I said, the police are handling it."

"Have you told Colin and Nikki?"

"Of course not."

"Why?"

"Because they'd worry. And Nikki's pregnant. She has enough on her mind."

"You have to tell them."

"No! And you can't say anything to them, either."

He could, and he would if he had to. "How can you expect me to keep this a secret?"

Her eyes widened, pleading. "Please, Shaun."

Damn, he was helpless against those eyes.

"All right," he agreed reluctantly. "I'll keep this quiet for now. But *I* want to know if you get any more letters."

She hesitated.

"I mean it, Arden. You keep me informed, or I call in the troops."

"I've been taking care of myself for a lot of years now," she said coolly. "And I don't need or appreciate your interference at this point in my life."

"Tough." Whether she appreciated his so-called interference or not, he had no intention of letting her handle this situation on her own.

Arden lay awake in bed later that night, puzzling over the situation with Shaun. She didn't want to get involved. She didn't think he wanted to get involved, either. He was attracted to her, he wanted to have sex with her, but it didn't go any deeper than that. And she resented that he thought he had a right to interfere in her life, as if he really cared. She was handling the situation, as she'd handled everything else in her life—alone.

But there were moments, like now, when she wished it didn't have to be that way. When she wished she had the courage to admit she was scared and ask for help. When she wished she could open up her heart and let someone in.

She rolled over and bunched her pillow beneath her head. She didn't want *someone;* she wanted Shaun.

She tried to forget about him, but it was no use. Her plan of avoidance was destined to fail if he insisted on showing up everywhere she went. She wanted to be annoyed that he'd intruded on her night with Carly, but secretly she was pleased. Touched that he'd given away prime theater tickets to be with her. No one had ever gone to such lengths just to spend time in her company before, and never had she enjoyed being with anyone as much as she enjoyed being with Shaun. It made her wonder if maybe there was a "right" someone for everyone. And maybe, just maybe, he could be right for her.

She rolled over again and sighed. There was no point in wishing for things that couldn't be. She'd never been able to make a relationship work. Even Brad, who'd professed to love her, had turned away when he'd learned the truth about her past. Shaun wouldn't be any different, and she'd have to be a fool to think otherwise. She wouldn't be such a fool again.

Yet, she almost wanted to be. She hadn't been honest with Shaun when she'd said she might want to have children someday. She *did* want children. She wanted to have a baby so much she ached with the longing.

She couldn't imagine anything more wonderful than carrying a baby in her womb, feeling it grow and move inside her. She wanted a child to lavish with love and affection; she wanted to be the kind of mother she never had. At the same time, she was desperately afraid that she'd end up being like her own mother.

She shook off the thought. It was unlikely she'd ever carry a child in her womb when she couldn't sustain a relationship with a man. Because as much as she wanted a baby, she wanted a husband, a family—the whole package. She wanted what Nikki and Colin had found and forged together.

Arden had been there for every step of Nikki's first pregnancy, she'd watched her belly swell with the child she carried, she'd held her hand through every minute of the sixteen hours of labor. She'd cradled Carly in her arms when she was only a few minutes old: a squalling, wriggling mass still warm from her mother's womb.

That single moment had changed Arden's life. She felt her lips curve as her eyes started to drift shut. Yes, she definitely wanted a child of her own.

When she finally fell asleep, she dreamed about a baby.

She was standing beside the crib, looking down at the sleeping infant. The baby was on its tummy, one arm tucked close to its little body, the other flung wide. She always put him to sleep on his back, as the books said to do, but he insisted on rolling over. His knees were tucked under him, his diapered bottom stuck up in the air.

She reached down and patted it gently, stroked his back, trailed a finger over the soft, downy hair. The baby's eyelashes fluttered a little, as if he was dreaming. One pink cheek was pressed against the mattress, the other round with the natural plumpness of a well-fed infant. His Cupid's-bow lips were slightly parted and subconsciously mimicking the gesture of nursing. Her breasts swelled in response, reminding her that he'd be awake soon for a snack. He wasn't yet sleeping through the night, but she didn't mind.

She sat in the rocking chair beside the crib, content to wait. She could spend hours just sitting and watching him sleep, this miracle of life. Her baby.

She heard something in the hall and glanced at the doorway. She saw the barrel of a rifle just before she heard the shot explode.

She woke up screaming.

Chapter 8

Arden was still out of sorts when she crawled, exhausted and bleary-eyed, out of bed the next morning. After she'd awoken from her nightmare, she'd given up on trying to sleep. She'd been plagued by similar nightmares since Denise and Brian Hemingway had been killed, but her role had always been limited to that of an observer. It had been years since she'd been a victim in her own dreams.

She moved into the kitchen and turned on the coffeemaker. She was going to need a lot of caffeine to get through the day on less than two hours' sleep. Or maybe she could just drown herself in the shower.

She padded into the bathroom and turned on the faucet, adjusted the temperature to cool, shivered as she stepped inside. Ten minutes later her skin was still covered with goose bumps but her mind was at least semifunctional. She followed the scent of coffee back into the kitchen, hoped a good jolt of caffeine would do the rest.

She was refilling her mug for a second cup when she was startled by a brisk knock at the door. She glanced at the clock on the microwave, saw it was only eight-thirty. She couldn't think of anyone who would be at her door at this early hour on a Saturday morning. Her heart leaped and lodged somewhere in the vicinity of her throat, as she recalled her nightmare of the previous evening and the anonymous letters she'd received. She walked resolutely toward the door, refusing to be a victim of her own overactive imagination. Most likely it was Greta Dempsey, needing to borrow one thing or another to bake more cookies.

But when she peeked through the peephole, she saw that it wasn't Mrs. Dempsey on the other side. It was Shaun.

Arden put a hand over her chest, where her heart had started to dance. Sooner or later, she promised herself, she'd stop reacting this way every time she saw him. She hoped it would be sooner rather than later. She turned the dead bolt and opened the door.

Before she could say hello, before she could say anything at all, Shaun had her in his arms, his mouth on hers.

Arden wasn't prepared for the onslaught of emotions, so she just closed her eyes and lost herself in the kiss.

Man, could he kiss.

His lips devoured her, devastated her.

She heard a low moan somewhere deep inside her, and everything else faded away. There was nothing but Shaun, and nothing else mattered.

"Good morning," he said, when he lifted his head.

She blinked, trying to put the world back into focus. "Good morning," she responded huskily.

"That," he said, brushing his lips over hers again, "was for last night."

"Last night?" she echoed, wondering why her brain didn't seem to be functioning.

"Colin and Nikki came home before I could steal a goodnight kiss," he told her.

She cleared her throat, tried to remember the boundaries. "I thought we agreed that there would be no more kissing."

He grinned. "I never agreed to any such thing."

She struggled to remember their conversation of the previous evening, but her mind was still reeling. Still, she was sure she'd objected to the kissing. There was no way they could establish a friendship if he kept kissing her like that, and friendship was all she was prepared to offer right now.

"In fact, I was hoping that you'd just gotten out of bed," he continued. "And that maybe I could talk you back into it."

She wouldn't admit that she was the least bit tempted by his proposition. Boundaries, she reminded herself again. "I was just on my way to the office."

"In that?" He gestured to the old terry cloth bathrobe she'd wrapped around herself when she'd stepped out of the shower.

Arden felt her cheeks color. She'd forgotten that she wasn't dressed. She'd forgotten everything when he'd kissed her. She tightened the belt on her robe, suddenly self-conscious.

"After I get dressed," she said.

"It's Saturday," he reminded her.

"A lot of my clients work Monday to Friday, so they come in on Saturday."

"What time's your first appointment?"

She eyed him warily. "Ten o'clock."

"So you still have lots of time to get to the office."

"I'm *not* going back to bed."

He grinned. "Of course not. The first time we make love, I want to spend hours just touching you."

She ignored the assumption implicit in his statement. She wanted to take issue with the arrogance of his words, but she was afraid any denial on her part might sound more like a challenge. And she wasn't sure that they wouldn't end up in her bedroom if he kissed her again.

"I was only thinking," Shaun continued, as if aware of

the internal battle she was waging. "That maybe we could go somewhere for breakfast."

"I'm not hungry."

"You'll get through the day easier if you fuel your body properly," he told her.

Her body was feeling plenty revved and ready to go after that kiss he'd planted on her. She probably wouldn't even need her habitual dozen cups of coffee this morning. "I appreciate the thought," she said. "But I don't need someone to take care of me."

He sighed. "Why is everything always a battle of wills with you, Doherty?"

"Why do you always think you know what I need?"

"Okay. Let's just say that I would like some breakfast, and I would appreciate some company."

Arden wasn't sure he was being forthright, but she didn't want to make his invitation into a battle. Was she always suspicious? Confrontational? Why couldn't she have just said yes and gone for breakfast? "I could use a cup of coffee," she said.

"That's what we call a compromise," Shaun said cheerfully.

Shaun ordered blueberry waffles with a side of bacon; Arden insisted she only wanted coffee. *Stubborn,* he thought, with a combination of amusement and affection. She challenged him, she intrigued him, and every time he was with her, he found himself falling a little bit more in love.

Love?

He choked on his coffee, nearly spewed it across the table.

Arden's brows drew together. "Are you all right?"

He coughed, nodded. "Yeah. Fine."

Of course he was fine. He was *not* in love. That was ridiculous. Yes, he enjoyed Arden's company. He was undeniably attracted to her. And he wanted—almost desperately—to make love with her. But there was a big difference between making love and being in love. His stomach lurched uncomfortably. He wanted to believe it was hunger pangs, but he knew better. He *was* halfway in love with Arden, and still falling helplessly.

It didn't matter that this wasn't what he wanted, that she wasn't what he wanted. As he'd told her last night, it wasn't about choice or preference. He still wasn't sure that two career-oriented people could make a relationship work, but he knew they had to try.

Arden sipped her own coffee, but she continued to look at him with a mixture of caution and confusion. She'd dressed casually for her office appointments today, in a pair of softly faded jeans that molded to her long legs and the curve of her buttocks. Tucked into the jeans was a peach-colored flannel shirt, of which the top two buttons were undone, revealing a tantalizing glimpse of creamy flesh. Her hair fell loose past her shoulders, like a soft wave of silk that his hands itched to dive into. Her eyes, he noted, were wary, and there were purplish smudges beneath them.

"Rough night?" he asked.

She seemed startled by his question, apprehensive. "Why do you ask?"

"You have shadows under your eyes."

"So much for the wonders of cosmetics," she muttered.

He didn't think he needed to tell her that she still looked beautiful. There was something about her fragile beauty that intrigued him. Her skin was flawless, almost translucent, like the porcelain dolls his mother used to collect. Her outward appearance gave no indication of the strength inside. She was steel wrapped in silk, but even steel had a breaking point.

"I'd like to think you laid awake all night thinking about me," he teased. As he'd done, thinking about her. But he sensed that whatever caused her sleeplessness was deeper in origin.

"Yeah, that's it," she agreed dryly.

"Are you worried about the letters?"

"No."

Any further inquiry was stalled by the delivery of his breakfast. His mouth watered as the plate was set in front of him: two thick Belgian waffles piled high with blueberries and dusted with powdered sugar, a half dozen slices of crisp bacon on the side. He picked up the syrup dispenser, poured a liberal helping of warm maple syrup over everything. Arden, he noted, was eyeing the plate with interest.

He cut off a piece of waffle, bit into it. The pastry was warm and fluffy, the berries plump and tart. He murmured with pleasure.

"This is so-o-o good."

Arden sipped her coffee.

"You have to try it." He cut off another piece and held the fork toward her.

She opened her mouth to accept the offering, then chewed slowly, savoring the rich flavor. "It is good," she admitted.

"Are you sure you don't want your own?"

She shook her head. "No, thanks." But she did nip a slice of bacon from his plate, munched on it while he continued to work his way through the waffles.

"Why do you always seem to be feeding me?" Arden asked.

"I'm trying to fatten you up."

"Why?"

"I like my women soft and cuddly."

Her eyes narrowed; Shaun grinned.

"Did I offend you?"

"Not at all," she said primly. "Because I have no interest in being one of your women."

He chuckled. Damn if he didn't want to haul her into his arms right now and kiss her senseless. As much as she might want to establish boundaries for their relationship, he knew they both wanted the same thing when she was in his arms. When he kissed her, when she kissed him back, nothing else mattered.

"You're not my usual type," he agreed, his tone as casual as if they were discussing the weather forecast.

Her eyes narrowed, but she didn't respond to his bait.

"What is my usual type?" he asked for her, in the same pleasant tone.

She picked up her coffee, sipped again, apparently uninterested. But he knew better.

He tilted his head, studying her. "Petite, blond, compliant. Someone who reads Stephen King and has more in her refrigerator than half a dozen cups of yogurt and diet cola."

"Everything I'm not?" Arden guessed, drawn into the discussion.

"Something like that."

"So why are you here with me?"

He shrugged. "Maybe I can't resist a challenge."

"Is that what I am?" She raised an eyebrow. "A challenge? Is there a pool in the courthouse to see if you can thaw the ice princess?"

"I don't know if there's a pool or not," he told her. "But I know that anyone who uses that name doesn't have a clue about you."

"And you do?"

"I think I'm starting to."

She dropped her eyes. "You're wasting your time if you think I'm going to fall into bed with you. I've already told you that I have no interest in being the latest in your long string of playthings."

"That's not what I want, either."

She stole the last piece of bacon from his plate, nibbled on it.

"Maybe it started out that way," he admitted. "But lately I've been starting to think you might be the one."

Her eyes widened a fraction, and he was sure he detected a hint of panic in their depths. "The one what?"

"The right person at the right time."

She shook her head, as if to deny even the possibility.

Shaun smiled, but didn't push. He'd said enough for one day, and he didn't want to scare her off. She'd figure it out for herself, when she was ready.

"Let's get you to the office," he said instead.

Arden pushed open the door of the little café and stepped into the cool morning. There was a bite in the air, as if winter was already on the doorstep and it wasn't even the middle of October. Shaun took her hand in his, linked their fingers together. The gesture struck her as strangely intimate, but comfortable, as if it was perfectly natural for the two of them to be walking along Court Street holding hands.

She was preoccupied with their breakfast conversation throughout the walk to her office. She didn't believe that Shaun's interest in her was anything more than a passing attraction. He'd admitted that she wasn't his type. She didn't imagine he'd want to spend the next couple of months with her, never mind the rest of his life.

And she wasn't in the market for a relationship, anyway. She wasn't comfortable with intimacy and she wouldn't set herself up for more rejection and heartache. She knew that Shaun McIver could break her heart, because as much as she tried to hold back, to distance herself from her feelings, she was already starting to fall for him. But as long as she was aware of that fact, she felt confident that she was still in control and could prevent herself from getting in too deep.

She unlocked the door of her office and disengaged the alarm. Shaun was right behind her as she walked through the reception area. The ever-efficient Rebecca had stacked the files for her morning appointments on her desk before leaving the night before.

Arden gestured to the pile. "I have to review these before my clients come in."

"Are you trying to get rid of me again?"

She nodded.

"All right, I'll go. I have to put the final touches on those bookcases, anyway." But he stepped closer to her, framed her face in his palms.

She knew he was going to kiss her again, and the anticipation was almost as devastating as the gentle pressure of his mouth on hers. Her eyelids lowered as his lips cruised over hers, slowly, expertly, completely seducing her.

She gave up trying to fight the attraction between them. What was the point in reciting words of denial when this was what she wanted? She knew it wasn't smart, she knew it might be a big mistake, but right now this was what she wanted.

She wound her arms around his neck, buried her fingers in his hair.

Maybe he wasn't so crazy to think that they might be able to build something special. Maybe this was what she'd been looking for, what she needed. Maybe…

"Arden, I have some questions about the separation agreement you asked me to— Oops." Marcy cleared her throat as Arden and Shaun sprang apart. Her lips curved. "Sorry."

Arden tucked a strand of hair behind her ear and stepped behind her desk, needing to put some physical distance between her and Shaun, and to remind herself that this was her office. She was a lawyer, for God's sake, not some hormonal teenager who couldn't control her most basic urges. "Mr. McIver was just leaving."

Shaun waited a beat, as if he wanted to take issue with her dismissal. But then he nodded. "I'll talk to you later, Arden."

"Okay." But she didn't look up from the appointment list on her desk.

"I am so sorry," Marcy said again, after Shaun had gone.

"There's no reason for you to apologize," Arden assured her. "This is a law office and what you walked in on was inappropriate and—"

"Arden," Marcy interrupted. "It's *your* office. You can have sex on the desk if you want." She grinned. "But you might consider locking the door first."

Arden managed a smile in response to the gentle teasing. "I don't do things like that."

"Why not, if that gorgeous hunk of a man is willing? And he seemed, from this perspective, very willing."

Arden felt the color in her cheeks deepen. "Shaun and I are friends." She needed to remind herself, as much as Marcy, of that fact.

"Yes, you did look rather...friendly."

"You had a question about the Randalls' separation agreement?" She needed to get things back on track. She'd spent enough time digressing and daydreaming about Shaun McIver.

Marcy passed her the thick document she'd drafted. "Mr. Randall hasn't given us all the financial information we need, and his company won't provide us with a pension valuation without a signed release from the employee."

"Have you contacted his lawyer?" Arden asked.

"I've tried," Marcy told her. "I've left no less than a dozen messages over the past week. Mr. O'Connor always seems to be in court or with a client."

"Of course he is," Arden agreed testily. "And he wouldn't set foot in his office on a Saturday." She dropped the document on top of the pile of files. "I'll give him a call first thing Monday morning. If we don't hear back from him, we'll go to court to get a compliance order."

"Do you want me to draft the documents?"

Arden shook her head. "No, he'll comply. He's just jerking you around because he thinks he can."

"I wish I could have handled it," Marcy said. "I'm not sure I've been all that much help to you."

Arden glanced up, surprised by the hesitant uncertainty she heard in her associate's voice. "You're kidding, right?"

Marcy shrugged. "You seem to spend so much time explaining things to me, I often wonder if it wouldn't be easier for you to do them yourself."

"Of course not," Arden denied, feeling guilty that she hadn't recognized Marcy's need for reassurance. The younger woman seemed so willing and capable, and Arden had been so preoccupied with everything going on in her own life, she'd never considered that Marcy might be nervous about the new job. "Not only have you been a big help to me, you're already building up your own clientele."

Marcy offered a tentative smile. "I love the work I'm doing."

"Good. Because now that you've been here a few months, I'm not sure how I ever handled things without you."

The smile widened a little. "Thanks."

"But if you don't butt out of my personal life, I'm going to have to fire you."

Chapter 9

"This is getting to be a habit," Lieutenant Creighton said when he strolled into Arden's office Tuesday afternoon.

Arden offered a weak smile. "I wouldn't mind if it stopped."

"I know." He lowered himself into one of the chairs across from her desk, his broad frame dwarfing the chair. "Where's the letter?"

Arden lifted her briefcase onto the desk, flipped the locks open. She lifted the envelope by one corner, hated that her fingers weren't steady.

"I just got this one," she said.

"When?"

She walked over to the bookshelf, wishing she could as easily distance herself from the letter she'd handed over, and crossed her arms under her breasts. "It was in my car when I got out of court this afternoon."

"*In* your car?"

She nodded.

"Was your vehicle locked?"

She nodded again, swallowed uneasily. "Always."

Creighton picked up the letter opener from her desk and sliced through the envelope. Unable to stop herself, Arden stepped toward him as he drew the single page out and unfolded it.

"THE DAY OF RECKONING IS NEAR."

Arden shivered, unnerved by the cryptic message spelled out in bold red letters.

"It sounds like he's getting ready to make a move," Creighton said.

As far as she was concerned, he'd already made a move. He'd been in her office, her apartment, and now, her car. He'd made it clear that he could get to her, he was just taking his time about it. She felt so victimized and vulnerable already, she almost wished he would come after her. Whatever he did couldn't be worse than the waiting and the wondering. But she knew that wasn't true, either, and she felt the helplessness overwhelm her. She didn't know how to deal with this nameless, faceless threat; she couldn't combat an enemy she didn't know.

"Am I just supposed to wait for that to happen?"

"I've requested round-the-clock surveillance, but the captain won't approve it until we know for sure that this isn't some wacko who gets his kicks sending threatening letters."

Arden nodded. She understood that with recent cuts to the police budget they didn't have the manpower to spare to appease her hysteria, and she had received meaningless threats before. But her gut told her that this time it was different. This time it was real.

"I wish you'd reconsider your decision to stay at your apartment. I don't think you should be alone."

"I'm not going to let him scare me out of my home." More important, she wouldn't subject anyone else to the potential danger.

"You should be scared," Creighton told her.

"You just said it might be some harmless wacko."

"No, I said my captain thinks it might be."

"What do you think?"

He hesitated briefly, then pinned her with his steely blue gaze. "I think he's dangerous."

While she appreciated his honesty, it did nothing to appease the tension inside her.

His words echoed in her mind, and the tension remained hours later when she returned to her empty apartment. Alone.

When Shaun called, as he seemed to be in the habit of doing every night now, she was absurdly relieved just to hear the sound of his voice. It made her wonder, not for the first time, if Shaun McIver wasn't potentially more dangerous to her peace of mind than some anonymous pen pal. Because just the sound of his voice, the deep, soothing timbre of it, made her forget about everything but him. The realization was more than a little disconcerting. She was, after all, an independent and self-sufficient career woman. She took care of herself—she always had. She didn't need anyone.

Except she wasn't entirely convinced of that anymore. She felt so helpless and out of control, and she wanted to lean on somebody. On Shaun.

"How was your day?" he asked.

She shook off the memory of the letter and Lieutenant Creighton's visit and everything else and allowed herself to be soothed by his voice. "Fine."

"Did you think about me?"

"Not at all," she lied.

"Yeah." She could hear the smile in his voice, felt her own lips curve in response. "That's what I figured."

"How was your day?" she asked.

"The same," he said. "Except that I've been thinking about you."

"Shaun." She tried to infuse a note of warning into her voice.

"What?"

"We're just friends."

"Of course," he agreed. "Do you have any plans for tomorrow night?"

No, was the response that came immediately to mind. But she knew better than to give him an opening. "Why?"

"Because I thought you might want to see the new Pierce Brosnan film."

"Are you asking me on a date?"

"Of course not. I'm just suggesting a movie with a friend."

"That's all?" she asked warily.

"Maybe some popcorn, too."

Arden laughed.

"Is that a yes?"

"Yes," she agreed.

So they went to the movies the following night. Then to the art gallery the night after that, and the Fairweather Fall Carnival two days later. Any time Arden expressed concern that maybe they were spending too much time with each other, Shaun would assure her it was natural for friends to want to be together. And because she enjoyed being with him, she let herself believe it was true. But every minute she spent with him, she found herself falling just a little bit more in…like, she decided firmly.

Tuesday night Shaun took her to DiMarco's for dinner again, ostensibly to celebrate his success in having a client acquitted. Arden didn't care what excuses he made anymore. She just enjoyed being with him. So they shared succulent chateaubriand, a wonderful bottle of cabernet sauvignon and stimulating conversation. It amazed her that they never ran out of things to talk about.

Shaun signaled the waiter for the check. "I'm going to Washington tomorrow for a seminar. I won't be back until

Friday, but you can reach me at the Courtland Hotel in Georgetown if you need me.''

Arden fought the instinctive surge of disappointment. It was, she assured herself, a natural reaction considering how much time they'd spent together. It certainly wasn't anything more personal than that. ''You don't have to clear your schedule with me,'' she said.

Shaun shook his head. ''You still don't get it, do you?''

She was almost afraid to ask. ''Get what?''

''This. Us.''

''It's not like we're dating. We're friends.''

''Yes, we are,'' he agreed. ''And more.''

''I don't want anything more.''

He picked up her hand and brushed his lips over her knuckles. She tugged her hand away, uncomfortable with the myriad of sensations the brief caress elicited.

Shaun's grin was quick, his gaze heated. ''Liar.''

She frowned but didn't comment.

''Have you been seeing anyone else over the past couple of weeks?'' he asked.

''Of course not, but—''

''Do you think I've been seeing anyone else?''

''Well, no, but—''

''Then I'd say we're exclusive.''

Arden exhaled slowly. How was it, she wondered, that she never managed to win an argument against Shaun? ''*Exclusive* implies a certain intention toward the relationship.''

''Uh-huh.'' He sounded almost amused as he scribbled on the credit card receipt the waiter had brought to the table.

''I have no objection to you going out with other women, if that's what you want.''

''Really?'' His lips twitched in the beginning of a smile.

Arden's frown deepened. She didn't *want* him to date other women, but she wasn't in a position to set down rules for their relationship when she was the one who kept insisting she didn't want a relationship.

"Well, I *do* object to you going out with other men," he told her.

"I'm not going out with other men."

"Good. Then we don't have a problem."

"But if I wanted to, that would be *my* choice."

"I don't think so."

"I'm not going to argue with you about this," Arden said. "It's irrelevant, anyway."

"Maybe it is. But you've missed my point."

"What was that?"

"I have no intention of sharing you, Arden." The confident assurance in his tone sent a quick thrill through her, even as it irritated her.

"I'm not yours to share."

"Yes, you are. You just haven't realized it yet."

"This macho attitude isn't very endearing."

"It isn't meant to be. I'm only telling you the way it is." He pushed away from the table and offered a hand to help Arden out of her chair. Deeply ingrained manners had her accepting, despite the fact that she was seething inside.

She didn't say anything to him on the way back to her apartment. There was no point, she decided, in trying to have an intelligent conversation with a man who was little more than a Neanderthal. Her silence didn't seem to bother Shaun, which only irritated her more, and when he pulled up in front of her building, she was out of the car before he could come around to help her.

Still, he was at her side before she reached the door, and he walked with her up to the third floor. If he thought that she was going to invite him inside for coffee, he was mistaken.

To her further irritation, he didn't attempt to wrangle an invitation. He just brushed a soft kiss on her mouth. It wasn't even a kiss, really, just a brief touch of his lips to hers. Just enough to make her want more.

"I'll pick you up Friday night at seven," he said, then turned away.

"Wait a minute," Arden called to his retreating form. "We don't have plans for Friday night."

He stopped at the top of the stairs and turned back to face her. "Sure we do," he insisted. "Judge Morrison's retirement party."

She frowned. "I'm not going with you."

"Why not?"

"Because."

"That's hardly a reasonable explanation," he chided, walking toward her again.

Arden sighed. "If we show up together, if we leave together, people will think we're a couple."

"Why is that a problem?"

"Because I'm not ready to have my picture posted in the ladies' room as Shaun McIver's flavor of the week."

"Flavor of the week, huh?" He sounded amused by the designation, which only annoyed her further. Then he bent his head to kiss her, stroking his tongue along the seam of her lips. "Mmm," he said. "I think it will take longer than a week to satisfy my craving for you, Doherty."

"That's hardly reassuring," Arden told him.

Shaun chuckled. "Will you go to Judge Morrison's retirement party with me if I promise to wear a badge that says 'Just Friends'?"

Arden felt the corners of her mouth tilt. "Maybe."

"I'll pick you up at seven," he said again.

She blew out an exasperated breath. "Do you always get your own way?"

"Always."

Arden prided herself on being a confident and successful career woman. She'd worked hard to earn the respect of her peers, to establish her professional reputation. After six years practicing as a family law attorney, she often still experienced nerves prior to a big court appearance. She'd never felt gargantuan butterflies kicking up a tornado inside her stomach before a date.

But that's what was happening Friday afternoon as she counted down the last few hours until Shaun was due back from his conference in Washington, until he would pick her up for Judge Morrison's retirement party.

So she wasn't sure if she was relieved or disappointed when Shaun called from the airport at six-thirty.

"I'm sorry," he apologized. "My flight was late leaving Washington and we just landed. I'm going to be at least another hour."

"That's okay," she said. "Marcy was about to head over to the courthouse, so I'll tag along with her."

"I'll be there as soon as I can," he promised. Then, more softly, "I missed you, Arden."

Her heart did a long, slow somersault in her chest. "You've only been gone three days."

"You didn't miss me?" The disappointment in his voice cut through her self-protective instincts.

"Maybe. A little."

"That's good enough," he said. "I'll see you soon."

Arden hung up the phone, completely unaware of the dreamy smile on her face, until Marcy spoke from the doorway.

"That must have been your...friend," Marcy said, tongue-in-cheek.

Arden felt her face grow warm. "Let's go drink to the judge."

They hadn't been at the Barristers' Lounge ten minutes when Marcy was whisked away by another colleague to discuss a proposed custody agreement between their respective clients. Arden didn't object to being abandoned by her associate. She was pleased by how well Marcy was fitting in with the Fairweather legal community.

So while Marcy was off talking shop, Arden mingled,

trying to keep herself occupied while she waited for Shaun to arrive. She made her way through the throng of people to Judge Morrison, offered her best wishes for his retirement, then moved on again.

She found herself hovering near the door, glancing at her watch every few minutes.

"Looking to make a quick getaway?" a masculine voice teased close to her ear.

Startled, embarrassed that she'd been caught watching the door, she turned to the speaker. "Hello, Warren."

He smiled at her, revealing perfect white teeth. He was a classically handsome man, with thick dark hair, strong features and pale blue eyes.

"Have you been here long?" he asked.

"Not really," Arden said. "But I was thinking I could use some fresh air. It's kind of stuffy in here."

Those pale eyes lit up with interest, and she realized—too late, obviously—how her words could be misconstrued.

"Would you like to take a walk?" he asked.

"Um…well…" *Hell,* she thought, berating herself for the slip. If she hadn't been so preoccupied thinking about Shaun, she wouldn't have found herself in this situation. "Sure."

He smiled. "Great."

She followed him out of the building. Warren took her arm to help her descend the concrete steps. It was a gentlemanly gesture, and yet Arden couldn't help but feel uncomfortable with the touch. He dropped her arm when they'd reached the bottom. Arden wrapped her arms around herself, surprised by how chilly it had turned in the past hour since she'd left the office.

"Would you like my jacket?" Warren asked solicitously.

"No, thanks." She forced a smile. "I'm fine."

He turned toward the park at the edge of the courthouse. It was almost dark, but she could make out the outline of the fountain at its center. It reminded her of Shaun and the day he'd found her there. She wondered again where he was, but she guessed he'd probably encountered some rush hour traffic.

She bit back a sigh. She hadn't wanted to come to this party with him anyway. So why was she so disappointed that he wasn't here?

She pushed him out of her mind, tried to focus her attention on the man beside her. Warren had been in Fairweather only since June, having moved from California to fill the vacant ADA position. "Now that summer's over, what do you think of Pennsylvania?"

Warren grimaced more than smiled. "It's cold."

"This isn't cold," Arden told him. "Wait till the snow comes."

"When should I expect that?"

"Usually the end of November until the end of March."

"I guess I'll have to get some boots."

"And trade in your surfboard for a snowmobile," she teased.

"That, too," he agreed.

"Do you miss it?"

"What…the sun, the sand, the surf?" He waved a hand dismissively. "What's that compared to all of this?"

She laughed softly as the dried leaves crunched under their feet. "Do you have plans to go back?"

"Not anytime in the near future," he said, as they turned back toward the courthouse.

"There you are."

She jolted as Shaun's voice carried through the darkness, an unexpected warmth spreading through her. The warmth chilled slightly when she stepped closer and saw his eyes narrow on the man by her side.

"McIver," Warren said tersely.

Shaun nodded. "Blake."

The apparent animosity between the two men wasn't entirely unexpected. After all, Warren was an ADA and Shaun was a criminal defense attorney, but Arden sensed that their dislike of each other went beyond professional differences.

What surprised her more was when Shaun leaned over and kissed her full on the lips. It wasn't a greeting, she realized with a mixture of shock and annoyance, so much as a brand.

Warren shifted, tension radiating from him. "I didn't realize you two were here together."

"Shaun just got here," Arden said, feeling a little overwhelmed by the testosterone in the air. She might have been amused at the way the two men circled each other like rabid dogs, if she didn't feel like she was the bone they were fighting over.

"I got tied up out of town." He slipped his arm around Arden's waist, splayed his hand over her hip. "But I'm here now."

"Warren and I were in the middle of a conversation," she said pointedly.

"It's okay," Warren said, surprising her with his easy withdrawal. "We can catch up another time."

Before she could agree or disagree, he'd walked away.

"What was that about?" Arden demanded when Warren was out of earshot.

"Why don't you tell me?" Shaun said.

Arden lifted an eyebrow. "It was stuffy inside, so I accepted Warren's offer to get some fresh air while I waited for you to show up."

He blew out a breath. "I'm sorry I was late. And I'm sorry if I overreacted. It's just that I've been looking forward to seeing you all day, and I didn't expect to find you with Blake when I got here."

"You did overreact," she agreed, more puzzled than angry now. Then she raised herself on her toes to touch her lips to his in a brief kiss. "But I'm glad you're here."

He wrapped his arms around her and kissed her again. Longer this time, lingering. "Let's get out of here."

"You haven't even seen the judge."

"Judge?"

Arden smiled. "Judge Morrison. It's *his* retirement party," she reminded him.

He sighed. "Five minutes. Then we're out of here."

"You have other plans for the evening?"

"You bet I do. And they don't include anyone but you and me."

True to his word, they circled the room for no more than five minutes. Shaun made a beeline for the judge, spoke a few words to him, then whisked Arden away so fast she knew more than a few eyebrows had been raised. And she knew she'd get a full interrogation from Marcy the following morning.

Right now she didn't care. Shaun had only been gone three days, but she'd missed him. It was disconcerting to realize how quickly he'd ingrained himself in her life. How much she'd looked forward to seeing him or talking to him every day. How much she was looking forward to some time alone with him. The depth of her own emotions scared her, but it scared her more to imagine her life without him in it.

He pulled into the parking lot of her apartment building, then helped her out of his vehicle. "You have five minutes to pack."

"Pack?" She halted her steps and turned to face him.

"Those plans I was talking about," he told her. "Just you and me and a little hotel by the lake."

"I can't go away," Arden protested. "I have appointments tomorrow and—"

"Marcy's already agreed to cover for you," Shaun told her. "We only have to drop your pager at the office on our way out."

Arden didn't know whether to be grateful or annoyed that he'd considered and taken care of her clients. "You've thought of everything, haven't you?"

He smiled. "I hope so."

"Except that it's the end of October," she felt compelled to point out. "It's going to be freezing by the lake."

His smile only widened. "I didn't figure we'd be doing much sight-seeing."

"Then why do we need to go away?"

Shaun brushed his hand over her hair, combed his fingers through the ends and tipped her head back. "Because you matter to me," he said. "And I want this weekend to be special for both of us. I want you to know how much you mean to me."

"It will be special, as long as we're together," she assured him.

He touched his lips to hers. "Let's go get you packed."

She led the way up to her apartment, her stomach knotted with nervous anticipation. She'd never gone away for the weekend with a man before. When she pulled her small suitcase out of the closet and began to pack, the contents of her wardrobe made that fact painfully clear. She had nothing appropriate for a romantic liaison. Her lingerie ran to white cotton rather than satin and lace. Simple, not sexy.

She sighed. Would Shaun be disappointed? Was he the type of man who went for frills? It had never mattered to her before. She'd never paid much attention to the things she wore closest to her skin. After all, no one ever saw them. Tonight, Shaun would see them. And she didn't want him to be disappointed.

Unfortunately, there was little she could do about her predicament on such short notice. If he didn't like her plain white cotton, too bad. He could sleep alone.

She hoped he liked white cotton. She didn't want to sleep alone anymore.

Chapter 10

The hour-long drive from Fairweather to Little Bandit Lake was a *long* hour drive. Every minute that passed, every mile they covered, brought them a step closer to their destination, and to the culmination of their mutual desire. It was, for Arden, like sixty minutes of deliciously excruciating fore-play. By the time Shaun turned into the long, winding drive that led to the picturesque hotel, her body was taut with expectation, the nerves along her skin fairly humming with anticipation.

She'd only ever seen pictures of Wallingford House, and although she was duly impressed by the exterior of the majestic four-story brick building with towering columns standing sentry over the ornately carved oak doors at the center, she was anxious to see the inside. Inside their room.

Shaun pulled up in front of the hotel, and before Arden could even reach for the door handle, it was opened from the other side by a uniformed attendant. He helped her descend, while another attendant took the keys from Shaun. A bellhop came out to take their luggage and escort them to

the front desk for check-in. Shaun dealt with the formaliti
while Arden admired the opulent decor of the lobby. The
were enormous chandeliers dripping crystal, real Itali
marble flooring, gleaming antique tables and fussy chai
and settees.

"What do you think?" Shaun asked, returning to her sid

"Wow." It was all she could manage.

Shaun grinned. "Yeah, that was pretty much my reacti
the first time I was here."

Had it been with another woman? She decided she didn
want to know.

"Come on," he said, taking her hand as the bellhop le
the way to the elevator.

The employee gave them a brief history of the hotel
they rode to their suite on the top floor. Arden didn't he
a single word. All she could think was that they were finall
here. Finally alone. Or they would be as soon as they coul
get rid of the chatty bellhop.

But he was not to be rushed. He slid the key card int
another ornately carved wood door. An interesting comb
nation of the modern and traditional, Arden mused. Then h
led them through the suite, turning on lights, opening cu
tains, demonstrating how the gas fireplace worked, recitin
the hours of the dining room.

Arden wandered through the suite. There were, she note
with some confusion, two bedrooms leading off from th
sitting area, each with its own ensuite. She wandered bac
into the other room in time to see Shaun pressing sever
bills into the hand of their uniformed chaperon as he steere
him back to the door.

"I didn't think he was ever going to leave," Shaun sai
flipping the lock on the door. Then he turned and held o
his hand to her.

She went willingly, if somewhat hesitantly. She sti
wasn't sure if she'd misunderstood his intentions in invitin
her here for the weekend. She'd thought they were going

consummate their relationship, but the presence of the two beds suggested otherwise.

Then he lowered his head to kiss her, and she tasted a hint of the passion he'd held in check over the past couple of weeks, and she met his need with her own. Mouths crushed together, tongues mated, bodies strained. She wanted him.

Oh, how she wanted him.

She didn't stop to think about the wisdom of her actions. All she'd done was think about her relationship with Shaun and where it was going, and she was still as confused as ever. But the wanting, that was real and compelling, and she wasn't strong enough to fight it anymore.

But Shaun pulled away, his breathing harsh and ragged. "I didn't bring you here to seduce you."

"Oh." She didn't manage to disguise the disappointment she felt. "Why did you bring me here?"

"Because I thought you could use a break from everything that's been going on. And because I wanted to spend some time alone with you."

"And if I don't want to have sex?" There was no reluctance behind the question, just simple curiosity.

"It's your call, Arden. Whatever you want."

Any lingering nervousness dissipated with those words. It wasn't just that he'd said them, but that she knew he meant them. He'd reserved a room with two beds because he didn't want her to feel pressured.

She hadn't realized how important it was to her to feel that she had some control over the situation, but Shaun had. It worried her, if she thought about it, how well he knew her already, how much he could see inside her. And it liberated her, to know that he understood her.

"I want you, Shaun. I want to make love with you," she told him.

His breath caught and his eyes darkened perceptibly, but he stepped back, away from her. He cleared his throat. "I'm trying to show some restraint here. I thought you might at least want to take a walk into the village or explore the hotel.''

His procrastination, his uncertainty, empowered her. "It's too late for a walk or a tour," she said. "And I think you've been restrained long enough."

She began unfastening the long row of buttons down the front of her jacket. The last of her doubts were cast aside by the flare of hunger in his eyes. He wanted her, hopefully as much as she wanted him.

He put his hands over hers, halting their progress. "Are you sure?"

She nodded. There was no hesitation in her response, none in her heart. "Yes."

He linked his fingers with hers, pulled her hands down by her sides. "Let me," he whispered the words against her lips. "I've been dreaming about this for a long time."

Me, too, she admitted to herself as his lips plundered hers again. There was more than a hint of passion in his kiss now, no evidence of his earlier restraint.

He slipped the jacket from her shoulders, tossed it carelessly onto the sofa, then moved on to her blouse. The back of his knuckles brushed against her skin as he worked his way down the front, and she shivered. He pushed the garment down, used the sleeves to pin her arms at her sides. His mouth left hers, skimmed down the column of her throat, lower to the curve of her breast. His tongue trailed along the edge of her bra, his breath warm and moist on her skin.

All her concerns about her lack of appropriate lingerie were forgotten as he closed his mouth over one cotton-covered breast.

She gasped as his teeth grazed the pebbled nipple, the pleasure arrowing so sharp and deep inside her it was almost painful. She hadn't even been aware of him unfastening the clasp at the back of her bra until he nudged it aside and continued the exquisite torture of her breast without the fabric barrier. His mouth was hot and hungry, fueling a matching hunger inside her.

Arden tugged at his tie, fumbled with the buttons of his shirt. She pushed it off his shoulders, needing to put her hands on his skin, to feel his flesh beneath her fingertips.

She hadn't realized he'd unfastened her skirt until she felt his hands work it over her hips. Of course, his lips were still doing wonderful things to her breasts, so it was a wonder she was cognizant of anything else. He quickly stripped away her underwear, leaving her naked before him.

"You are so beautiful." His words were little more than a breathless whisper, and Arden felt the last of the barriers around her heart begin to crumble. It wasn't just the words—she'd heard them before—but the way he said them. She knew he meant them and that made her feel beautiful.

Then he lifted her off her feet and carried her into the closest bedroom. He laid her down on top of the covers, then stood beside her, just staring down at her. She didn't feel at all self-conscious. She felt wanted. And she wanted in return.

She raised her arms to him in silent invitation. He paused only long enough to strip off the rest of his own clothes before lowering himself onto the bed beside her. She turned to him, met his mouth with her own as her hands moved over him, eager and searching, reaching for the evidence of his desire, wanting to give him even a fraction of the pleasure he'd already given her.

She wrapped her hand around the hard length of his shaft, heard the groan rumble deep in his throat. Smiling, she stroked her hand downward, then up again. He grasped her wrist in his fingers, raised her hand up over her head and held it there.

"I want to touch you," she told him.

"Honey, if you keep touching me like that, it's going to be all over before we get started," he warned.

Any response she might have made was lost when he slid down her body. The friction of his skin on hers caused all kinds of sensations to run rampant through her system. Everything was so sharp and close and she felt an incredible pressure starting to build inside her, coiling low and tight in her belly. His hands were on her breasts again, his thumbs rasping over her peaked nipples, as he trailed hot, hungry kisses down to her navel, then lower still.

She screamed out as his tongue delved inside her, her hips arching off the bed instinctively as the first climax ripped through her. She hadn't been prepared for the intensity of the explosion, the aftershocks that rippled through her body. She'd never experienced anything like it before, wasn't sure she'd live through it. She was certain she couldn't survive a second time.

But Shaun had other ideas. He waited until her shudders subsided, then he drove her up again. She wanted to protest, to beg him to stop, but she could hardly even breathe, never mind speak. And she was rushing toward that peak again, and she didn't want him to stop.

She was gasping, her body quivering, when he finally covered himself with a condom and slipped inside her. She wrapped her arms and legs around him, clinging to him, drawing him deeper inside.

Then he began to move. Slow, steady strokes that seemed to touch the very center of her being, driving her again to the edge of that desperate, greedy pleasure. She matched his rhythm, their bodies moving in tandem, their hearts beating as one, until they finally leaped over the edge together.

Afterward, as Arden lay quietly in his arms, Shaun was stunned, overwhelmed, by the emotions that coursed through him. None of his fantasies had prepared him for the reality of making love with Arden. Nothing had prepared him for an experience that was as satisfying emotionally as it had been physically. It was so much more than the culmination of desire. It was a life-altering experience. He stroked a hand down her back, tracing along her spine. He loved to touch her, the feel of her warm, silky skin beneath his hands, the passion of her responses.

"Thank you," she murmured sleepily.

He lifted his head to look down at her. Her eyes were closed, her lips curved in a satisfied smile. And he wanted her all over again.

"What are you thanking me for?"

"For showing me how incredible making love could be."

Her words stunned him, humbled him. He hadn't shown her anything. It was she who had opened him up to a whole new experience.

"I've never felt so..." Her words trailed off, her eyelids flickered open. "I've never felt like that before. I didn't believe it was possible."

"Are you telling me..." He hesitated, looking for the right words to phrase the question, failing.

"I've never had an orgasm before," Arden admitted. She glanced away, her cheeks flushing.

Never? He was speechless.

"I never understood what the big deal was...about sex." Her eyes were soft, her smile warm, as she looked up at him again. "Now I know."

"I never understood the difference between having sex and making love," he told her, meaning it. "Now I know."

Her smile widened. "That's a really sweet thing to say."

He winced. "It's not sweet, it's true."

"I'm glad. I wasn't sure if—" she blew out an impatient breath "—I didn't want you to be disappointed."

"I'm not disappointed," he told her.

"Good."

She took another condom from the box he'd left on the bedside table and removed the wrapper. He was almost embarrassed by the enthusiasm with which his manhood stood up again to be sheathed. She rolled the condom onto his erection, and his eyes practically rolled back into his head.

"I am sorry that I didn't take my time with you," he said, trying to focus on conversation rather than the impatient demands of his body. "I wanted to give you romance and seduction."

He pulled her on top of him, kissed her slowly, thoroughly.

"You can make it up to me later," she said, pulling her knees up so that she was straddling him. She rocked forward slightly and took him inside her in one long, deep thrust.

Now his eyes did roll back in his head. Heaven help him, he thought, if she ever figured out the power she had over him. Then she was moving her hips, and he wasn't thinking at all.

Arden woke early Sunday morning, but she wasn't in a hurry to get out of bed. She felt comfortable with Shaun, more so than she would have expected. She'd always been a little self-conscious about her body, more than a little uncomfortable with her own nakedness. Not with Shaun. During the past thirty-six hours he'd touched every inch of her bare skin with his hands, caressed every curve and angle with his lips, and loved her body with his own.

He'd taught her so much in such a short period of time about the giving and receiving of pleasure, and she knew that, regardless of whatever else might happen between them, she'd always be grateful to him for that.

A low murmur of pleasure hummed in her throat as his hand skimmed over her hip to cup her breast.

"You are awake." His voice was still rough with sleep, his breath warm on her ear.

"Mmm-hmm." But she closed her eyes again as his thumb brushed over the tingling peak of her nipple. She felt the familiar tension already beginning to build deep in her belly, the aching warmth spread between her legs.

"Good." He rolled her onto her back and levered himself

over top of her, the hard length of his shaft pressing against her leg.

She shifted to position him more firmly between her thighs, her hips arching instinctively off the mattress, her body seeking the fulfillment of his.

"Not yet," he said. He combed his fingers through her hair and touched his mouth to hers. A teasing caress more than a kiss. Gentle, fleeting. Then his lips skimmed over her cheek, nibbled down the column of her throat. His hands moved over her skin softly, slowly.

Arden thought she knew by now what it was like to make love with Shaun. She was wrong. Everything was different this time. The very air she breathed seemed richer, intoxicatingly sweet. Every moment stretched into an eternity, drawing her inexorably deeper into a swirling vortex of building desire. Each kiss was agonizingly tender, every touch gloriously gentle.

When he finally sheathed himself in a condom and slipped between her thighs, filling her, fulfilling her, nothing else in the world mattered.

He kissed her again. "I don't ever want to leave here."

"We have to," Arden said, with more than a little regret. She glanced over at the glowing numbers of the alarm clock on the bedside table. "Very soon, in fact. We have less than an hour before checkout."

"It would be worth paying for an extra day to hold you in my arms just a little while longer."

Arden's heart sighed. Gorgeous, sexy, and charming. "You could come back to my place and hold me for free."

She hadn't intended to issue such an invitation. She didn't want to assume anything beyond the right now; she didn't want to think about what would happen when they had to return to the real world.

"Or you could come home with me," Shaun countered. "I have a king-size bed."

"How do you know I don't?" Arden demanded, both pleased and relieved by the reciprocal invitation.

"You're a very practical woman, and a king-size bed is impractical for a woman sleeping alone. Besides, I peeked into your bedroom while you were packing."

"Practical," she echoed. "As in boring?"

Shaun smiled. "No. One thing you're not is boring." He nuzzled her throat. "What do you say, Doherty? Will you come home with me?"

Arden hesitated, not because she didn't want to, but because she did. Maybe too much.

"Please," he said.

"Okay."

A short while later he pulled into the driveway beside the two-story Georgian-style house that was his home. It wasn't the first time Arden had been there. In fact, she'd attended a barbecue at his house a few months earlier, but that was with Nikki and Colin. This time it was just her and Shaun, and she was nervous. Terrified, even. Not of what would happen when she walked through the door with him, but of what had already happened.

How could she keep sharing her body with this incredible man and expect to keep her heart intact?

Then he pulled her into the house and closed the door behind them. Arden met him eagerly, lips meshed, bodies aligned. He backed her down the hallway and into the kitchen, then lifted her onto the table. She wrapped her legs around him, drawing him closer to the heat pulsing inside her. He tugged on her bottom lip with his teeth, then his tongue soothed the gentle ache, slipped between her parted lips. Arden sighed, leaning into him, losing herself in his kiss.

She felt his hands at the front of her blouse, slipping the buttons free. His movements were steady, quick, determined. Then the garment was gone, and his hand covered her breast through the thin fabric of her bra. She gasped as his thumb moved over the already taut peak, enticing, teasing. She felt her blood heat, pulse, and she went to work tugging his shirt out of his jeans.

His lips skimmed along her jaw, down the column of her throat, and she shivered with anticipation. His mouth moved lower, over the curve of her breast, to fasten over the straining nipple. "I seem to recall you promising me a king-size bed," Arden managed to get the words out between gasps and moans.

"In a minute," he promised, pushing her skirt up over her thighs.

Just as the doorbell chimed.

Shaun hesitated, swore under his breath, then lifted Arden into his arms and moved decisively to the stairs.

"I'm not answering that," he said, when the bell chimed again.

"It might be important," Arden said.

"Not as important as getting you upstairs," Shaun told her.

Arden smiled. "Go to the door to get rid of your visitor, then we can go upstairs."

He set her feet back on the ground, pressed a brief but firm kiss on her already swollen lips. "Don't move."

"I'm not going anywhere," she assured him.

He pulled open the door, his most ominous glare in place. He didn't want to give his uninvited visitor any hope that he was in the mood for company. The only person he wanted to be with right now was Arden, naked and sweaty.

He swore again when he found his brother on the doorstep. "Don't you have a wife to go home to?" Shaun asked testily.

Colin didn't wait for an invitation but pushed past his brother and into the house. "She's having some kind of candle party tonight—told me not to rush home."

"Well, find somewhere else to hang out," Shaun advised. "I'm busy."

"Busy?" Colin's confusion edged away as he smiled in understanding. "Hot date?"

Before Shaun could confirm, as he intended to do in order to speed his brother out the door, Arden stepped into the kitchen. The buttons on her blouse had been refastened, the hem tucked back into her skirt, but her lips were bare, swollen from his kisses, and her hair sexily disheveled.

She looked as if she'd just rolled out of bed, and he couldn't wait to roll her into his. It didn't matter that they'd already made love more than half a dozen times this weekend, he wanted her again, wanted her with an intensity that shook him to the very core.

"Just me," Arden told Colin, forcing a smile.

"Arden." Colin looked from his wife's cousin to his brother, and back again.

"Shaun, um, offered to lend me some research...for a case I'm working on."

The words spilled out of Arden's mouth in a rush, and with them came a stab of pain, quick and unexpected. He hadn't realized it would be so easy, so effortless, for her to hurt him.

He knew that she was reluctant to let Nikki and Colin know they were involved, and he thought he understood. But he also thought if she was willing to take their relationship to the next level, she'd be willing to admit to others that they were a couple. Obviously, he'd been wrong.

Arden turned back to him, but she wouldn't quite meet his eyes. "If you can't find the book, maybe it's at your office. I'll give you a call on Monday and pick it up there."

Hurt turned to anger, began to churn hot inside him. "Fine," he agreed abruptly.

She grabbed her purse from where she'd dropped it on the counter, just minutes before she'd ended up panting and breathless beneath him on the kitchen table, her blouse open, her skirt up around her hips. Now she was acting as if none of that had meant anything, as if the weekend hadn't meant anything.

She pulled her keys out of the little purse, then realized she was stranded. "If I could just borrow your phone, to call a cab."

"That's not necessary," Shaun said tightly. "I'll take you home."

She shook her head, almost desperately, he thought. "It's out of your way."

"It's not out of mine," Colin said, a slight edge to his voice as he glanced accusingly at his brother.

"I thought you wanted to visit with Shaun."

Colin shrugged. "He doesn't seem very sociable tonight."

Shaun could tell his brother knew exactly what he'd interrupted, and that he wasn't the least bit sorry. He wasn't sure who he should be angrier with—Colin for bad timing, or Arden for her complete about-face. He'd never known a woman who ran hot and cold the way she did. If she didn't know what she wanted, that was her problem. There were plenty of other women in this town.

The thought was hardly reassuring. He only wanted Arden. And that was *his* problem.

Arden cast a quick, hesitant glance in his direction before turning to Colin. "I'd appreciate the ride home, if you're sure you don't mind."

"Of course not." Colin nodded at him. "I'll talk to you later."

Shaun didn't bother to respond; Arden didn't even say goodbye.

Chapter 11

Arden was more than a little distracted Monday morning. She went through the motions of meeting with her clients, asked all the right questions more out of habit than concentration. She knew she had to see Shaun, had to explain what had happened last night. He'd been angry when she'd left with Colin, and she didn't blame him. One minute they'd been engaged in the most intimate act of a man and a woman, and the next she'd bailed on him.

Marcy, sensing her mood, didn't ask about her weekend with Shaun. Arden knew she should be grateful for her discretion, but she needed to talk to someone about what had happened. In the past, if she'd been bothered by anything, she wouldn't have hesitated to call Nikki. She didn't think that would be wise under the circumstances.

She knew she'd messed things up with Shaun. He might not understand what had caused her abrupt turnaround the night before. She wasn't sure she understood it herself. She'd never been good at the games men and women played, but she did know that she owed Shaun an explanation.

Still, her heart was in her throat as she left the office to drive across town to the tidy little suburb where Shaun lived. She'd thought about calling first, but this way, if she lost her nerve, she could just turn the car around and go home.

Wimp.

She nodded. Yes, she was a wimp. And she was terrified to think that she might have ruined the best relationship she'd almost ever had.

She turned onto Meadowvale Street, half hoping that Shaun wouldn't be home.

She eased up on the gas pedal as his house came into view, braking lightly when she spotted his car in the driveway. She pulled into the lane behind the Lexus just as the front door opened and Shaun stepped outside.

He was wearing black jeans and a leather jacket open over a dark green shirt. Her heart tripped, raced. She got out of the car, moved determinedly toward the front step.

"You look as if you're on your way out," Arden tried to sound casual, although her stomach was a mass of nerves.

"I have a few minutes," he said, after a brief hesitation.

Arden nodded. "I wanted to explain. About last night."

He waited.

The expression on his face was as stern and unyielding as that of Judge Baldwin in youth court. She'd never been so nervous facing Judge Baldwin; she'd never had so much at stake. "Can I come in?"

He shrugged. "You might want to move your car down the street," he said. "Before someone you know drives by and sees it parked in my driveway."

Arden knew the comment was no less than she deserved.

She ventured into the kitchen, tried not to look at the table. Tried not to remember that she'd been half-naked on top of it, her body tangled with his.

"Can I get you anything?" he asked, as politely as he would offer refreshment to a stranger.

She folded her arms at her waist, bracing herself. This was already harder than she'd expected. The distance that had grown between them in less than twenty-four hours seemed insurmountable. "No, thank you," she responded to the question in a tone that matched his.

"You said you were going to explain," Shaun said, after a minute of very tense silence had passed.

She nodded, but still she hesitated. She'd never been good at talking about her feelings, about expressing what she wanted, what she needed. It had been easier to hide behind a smile, pretend everything was okay. But she couldn't do that with Shaun.

"Everything just happened so fast," she admitted at last. "When I heard Colin's voice, when I remembered that the man I was having sex with was my cousin's husband's brother, I panicked. I knew Colin would go running home to tell Nikki that something was going on between us."

"So?"

She sighed. "You don't understand what Nikki would do with this information."

"What would she do? Rent a billboard? Put an ad in the paper?"

"Send out wedding invitations," Arden muttered.

Shaun frowned.

"Nikki's in love. She's happy. So she wants everyone else to be happy. And if she found out that you and I were…involved, she'd jump to all kinds of conclusions."

"You don't know that," he said.

"I know Nikki."

"Are you saying that you wouldn't ever tell her the truth?"

"I don't know what the truth is," she said. "How can I explain our relationship to her when I'm not sure I understand it myself?"

"Yesterday I could have answered that question," he said. "Now I have no clue."

"What would you have said?" she countered. "What would you have told Colin if he'd asked about me?"

"I would have told him that, for the first time in a long time, I'd found a woman who really mattered to me."

"Oh." His words humbled her. "I'm sorry."

"Sorry that I care about you?"

"Sorry that I walked out on you."

"I'm not going to pretend I understand," Shaun said.

"Sex is supposed to be simple."

Now he smiled. "Not if it's done right."

"I wanted it to be simple. But I..." She looked away, uncomfortable admitting her own feelings. "I...I care about you, too."

"Then what's the problem?"

"*That* is the problem."

"So far this explanation is only confusing me more."

"I'm sorry. I'm not used to talking about my feelings."

He frowned. "Isn't that what the man's supposed to say?"

"It's the truth." She hesitated again before confessing, "I've got a lot of emotional baggage, Shaun. You shouldn't get involved with me."

"I know your parents died when you were young, and that's why you grew up with Nikki."

"That's part of it," she admitted.

"But what does that have to do with us?"

"I can't lie to Nikki. I wouldn't be able to tell her that we were dating without her asking all kinds of questions. Without her somehow realizing how I feel about you. I love her to pieces, but I don't need her interfering in my life and trying to make it into some happily-ever-after fairy tale like what she's found with Colin. And I don't want her to be disappointed when it doesn't work out the way she'd hoped."

Shaun's eyes narrowed. "You don't want Nikki to know we're dating because you don't want to disappoint her?"

Arden frowned at the way he'd summarized the situation, but she nodded.

"Okay, even if I accepted your explanation, it fails to take into consideration the possibility—as far-fetched as it may seem—that it might work out between us."

She wanted to believe that was possible. She wanted to let herself hope that she might be able to make a relationship with Shaun work. But, "It's just too soon," she told him. "Everything's happening too fast."

"You didn't seem to have any trouble keeping up on the weekend."

She nodded. "I just think that if we're going to continue…having sex…we should talk about the situation."

"Why?"

"Because I want to make sure we both know what to expect."

"What do you want—to negotiate terms and conditions?" Shaun's voice was tight.

He was annoyed again, but she didn't let it sway her. She needed to believe she had some control over the situation. "It seems reasonable."

"No."

She frowned.

"We're talking about making love," he told her. "Not writing a damn contract."

"I'm only trying to be practical."

"How can you expect to be practical about your emotions?"

"I don't know," she admitted. "I just know that I need some time to figure this out."

He sighed. "Okay."

Despite his obvious reluctance, she knew she was forgiven when he slipped his arms around her and pulled her close. It wasn't a passionate embrace so much as a comforting one, and still her body responded immediately to his nearness.

She put a tight rein on her hormones. After all, that was what had gotten her into trouble last night. But she let herself lay her head against his chest, where she could hear the pounding of his heart. It was steady and strong, so much like Shaun.

"I wasn't going to call you," he told her.

"I know."

"I'm glad you came by."

"Me, too."

"I never meant to rush you. I didn't want to push you into something you weren't ready for. I just—" his breath blew out in a rush "—I still want you, Arden, but we can take a step back if you want. If you need to."

She shook her head. "I want to be with you," she told him. "I just need some time to get used to our being together."

"I can give you time," he promised.

But how much? she wondered. How long would he be satisfied with what she could give him? And what would happen when he found out about her?

Arden was in court all day Tuesday. The only break she had was for lunch at one-thirty. She left her briefcase in the courtroom while she went to the cafeteria to grab a sandwich. Ten minutes later, when she returned to review her file for the afternoon, she found the letter.

Just the presence of the envelope had shaken her so much she'd considered asking the judge for a postponement of the proceedings. Instead she'd squared her shoulders and called Lieutenant Creighton to get rid of the damn thing. She refused to let her stalker have that much control over her life.

Somehow she made it through the rest of the day without anyone seeing how she was trembling inside. Now court

was finished and she was back at the office, having to face
Lieutenant Creighton and the letter again.

"This was in your briefcase?" Creighton asked, holding
up the letter she'd passed off to him earlier.

Arden nodded, trying not to look at the carefully printed
message. Not wanting to see the words spelled out in blood-
red ink.

"YOU'RE GOING TO BURN IN HELL."

She drew in a deep breath. It's just a letter, she reminded
herself. A piece of paper. It couldn't hurt her. But she could
almost feel the hatred, the loathing, in the person who'd
penned those words, and that scared her.

"In the courthouse?"

She nodded again.

Creighton shook his head. "He's either extremely stupid
or too damn cocky."

Arden would have bet on the latter. Every step her mys-
terious pen pal had taken thus far indicated a carefully orchestrated plan. He was confident and determined and smart.
And for reasons still unknown, she was his target.

"You need to consider some kind of protection," Creighton said.

She managed a smile. "I know a cop who sometimes
sleeps in his car outside my apartment building."

The lieutenant shifted self-consciously, as if embarrassed
that she'd caught him watching out for her. "I can't be there
all the time."

"I appreciate that you've been there at all. I know you're
not pulling any overtime for your surveillance."

He shrugged his broad shoulders. "I can not sleep in my
vehicle as easily as in my bed."

She didn't ask for an explanation. She knew of the tragic
circumstances under which Creighton had lost his wife several years earlier, and she knew that beneath the tough exterior, he was still hurting. And she wondered if his willingness to go the extra mile to protect her was an innate

part of his nature, or perhaps an attempt to save her because he hadn't been able to save the woman he'd loved.

"If you know I've been watching your apartment, your stalker probably knows it, too," he warned. "And if he's going to make a move, it will be when my car's not parked in front of your building."

Arden nodded.

"This is getting serious, Ms. Doherty. You can't just sit back and wait for him to follow through on his threats."

"We don't know that he will," she said. "I've been threatened before, and nothing has ever come of it."

"I don't like this," Creighton muttered.

She didn't, either, but she didn't see that there was anything she could do about it—except wait and hope that the threats were simply that.

"I'll put in a request for round-the-clock surveillance on you," he said, "but I don't expect it to be approved. We don't have the manpower for that kind of thing."

"I'll be okay," Arden said, determined to hide the fact that she was a bundle of nerves inside.

Creighton nodded and bagged the letter. "Is there anyone you can stay with until we catch the perp? Family? Friends?"

She shook her head again, more vehemently this time. If the threats were real, the last thing she was going to do was subject her family to that danger.

"I'll let you know about the surveillance," he said, rising from his chair.

"Thank you."

She followed him to the door, anxious for him to go. Once he was gone, she could try to forget about the letter or at least put it out of her mind for a while by burying herself in work.

Unfortunately, Lieutenant Creighton was walking out as Shaun was walking in. Arden pasted a smile on her face and steeled herself for the next round of interrogation.

* * *

"What was Creighton doing here?" Shaun asked without preamble as he stepped into Arden's office.

She closed the door behind him.

"How do you know Lieutenant Creighton?" Arden asked.

The fact that she hadn't answered his initial question confirmed the uneasy suspicion in his mind. "You got another letter, didn't you?"

She exhaled wearily, nodded.

"What did it say?"

"More of the same. They've just been vague threats."

"Have the police got any leads?"

"Not yet," she admitted.

He knew the police were doing everything they could, and it frustrated him that they had nothing to go on. He wanted this to be over. He didn't want Arden to be afraid anymore.

"How do you know Creighton?" Arden asked again.

"He's a cop, I'm a defense attorney."

"Professional adversaries."

"I don't have to like him to respect him. He's a hell of a good witness on the stand. Almost unshakable," he admitted with grudging admiration. Which gave him a small measure of reassurance. If Creighton found whoever was writing the letters, he'd put him behind bars.

"I don't want to talk about it anymore," Arden said, sinking into the chair behind her desk.

He fought back the surge of annoyance. He knew she preferred to deal with things on her own, to prove to herself that she could, and he knew he wouldn't get anywhere with her by forcing the issue. She would neither welcome nor thank him for his interference. But eventually he would make her realize that she wasn't on her own.

He walked behind the desk, settled his hands on her

shoulders and started to massage gently. "Do you want to cancel for tonight?"

"Tonight?" she echoed blankly.

"The theater. *Rosencrantz and Guildenstern are Dead.* The tickets I bribed you with to be my date for the Law Ball." He knew she'd been looking forward to the production, and the fact that she'd forgotten about their plans didn't so much annoy as concern him.

"Oh." She let her head fall back against the chair, her eyes closed. "No. I think I need to get out and just forget everything for a while."

He turned her chair around, tugged on her hands to draw her to her feet. "Let me help you forget for a while."

He touched his lips to hers, intending to offer her comfort, and found solace for his own heart in her response.

"Better?" he asked, when he'd at last eased his mouth from hers.

"Much." She pulled out of his arms and sighed. "And that's half of the problem."

"What are you talking about?"

She wrapped her arms around herself, something he'd learned she did when she was nervous or upset about something. "I need to deal with things on my own."

Her response irritated him. "Fine. But one of the things you have to deal with is me."

"Dammit, Shaun. This is exactly what I *didn't* want."

"Tough."

"I've changed my mind," she said. "I am canceling our plans for tonight."

"No."

She whirled back to face him. "What?"

"No." He closed the lid on her briefcase and picked it up. "Let's go."

"I'm not going anywhere with you."

"Sure you are. We have a date."

"Which I just canceled."

"I could sue you for breach of contract." It was, he thought, an inspired argument.

"What contract?"

"Our date."

"A date is *not* a contract."

"*Cummings* v. *Wilson*. Massachusetts Supreme Court, 1978."

She frowned. "That doesn't sound familiar."

He made a clicking sound against the roof of his mouth with his tongue and shook his head. "Rita Cummings sued her fiancé for the cost of her wedding dress and deposit on the reception hall when he backed out of their wedding. The court ruled that his proposal was a contract, and his breaking of their engagement a breach of that contract."

She didn't look convinced. "We're not engaged."

"We had a date."

"You can't sue me for breaking a date. You haven't suffered any damages."

"Disappointment, loss of companionship, the price of your ticket."

"You're trying to blackmail me again." But she sounded more exasperated than angry.

He leaned over and brushed his lips gently against hers. "Whatever works."

She exhaled slowly. "Are you that desperate for a date, McIver?"

"I'm that desperate to spend time with you."

"I'm going to be miserable," she warned.

"I'll take my chances."

"Fine."

He bit back a smile as he followed her to the door.

As much as she hated being maneuvered, Arden had to admit that spending time with Shaun was just what she needed to get her mind off the letter she'd received that afternoon. The play had been entertaining and enjoyable, and she'd managed to lose herself in the action onstage for a couple of hours. Afterward, they'd gone to DiMarco's for a late dinner, then Shaun had taken her home.

"I'm glad you decided not to stay mad," Shaun said.

"I'm not still mad," she agreed. "But I do have a question."

"What is it?"

"*Cunningham* v. *Watson*. Was there ever any such case?"

"Of course," he said.

She shook her head. "And *Cummings* v. *Wilson?*"

She saw him flinch as the trap she'd set neatly ensnared him.

"I'm not good with case names," he hedged.

Arden laughed softly, but she let it go. How could she stay annoyed with a man who went to such lengths to spend time with her? Especially when all she wanted was to be with him, too.

Chapter 12

"You're a difficult woman to catch up with lately," Nikki said as she tucked her feet beneath herself on Arden's sofa Wednesday night.

Arden knew she should have been prepared for the third-degree. She and Nikki had always been close, and it was only a matter of time before her cousin clued in to the fact that there was something going on in Arden's life. In fact, she was surprised it had taken Nikki this long to get around to her interrogation, and yet she still didn't know what to tell her cousin. She didn't want to lie to her, and anything less than the truth would be a lie. But how could she tell Nikki that she'd had the most incredible sex of her life with Nikki's brother-in-law?

"I've been busy," she hedged.

"Obviously. I tried calling you all weekend."

"I was away."

"Really?"

Arden couldn't blame her cousin for sounding so surprised. It wasn't like Arden to go out of town without letting Nikki in on her plans.

"By yourself?" Nikki prompted.

Arden sighed. "No."

"Hmm."

"Don't 'hmm' me," Arden muttered. "I can practically hear the gears in your brain clicking away."

Nikki grinned. "Then you must know that I'm happy to see you happy."

"I can't talk to you about this."

"I'm not asking any questions."

"That only makes it harder," Arden told her. "If you were badgering me for details, I could tell you to mind your own business. But you're just sitting there with that smug smile on your face, and I feel like I'm deceiving you."

"Why?"

"Because I haven't told you who I was with this weekend."

"I'm guessing it was Shaun," Nikki said easily.

Arden felt her jaw drop open.

Nikki shrugged. "Did you really think I didn't know?"

"Well...yeah."

Now her cousin smiled. "I'd have to be blind not to see the vibes that have been passing between the two of you lately."

"Are you...okay...with this?"

"Why wouldn't I be?"

"Because I spent the weekend—" and both nights since then "—having wild sex with your brother-in-law."

Nikki's smile widened. "Wild, huh?"

"You're missing my point," Arden said dryly.

"I don't think so. The only thing that matters is that you had a good time."

"It was amazing," Arden admitted. "But—" she blew out a breath "—I just don't know what's going to happen now. Where things are going from here."

"What do you mean?" Nikki demanded. "Did he imply that it was over? Thanks for a good time and so long?"

"No. Of course not." Arden was anxious to divert any potential tirade on her behalf. "But we've just kind of been taking it one day at a time, and this was a big step for me. For us. And…" She smiled again, still awed by what she'd found with Shaun. "I never knew making love could be like that. So…everything."

"It is when it's with the right person," Nikki said knowingly.

Arden's smile slipped, and she shook her head. "Don't start thinking about orange blossoms and wedding gowns," she warned.

"I just want you to be happy," Nikki told her.

"I am happy."

"Then I'm happy," Nikki said. "Although I can't deny that I am a little worried, too."

"I can handle this," Arden said, not certain whether she was trying to convince her cousin or herself.

Nikki nodded. "I know. I'm worried about Shaun."

"Shaun?"

"He's the sweetest guy I know," Nikki said. "He puts it all on the line. If he's not already in love with you, he will be. And I don't want you to hurt him. If you're not willing to follow through, to see where this goes, tell him now."

"He knows what I want from this relationship," she said. At least, as much as she herself knew.

"I'm not suggesting you've been dishonest," Nikki said gently. "I am concerned that he'll think he can change your mind. That he might be thinking forever, while you're thinking for the next few months."

"I care about him," Arden said. "I wouldn't have gone away with him this weekend if I didn't."

"I know." Nikki sighed.

Arden knew her cousin was still going to worry, which

made Arden worry. She wouldn't regret the weekend, but she was once again reminded that nothing this good could last forever. And she hated to think that Shaun might get hurt when everything fell apart.

While Arden was being interrogated by Nikki, Shaun was subjected to a similar, if slightly more subtle, questioning from his brother. He endured it graciously, only because he knew Colin's questions were motivated by his concern for Arden.

"I don't want any details," Colin said, helping himself to a bottle of beer from his brother's refrigerator. "I just want to know if the two of you are still on speaking terms."

Shaun decided that he might be willing to endure the interrogation, but he didn't have to make it easy. "The two of who?"

Colin took a long swallow of beer. "Cut the crap. I know you spent the weekend with Arden."

"How do you know that?"

"Because both you and Arden were out of town on the weekend, and I obviously interrupted something hot and heavy when I stopped by Sunday afternoon."

"You should have been a rocket scientist instead of a hockey player," Shaun said dryly.

Colin shrugged. "Just confirm that everything went okay, so that I don't have to worry about Nikki worrying about Arden."

Shaun couldn't prevent the grin. "Everything went okay."

"Geez, Shaun. I don't need to know that kind of stuff."

"I didn't say anything."

"It was the look." Colin shook his head. "Man, I never thought I would see the day that you fell again."

"Fell?"

"In love."

"I'm not—" The denial had risen immediately to his lips,

but he couldn't speak the words. And he wondered if maybe his brother wasn't right. He remembered how he'd felt when Arden had walked out Sunday night. He'd never minded living alone in the four-bedroom house—he liked the space, the solitude. But after spending the weekend with Arden, the house had seemed emptier than usual. He'd felt alone. Incomplete.

"Maybe I am in love," he admitted at last.

Colin raised his glass, drank. "It happens to the best of us," he said. Then, "What does Arden have to say about it?"

Shaun didn't have to think about the question. "She'd panic."

"She doesn't know?"

"No."

"You plan on telling her anytime soon?"

"I think I need some time to get used to it myself." Then he'd figure out some way to ease her into it. To help her realize that she loved him, too.

Colin shrugged. "It's your life."

It was, Shaun realized. And nothing in his life mattered to him more than Arden.

He continued to ponder the situation long after Colin had gone. He hadn't been joking when he'd said Arden would probably panic if she knew how he felt. The realization had almost sent him into a tailspin.

He'd only ever been in love once before, with Jenna. But what he'd felt for his former fiancée was different from what he felt for Arden. He'd been a lot younger when he'd known Jenna, easily dazzled by her effervescent personality. No one would ever describe Arden as effervescent. She was, however, as committed to her career as Jenna had been. And that worried him.

Was he destined to fall in love with women who subjugated their personal lives to professional obligations?

Arden had made it clear that her clients were her priority.

But with Jenna, it had all been part of a master plan to get ahead—to become the rich and successful attorney. Arden's motivation went deeper. Her law practice wasn't just a business to her, she cared about her clients. She fought for them, not because she was being paid to do so, but because they needed her. And because she needed to know that she could make a difference.

She'd already made a difference in his life. She was the strongest woman he'd ever known, almost fiercely independent. He'd thought he wanted a woman who needed him. A wife who would be content to stay at home and have his meals on the table at the end of the day. Okay, so maybe it was chauvinistic and old-fashioned, and he knew now that it wasn't what he was looking for. He wanted a partner in every sense of the word.

And he knew that Arden could be that partner.

Now all he had to do was convince her of the fact.

Less than half an hour after Nikki had gone, Arden pulled open her door to find Shaun on the other side. Her heart jolted, did that long, slow somersault in her chest. She couldn't believe his mere presence still had this effect on her.

"How do you always manage to get into the building without using the intercom?" she asked.

Shaun grinned. "Mrs. Dempsey. She likes me."

Arden shook her head despairingly, but she couldn't deny the truth of his statement.

"Can I come in?" he asked.

Arden stepped back, and he stepped into her apartment. Before she'd even closed the door, he had her in his arms, his mouth on hers. His kiss was long and lingering.

"I've been thinking about you all day," he admitted.

It worried her that his words so clearly mirrored her own feelings. She'd been convinced that she could enter into a consensual sexual relationship with Shaun with her eyes wide-open, that nothing would happen that she didn't want to happen. But somehow her emotions had spiraled wildly out of control.

It hadn't scared her so much on the weekend because she'd convinced herself that it was the romantic atmosphere of the hotel. But this was the real world, and still, he made her feel things she'd never thought she would feel. He made her want things she knew she could never have.

Making love with Shaun was unlike anything she'd ever experienced. Not just because of the mind-blowing orgasms, although those were worth the price of a ticket themselves. But it was so much more than the physical. Being with Shaun, having him beside her, made her feel complete. Fulfilled.

And it terrified her, because she knew she was falling in love with him. Everyone she'd ever loved had left her. From her father, when she was only four years old, to Brad Fullerton, in her last year of law school.

But she'd never had a relationship like this. So easy and relaxed. So comfortable. With anyone else she'd dated, she'd always felt as if she had to be on her best behavior, that she had something to prove. Shaun had never asked her to be anyone but herself. He accepted her, completely and without question.

Of course, he didn't know everything there was to know about her. Would it make a difference to him? She didn't want to think so, but she didn't know. And she was afraid to find out. Afraid that if she did tell him, it would matter, and he wouldn't want to be with her anymore.

His kiss pushed her concerns aside. When he carried her down the hall to her bedroom, she couldn't think about anything but how right it felt to be with him. And when his body joined together with hers, she knew she'd finally found the place where she belonged.

After their bodies were thoroughly sated, Arden sighed and snuggled against him. It was so much more than the sex. It was Shaun. She closed her eyes, finally acknowledging that she was in over her head and helpless to do anything about it. But she didn't have to let him know it. As long as she kept her feelings to herself, she could maintain the illusion of having some control over the situation.

She cared about Shaun, and the affection she felt intensified the experience of their lovemaking. But that didn't mean she was *in* love with him. She certainly didn't *want* to be.

It's not a matter of choice or preference. Shaun's words echoed in her mind, taunted her. Arden banished them to the back of her mind.

Love complicated things. Emotional attachments made people vulnerable. It opened them up to heartache and disappointment. She would enjoy her relationship with Shaun for as long as it lasted, but she would *not* fall in love.

So resolved, she let the strong and steady beat of his heart beneath her cheek lull her into a deep, contented sleep.

Shaun had never given much thought to his morning routine. He got up when the alarm went off, stumbled downstairs to the kitchen to turn on the kettle, then jolted himself into wakefulness with a cold shower. He'd been doing the same thing for too many years to count. But waking with Arden in his bed—well, that was still a new and exciting experience.

She wasn't a morning person. She didn't offer much in the way of conversation until she'd had a shower and at least one cup of coffee. The first night she'd stayed over, she'd been appalled to realize he didn't even own a coffeemaker.

He'd gone out that same day and bought one. Now, when Arden spent the night, he'd turn on the coffeemaker at the same time he put on his kettle. He enjoyed the routine they'd established when she spent the night at his house, or he at her apartment.

It mystified him, how easily she fit into his life, how firmly she'd established a hold on his heart. He knew she wasn't ready to hear how he felt about her, and he was trying to be patient. There was no need to rush when he knew they'd have the rest of their lives together.

"Do you want to catch a movie tonight, or would you rather stay in?" Shaun asked her Friday morning.

"Oh, um, actually, I have other plans." Arden was leaning against the counter, sipping her coffee.

"Other plans?" Shaun frowned, not comfortable with her response, or his instinctive reaction to it. "What kind of plans?"

"I have a dinner meeting."

"With whom?"

"Warren Blake."

He dropped his toast onto a plate, carried it over to the table. There was no point in overreacting, he told himself. If Arden was having dinner with Blake, there was a logical explanation. But he wanted to know what the hell it was. "Why are you going out with the assistant district attorney?"

She refilled her mug with coffee. "It's not a date, Shaun. It's a sentence negotiation."

"Why can't you negotiate during regular business hours?" he grumbled.

"Because he's been tied up in a trial for the past two weeks, and we're back in court early next week for sentencing."

"I'm not going to pretend I like this arrangement."

Arden straightened her shoulders. "This is my job, Shaun."

He sighed. "I know. And if it was anyone but Blake, I wouldn't say anything about it."

"What do you have against Warren?"

"I don't trust him," he admitted.

She frowned. "It's a business dinner."

Sure, he thought. And all he'd wanted was to be her friend. "Be careful."

"Don't you think you're overreacting just a little?"

"No, I don't." He pushed away from the table.

"I can take care of myself."

He smiled and brushed his thumb over her bottom lip. "Make sure you do."

Her tongue traced the path of his thumb, a subconsciously erotic gesture that almost made him forget he was due in court in twenty minutes.

"I'll call you tomorrow," Arden said.

"Call me when you get home."

"I'll call you tomorrow," she said again.

Shaun touched his mouth to hers, nibbled gently on the fullness of her bottom lip until he heard her soft sigh, felt her body yield against him.

"Maybe I'll call you when I get home," she relented.

He walked out of the house with his briefcase in hand, a satisfied smile curving his lips.

When Arden pulled into her designated parking spot outside her apartment building early Saturday morning, she was starting to lose the battle to keep her eyelids open. She was looking forward to a long hot shower and a few hours of sleep—not necessarily in that order. She grabbed her purse off the passenger seat and stepped out of the car. The cold wind slapped her in the face. She wrapped her coat more tightly around herself and headed for the front door.

"Where the hell were you last night?" Shaun demanded.

Arden glanced up, surprised to find him standing there, waiting for her. It was proof of just how tired she was that she hadn't sensed his presence, didn't know how to respond to his confrontational greeting.

"What are you doing here, Shaun?"

"What am I doing here?" he echoed, his tone a mixture of anger and incredulity. "I've been looking for you."

She stifled a yawn. "Why?"

"Because I tried calling you last night. All night. And you never picked up the phone."

"I've been out all night," she said wearily.

"Obviously."

She frowned as she located the front door key on the ring. "For some reason that seems to annoy you."

"For some reason that seems to surprise you," he said sarcastically.

"Do you want to come inside and talk about this, or would you like to continue yelling on the front lawn where all my neighbors can overhear?"

His lips thinned as he came up the front steps. He pulled the door open when she released the lock and stalked down the hall ahead of her. He was waiting outside her apartment when she made her way up the stairs, his expression murderous.

"I need caffeine," Arden said, automatically moving into the kitchen to start brewing a fresh pot of coffee. The shower and sleep would have to wait.

"Didn't get much sleep last night?"

Arden frowned. She hadn't managed to get *any* sleep last night, but somehow she knew that she was missing something here. For some reason that she had yet to understand, Shaun was annoyed with her. Okay, maybe she should have taken a few minutes to call him, to let him know where she was. But it wasn't as if they'd had any plans.

She measured grounds into the filter, remembering that Shaun hadn't been thrilled when she'd told him about her meeting with Warren Blake. Now he was here, and ready to blow a gasket. She slid the basket into place, flipped the switch and turned to him.

"Where do you think I was last night?"

He folded his arms over his chest. "Why don't you tell me?"

She felt her heart sink, just a little. It shouldn't matter

what he thought of her. She'd learned a long time ago not to measure herself by anyone else's expectations. But she'd thought Shaun was different. She'd wanted to believe that he was different.

But she knew now that his macho routine wasn't because he was worried about her or because he'd wanted to be with her. He was angry because he thought she'd spent the night with Warren Blake. As if the ADA was even her type. She felt the sting of tears behind her eyes, fought against them. No way in hell was she going to cry over a man who would think so little of her.

"Apparently you have this all figured out, so why don't you make this easy on both of us and leave? I'm not in the mood to fight with you."

She could tell that her response surprised him. That he'd expected her to deny his accusations. What was the point? If he didn't know her well enough to know that she wouldn't have spent the night in another man's bed, he didn't know her at all.

"Is that what you want—you want me to leave?"

She nodded. "Yes. Please."

He took a step toward the door, then turned back again abruptly. "No."

"No?"

"No," he said again. "I'm not going to make this easy for you."

Her eyes were burning with fatigue, and she let them drift shut for half a minute. She was too exhausted, mentally and physically, to handle a confrontation right now, but she knew he wouldn't give her any choice.

"Dammit, Arden. I was worried about you."

"Because you thought I was with Warren?"

"Because some nutcase has been sending you threatening letters and I had no idea where you were last night. I tried your cell phone, almost every hour all night, but I kept getting your voice mail. I tried to page you, but you neve responded. I was frantic.''

She felt the first nudge of guilt at her subconscious. She' been so wrapped up in what was happening that she hadn' thought about the letters or Shaun or anything else. She wasn't used to having people worry about her. ''I didn't as for this,'' she said defiantly.

''I didn't either,'' he said. ''But this is what we've got.'

''If you have a problem with the way I conduct my life maybe you shouldn't be a part of it.''

''Nice try, Arden.''

She rubbed at the center of her forehead, trying to mas sage away the building pain. ''Why are you doing this?''

''Because I care about you.''

The simple honesty of the statement, the heartfelt emotio in his eyes, dissipated the last lingering vestiges of annoy ance. Still, she sighed. ''I'm not good at this.''

''What 'this'?''

''Relationships.''

He set his hands gently on her shoulders, rubbed then down her arms. ''You'll get better.''

''I'm not used to having to explain myself.''

''I'm not used to pacing a hole through my carpet a 3:00 a.m.''

''I'm sorry. I was paged by an intake worker at the shelte before Warren and I had even finished dinner. She aske me to meet her at the hospital to speak to a woman who' been beaten unconscious by her husband. I went straight t the hospital, and I left my briefcase, including my pager an my cell phone, in the car.

''I spent most of the night with her, explaining her op tions, then I went to the office to draft the documents to ge a restraining order, then I went back to the hospital to ge her to sign them, then I came home.''

''It sounds like you had a rough night.''

''Yeah, I did.''

"And the last thing you needed was for me to jump all over you when you got home this morning."

"Just about," she agreed.

Shaun took a deep breath, prepared to grovel. "I'm sorry."

Arden just nodded wearily, and her obvious fatigue made him feel a million times worse than if she'd yelled and screamed at him. He put his arms around her, breathed a silent sigh of relief when she leaned into him, because he knew it meant that he was forgiven.

When she tried, unsuccessfully, to stifle a yawn, he lifted her off her feet and carried her toward the bedroom.

"What are you doing?" Arden demanded.

"I'm taking you to bed."

"Make-up sex?"

"To sleep," he corrected.

"Oh."

He grinned. "Don't sound so disappointed. I think your body needs rest more than stimulation right now."

She yawned again. "You're probably right."

"After you've had a few hours of shut-eye, then we'll see what happens."

"You're going to stay?"

She sounded surprised, which made him frown. Was he only here when he was getting her naked? Did she think that was all he wanted from her? He pulled back the covers on her bed and laid her down gently. "Yes, I'm going to stay."

Her lips curved, her eyes already closing. "I like having you here."

It was as big an admission as he was likely to get from her, and it pleased him. He lay down beside her, slipped his arm around her to hold her close. "I like being here with you."

* * *

When Arden awoke, the sun was filtering through the blinds, painting horizontal lines of light across the bed. She felt the weight of Shaun's arm across her waist, took comfort in his presence. After a week of going to sleep beside him almost every night, waking in his arms, it still boggled her mind that he wanted to be with her.

When she'd first decided to become intimate with Shaun, she'd based the decision on logic and reason. It was a natural progression of the attraction between them. She didn't expect it to last.

She still knew it wouldn't, it couldn't. But she was determined to savor every moment so long as it did. He'd become more than just a lover. He'd become a friend, a confidant. And she knew that—for the very first time in her life—she was starting to fall in love.

The realization terrified her. Love made rational people do crazy things. Love made people hurt each other, and forgive each other, and open themselves up to more hurt and heartache.

Shaking off the thought, she cast a quick glance at the clock on the dresser. It was just past noon, which meant that she'd slept for almost three hours.

"Sleep well?" His lips cruised over her earlobe, causing shivers of anticipation to dance over her skin.

She turned to him willingly, slid her arms around his neck, and pulled his head down to meet his lips with her own. It was easier to accept the physical aspects of their relationship than the emotional ones, so that was what she focused on now.

She felt his hands skim under her blouse. His touch was warm and familiar, although the intensity of her reaction continued to surprise her. He skimmed a hand over her hip, upward to toy with her breast. She felt her nipple pebble beneath his touch, and the heat coil in her belly.

"Are we going to have make-up sex now?" she asked breathlessly.

She felt his smile against her lips. "Have you forgiven me?"

"Yes," she said.

"Yes," he responded to her question in turn.

Chapter 13

Arden heard the sirens in the distance. She pushed open the courthouse doors, stepped into the night. The fire trucks whizzed past—a blur of flashing lights and screaming alarms. Icy fingers of trepidation trailed down her spine. She could smell the smoke. Its acrid scent hung in the air like a noxious perfume. Assaulting her nostrils. Churning her stomach.

She clutched the handle of her briefcase tighter as she slowly moved across the parking lot to her car. Traffic on the street was at a standstill. Pedestrians clogged the sidewalk. She dumped her research into her car, then made her way through the crowd to stare, horrified, fascinated, as the fire department battled against the flames that poured out of the third floor windows of the apartment.

Her windows.

YOU'RE GOING TO BURN IN HELL.

She could see the bold red ink, the menacing message, as clearly as if the letter was in her hand.

Arden shook her head, tried to shake off the thought. It was a coincidence, nothing more.

She so desperately wanted to believe that, but she knew better.

This was personal.

And she was terrified.

She'd seen enough reports of fires on the eleven-o'clock news, but nothing she'd watched in the safety of her living room had prepared her for this. Nothing had prepared her for the shock of seeing her own home engulfed in flames. The heat was staggering in its intensity; the air was heavy with smoke, burning her eyes, her nose, her throat. Greedy tongues of flame licked at the building, ravenous, devouring.

She scanned the gathering of spectators, breathed a sigh of relief when she saw Mrs. Dempsey dressed in a neon-green housecoat with Rocky tucked under her arm. She also spotted Kelly and Rick Larsen, the newlyweds who'd recently moved in on the second floor, and Mr. Fitzsimmons, the first-floor tenant who was older than the building itself. At last she spotted Gary Morningstar, the landlord, and she slowly meandered through the maze of people toward him.

"Is everyone out of the building?" she asked, shouting to be heard over all the other noise.

Gary turned, the relief on his face palpable. He nodded. "Now that we know you're here, everyone's accounted for." His eyes were tired, his face strained.

"Any idea what happened?"

He shook his head. "It looks like it started upstairs, but it escalated so quickly it's hard to say for sure."

Arden could only nod, her eyes stinging with smoke, with grief, with guilt. All she had left were the clothes on her back: a faded pair of jeans and her University of Michigan sweatshirt, a battered pair of sneakers, jacket, and her cell phone. But it wasn't the loss that bothered her—it was the fear. Not just for herself but for everyone who had been in the building. She knew the fire had started in her apartment.

She knew it had been deliberately set. And she knew that she would have been responsible if anyone had been hurt.

She was jostled aside by a television crew moving in for better footage of the fire. To them it was news. To her it was her life.

A life that was so completely out of her control.

Arden went to Nikki's. She knew her cousin would worry if she saw reports of the fire on the news, so she preempted her concern by going over there. Nikki made a fresh pot of coffee for her, and Colin liberally laced her cup with whiskey. Their care and concern made her smile in spite of everything.

A brief knock sounded at the back door, but before either Nikki or Colin could get up to respond, Shaun came into the kitchen. He ignored his brother and sister-in-law, pulled Arden off the chair and into his arms. He held her so tightly she couldn't breathe, but it felt good to have him there.

"Why didn't you call me?" he demanded.

She swallowed, not certain how to respond to the raw hurt she could see in the depths of his green eyes. Not willing to admit that it had been her first instinct to do so. She'd ignored the impulse to turn to him for comfort and support. She'd been relying on him too much. She prided herself on her independence, her ability to be strong and self-sufficient. She was afraid of losing that to Shaun. She was more afraid that she'd relinquish it willingly.

"I went by your building. Your apartment—" He couldn't complete the thought. "God, Arden. I thought you might have been in there and—"

She laid her palm against his cheek, reassuring him with the comfort of her touch. "I wasn't. I'm fine." Her lips twisted into a wry smile. "Homeless, but fine."

"Of course you're not homeless," Nikki interrupted. "You can stay here as long as you need to."

Arden dropped her hand from Shaun's cheek and turned

to her cousin, embarrassed to realize she'd forgotten, however briefly, that she was there. "I can't stay here," she
protested. "You've just started redoing the spare room for
the baby."

Nikki waved a hand dismissively. "We have plenty of
time for that. And I'm not going to have you living at some
motel when we have more than enough room for you here."

"It used to be your room, anyway," Colin reminded her.

"I appreciate the offer," Arden said, meaning it.
"But—"

"I have more room at my place," Shaun said, surprising
all of them with the statement. Arden especially. She gaped
at him.

"I'm *not* moving in with you," she said. "No matter how
temporarily."

"Why not?"

"B-because." She was sure there was a reason. Probably
half a dozen good reasons. But she couldn't think of a single
one when he was looking at her like that.

"Maybe we should let them talk about this privately,"
Colin suggested, nudging his wife toward the doorway.

"There's nothing to talk about," Arden said. "Because
I'm not staying at Shaun's."

But Nikki and Colin had already disappeared, leaving her
to face off against Shaun alone.

"Why not?" he asked again.

"It's not a good idea," she said, even though she wanted
to take him up on the offer.

"It's the best idea," he argued. "You don't want to im-
pose on Nikki and Colin, but you know Nikki will worry
about you if you're on your own."

"I've been living on my own for a while now," she said
dryly.

"She'll still worry," he reminded her. "Besides, you've
been sleeping at my house most nights, anyway."

It was true, but having a toothbrush in his bathroom

wasn't the same as having her clothes in his dresser. She knew his offer was dictated by circumstances, but moving in with Shaun seemed like such a leap, and she wasn't sure if she was ready.

"Why don't we at least try it for a few days?" Shaun suggested. "If you're not comfortable with the arrangement, I'll help you find someplace else to stay."

"What if *you're* not comfortable with the arrangement?"

"Then I'll let you know."

She was skeptical. "Promise?"

"Yes, I promise." He slipped his arms around her waist and drew her closer. "To be honest, I'm kind of looking forward to having you under my roof for a while. These aren't exactly the circumstances under which I would have hoped for this to happen, but I'm learning to take what I can get."

"You're sure you're okay with this?"

"I offered, didn't I?"

"Okay," she agreed finally.

"Have you guys come to any kind of agreement?" Colin asked, poking his head into the kitchen.

"Yeah. Arden's going to come home with me," Shaun said.

"Good," Nikki said.

Arden raised an eyebrow.

"Come on," Nikki said. "I'll let you raid my closet until you can replace your own things."

"I'd appreciate that," Arden said, following her cousin up the stairs. "The only clothes I have are those on my back." She sniffed, inhaled the acrid scent of smoke that had permeated her attire. "And they don't smell very good."

"Help yourself." Nikki gestured to her closet. "Nothing fits me right now, anyway."

Arden glanced at her cousin's slightly protruding belly and smiled. "You look great," she said honestly, enviously.

What would it be like, she wondered, to carry the child of the man you loved?

"I feel great," Nikki admitted. "We're all so thrilled about the baby. Carly can't wait for her baby sister. No matter how many times we tell her it might be a boy, she keeps insisting otherwise."

"Are you going to ask about the baby's gender?" Arden asked.

"I don't think so. Colin wants to be surprised."

"And you?"

"I just want a healthy baby."

"She will be," Arden said. Then, "Everything's different this time around, isn't it?"

"Yeah." Nikki's smile was luminous. "But shouldn't we be talking about your situation now?"

"What's to talk about? My apartment burned down, and I'm going to stay with Shaun for a few days until I find somewhere else to live."

"Are you sure you don't want to stay here?" Nikki asked. "I was kind of looking forward to having my former roommate back."

"You have your family together now. You don't need me underfoot."

"You're family, too," Nikki reminded her. "And I like having you underfoot."

Arden took a sweater out of the top drawer, tossed it on the bed. She added a couple of T-shirts, a sweatshirt, and a pair of jeans before moving to the closet.

"Do you want to stay with Shaun?" Nikki asked.

Arden sighed. "Yeah, I do."

Nikki smiled. "Those orange blossoms might not be so far off."

"He offered his spare room, he didn't propose."

"Spare room," Nikki scoffed.

"The invitation never would have been issued if my apartment hadn't burned down," Arden said.

Her cousin just smiled. "I guess time will tell."

Arden turned her attention back to the contents of Nikki's closet. She didn't know how to respond to her cousin's teasing. She hadn't allowed herself to think that far ahead. Her relationship with Shaun had already been so much more than she'd expected, so much more than she'd hoped. If she allowed her thoughts to wander, she sometimes found herself thinking that they could have a future together. She wanted to believe they could. But there was still so much they didn't know about each other. So much he didn't know about her.

She pulled a navy skirt out of the closet and tossed it onto the bed. She selected a few more items, blinked back the sudden sting of tears. "I don't even have a spare pair of underwear."

Nikki pulled open a drawer, but Arden shook her head. Nikki's taste ran more to satin and lace than she was accustomed to.

"I'll wash out the ones I have on, so I can wear them again tomorrow. Then I'll have to go shopping."

"Is everything gone?" Nikki asked gently.

Arden shrugged. "I can only assume so," she said. "It wasn't as if I was allowed to go inside and take inventory." She didn't tell her cousin that most of the damage seemed to be focused on her apartment. She didn't want to think about that fact, and wonder, and worry.

It was possible that she'd been wrong to connect the fire to the letters she'd been getting. The fire could have started for any number of reasons—maybe it was faulty wiring or something like that.

And maybe her twisted pen pal had meant it literally when he'd said she would burn in hell.

Shaun had no doubts about why he'd offered to open his home to Arden. When he'd gone by her apartment and found the street blocked off by police barricades and fire trucks, he'd experienced a moment of bone-deep, paralyzing fear unlike anything he could ever have imagined. And in the split second that he'd considered she might be in that burning house, emptiness had threatened to swallow him whole.

It was then he knew, without any doubt or qualification, that he loved her.

And he would do anything to keep her with him.

He knew she wasn't ready to hear how he felt. For whatever reason, he knew she was reluctant to acknowledge the growing emotional ties between them. The sex was great, they laughed and talked and enjoyed being together. But whenever he tried to talk to her about the future of their relationship, she diverted the conversation to other matters.

It intrigued him. Most women he knew were the ones pushing for commitment, wanting to know what was in the future. Arden was unwilling to consider anything beyond tomorrow.

He hoped that having her under the same roof might encourage her to open up to him, to confide in him about whatever it was that had her running scared. Only when he knew what he was up against would he be able to consider his course of action. Because he had no doubt that Arden was the woman he would spend the rest of his life with.

He pulled into the driveway of his home in front of Arden. When she stepped out of her car and into the light, he noticed how exhausted she looked. Her usually immaculate hair was tousled, her shoulders sagged. Her deep-brown eyes were shadowed with fatigue, but she offered him a weak smile.

He took her hand and led her into the house, then set the suitcase down and took her in his arms.

"Are you okay?"

She drew in a deep, shuddering breath, nodded. "Yeah. I think so."

"It's okay to be upset. Everything you owned just went up in smoke."

"I didn't own very much."

"That's not the point." He couldn't have said why, but he would have felt better if she'd cried. Generally he hated a woman's tears; he felt helpless around them. Which was why it still surprised him that he'd stopped to sit with Arden that day in the park. But he was glad that he had, because that was the day their relationship had changed. And that was why her calm determination seemed unnatural to him now, and why he was so worried about her.

"My bookcases." Her eyes widened with distress.

"Are probably ashes now," he said gently.

"You did such a beautiful job on them."

"I can build more."

She managed a weak smile. "I have to find somewhere to live first."

"Don't worry about that right now," Shaun told her.

If he had his way—and he intended to—Arden wouldn't be living anywhere but with him. He hoped that being together under the same roof might be just the thing to convince her that they were meant to be together.

"I have court first thing in the morning," she told him, forcing his attention back to more immediate matters. "So, if you don't mind, I'd just like to take a shower and go to bed."

He nodded.

Arden followed him up the stairs, into the master bath, watching silently as he got fresh towels out of the cupboard for her.

"Do you have something I could sleep in?" Arden asked. "I forgot to grab a nightgown from Nikki."

"Sure. I'll get you a T-shirt."

"Thanks." She smiled, but he could see the strain around her mouth, the shadows under her eyes. She was worried about something. The fire was the obvious explanation, and he couldn't blame her for being upset about that. But it went deeper than wariness or loss. There was fear in her eyes. He didn't understand it and he didn't like it.

Could the fire in her apartment building somehow be linked to the letters she'd been getting? He didn't want to believe it, but it wasn't much of a stretch to think that the two events might be connected.

His mind drifted back a few weeks, to the gunshots that had shattered her kitchen windows. The police were convinced it had been a random act. Shaun wasn't so sure. And it terrified him to know that Arden's life could be in real danger.

He poured himself a generous glass of scotch while he waited for Arden to finish in the shower. She was holding something back, and that bothered him. He wanted to be there for her. He wanted her to know that she could count on him. But she was so determined to stand on her own, to prove that she could. He didn't want to hold her up. He knew she didn't need that. But he wanted to stand beside her, to offer his support, to have her accept it.

He heard the water shut off, and ten minutes after that she came down the stairs.

"Where—" she cleared her throat "—where do you want me to sleep?"

He turned to study her. Her face was scrubbed free of makeup, her long dark hair still damp from the shower. His T-shirt covered her adequately, enticingly. The hem rode high on her thighs, the soft cotton hugged the curve of her breasts. He finished the last of his scotch and set his glass down on the table. "Where do you want to sleep?"

"With you," she said without hesitation.

Shaun's lips curved into a slow, satisfied smile. "I didn't invite you to stay just so that I could take advantage of the situation."

She came into his arms willingly, pressed her lips to his.

"That doesn't mean we can't take advantage of the situation, does it?"

"I love the way you think," he murmured.

She nipped his earlobe. "I love the way you..." She whispered an incredibly vivid suggestion in his ear that had all the blood rushing out of his head.

"Well then," he said, swinging her into his arms. "We'd better get started."

Things did look better in the morning. Arden got up and put on some borrowed clothes, made her court appearance, then went to the office and buried herself in work. In fact, she was so preoccupied with preparing court materials she almost forgot about the fire that had devastated her apartment and left her and several other tenants homeless. She thought of Greta Dempsey and her dog, wondered where they would go. Arden knew she'd been lucky. As much as she often felt alone, she knew she wasn't. She had family, people who cared about her.

And now she had Shaun. She still had her doubts about the wisdom of their current arrangement. Not that she had any real objections to sharing his home. She and Shaun were each so busy with their own lives, it was sometimes difficult to find time for each other. Now, no matter how late she had to work, she knew she could go home to him. At least for a while.

She frowned. They hadn't talked about how long she would stay with him. She knew he didn't intend for it to be any more than a short-term arrangement, until she could find something else suitable. A week? A month?

She pushed the thought aside and focused on the pretrial memo she was finishing up.

At least until Lieutenant Creighton showed up at her office.

Chapter 14

"I assume there's a reason for this visit." Arden forced a smile even though her stomach tightened.

"There is," Creighton agreed. "Preliminary reports indicate that the fire in your building was deliberately set, and that it started in your apartment. In your bedroom, to be precise."

She exhaled slowly as his words confirmed her suspicions. Her fears. Someone had to have been inside her apartment to start the fire there. In her bedroom. "And you think the fire is related to the letters."

"I do," he agreed. "We're investigating the owner of the building, of course. Most often, arson is implemented for financial gain, so we're following all leads. But we can't discount the possibility that this attack was directed at you, especially considering the content of the last letter.

"You've pissed somebody off," he continued, "and it makes sense that this was directed at you. If whoever set the fire knew you were out of the building, it might just have been an attempt to scare you. If he didn't know, he might have been trying to kill you.''

She felt the color drain from her cheeks. She'd known that she was the target, no matter how hard she tried to deny it, but she'd never thought that someone—some nameless faceless person that she didn't even know—could want her dead.

''Sorry to put it so bluntly,'' he apologized. ''But I want to make sure you know what's going on here.''

''I don't know what's going on,'' she protested, hating the helplessness that threatened to overwhelm her. ''I have no idea who could be doing this.''

''You represent a lot of women who are the victims of domestic violence. It isn't a stretch to think that a man who beats his wife would exhibit other forms of deviant behavior.''

''Men who batter their partners rarely act violently toward third parties. They usually try to hide the darker side of their personality.'' Everything she'd ever read about domestic violence confirmed this fact.

''Statistically, you're probably right,'' Creighton agreed. ''But you know that not every perpetrator can be slotted into a designated mold.''

She nodded, but she still couldn't imagine who would target her.

''If you think of anyone at all who might have reason to threaten you, call me,'' the lieutenant instructed.

Arden nodded.

''I'll get in touch with you as soon as we have any more information. Where are you staying?''

''With a...a friend.''

''McIver?''

Arden frowned. ''How did you know?''

Creighton grinned. ''I am a detective,'' he reminded her. ''And I didn't figure he would have hired a P.I. if he didn't have a personal interest in the situation.''

Arden felt her blood chill. Shaun had hired a private investigator? Why? And why hadn't he told her about it? She shook her head. No, Lieutenant Creighton must have made a mistake. Shaun wouldn't do something like that. Not without her permission. Not without discussing it with her first.

She forced her voice to remain casual as she asked, "What makes you think he hired an investigator?"

"Joel Logan contacted me to get copies of the incident reports. He's a good guy," Creighton assured her. "Used to be a cop."

Arden nodded. She didn't care about Joel Logan, but she sure as hell intended to find out what Shaun was up to.

She sat for a long while after Lieutenant Creighton had gone, thinking about the situation, but she still couldn't believe Shaun would do something like this without first discussing it with her. It was *her* life that had been threatened, after all. What right did he have to interfere?

Fueled by righteous anger and indignation, she pushed through the heavy paneled doors that led into Madison & McIver Law Offices.

"Can I help you?" The pretty young woman behind the front desk asked in a sweet voice.

Arden vaguely remembered the receptionist from her first visit to Shaun's office, but she walked straight past the desk. She was a woman on a mission, and she would not be diverted.

"Excuse me, ma'am. You can't just go back there."

Arden continued to ignore her. Shaun's door was open.

"What the hell did you think you were doing?"

Shaun glanced up, then from Arden to the receptionist, who was hovering nervously behind Arden.

"I'm sorry, Mr. McIver," she said in a tremulous voice. "I tried to stop her, but—"

Shaun waved off the apology. "That's okay, Claire."

Arden noted, with increased annoyance, that the woman

practically bobbed a curtsy before scurrying back
her desk.

"Hello, Arden," Shaun said politely. "Is there somethin
you wanted to talk—"

"Damn right there's something I want to talk about,
Arden snapped. "Who the hell is Joel Logan?"

"Joel Logan is a private investigator," Shaun explaine
calmly.

"I know that," she admitted. "Although not through an
revelation on your part."

"I should have told you," he agreed, his tone placating

Arden was not to be placated. "No, you shouldn't hav
told me. You should have discussed it with me *before* yo
hired someone to pry into my life. You might even hav
considered whether or not I wanted your interference."

"That's exactly why I didn't discuss it with you."

"Why?"

"Because you would have said that it was your problem
and you would deal with it."

Arden blew out an exasperated breath. "Well, it is m
problem, and I would have—I will—deal with it."

"Uh-huh," he agreed.

"Dammit, Shaun. I don't want you involved in this."

"Too late."

She narrowed her eyes. "When did you hire this privat
investigator?"

"A few weeks ago."

"Why?"

"Because I was concerned about you."

She crossed her arms over her chest. "How concerne
were you?"

He frowned. "What kind of question is that?"

"Were you concerned enough to have sex with me?"

She hated to think that it might be true, that Shaun'
interest in her stemmed from a desire to protect her rathe
than a desire for her. But she couldn't deny the possibility

"After all, if I'm sleeping in your bed, you know where I am."

"I won't deny that I'm more comfortable having you stay in my home. I know you're safe there."

She felt betrayed by his response, by his admission that he had ulterior motives for pursuing a physical relationship with her. And it hurt, so much more than she'd expected it to. She'd been let down often enough that she should have been expecting it. But she'd thought Shaun was different. She'd believed he cared about her.

"Stop it," he said gently.

She lifted her chin. "Stop what?"

"Jumping to all kinds of unwarranted conclusions about our relationship."

"Are they unwarranted?"

"Yes," he insisted. "I'm not pretending to care about you because I'm concerned about you. I'm concerned because I care."

She wanted to believe him, but she was afraid to trust him, afraid to trust her own feelings for Shaun. And she was even more afraid of what kind of information his investigator might turn up. There were still things she didn't want Shaun to know. Things she might never be ready to tell him. Things she definitely didn't want him learning from a third party.

"Lieutenant Creighton is handling this."

"And I'm sure he's doing everything he can. But he's only one man, and this is only one of his cases. I need to know that someone is making it a priority to find this guy. I can't just sit around and wait for him to make his next move."

She dropped her eyes, unwilling to let him see her fear.

"Did you think I wouldn't find out that the fire in your apartment was deliberately set? Did you think I wouldn't connect this arson to the last letter you received?"

Arden didn't dare admit that she had hoped he wouldn't find out it had been her apartment that had been torched.

"Where were you when the fire started?" he asked.

She frowned. "I was at the library doing research."

"But you had been home."

"Yes."

"How long were you gone?"

"Why all the questions?"

"How long were you gone?" Shaun repeated the question slowly.

"I'm not sure."

"You're lying."

"I'm not lying," she snapped. "I didn't check my watch when I left."

"You must have an idea what time it was when you decided to go to the library."

"Why are you cross-examining me?"

"What time?" he repeated.

Arden turned away from him. "It was about seven o'clock."

"And what time did you leave the courthouse again?"

"Around eight."

"So you were gone less than an hour, and in that time, your apartment was destroyed."

"That doesn't prove that I was a target."

"Maybe it doesn't prove anything," he admitted. "But it sure as hell concerns me."

"I'm sorry. I didn't...I don't—" She blew out an exasperated breath and stepped away from him. She remembered his reaction after the fire: his fear and concern, and the way he'd made love with her, slowly and tenderly, until she felt as if she were really cherished. "I'm not used to having people worry about me."

"Then you'll have to get used to it," Shaun said. "Because I'm not going away."

* * *

Shaun tried to convince Arden to go to bed early that night. After everything she'd been through in the past week, he knew she had to be exhausted. But she insisted that she had reading to catch up on, and she settled down on the sofa with a stack of legal journals. He wasn't surprised that she'd fallen asleep less than half an hour later.

He *was* surprised when he heard her scream.

It was a deep, blood-curdling sound wrenched from somewhere deep inside her. He dropped the book he'd been reading and leapt from his chair. She sucked air into her lungs, prepared to scream again. He wrapped his arms around her, and she fought against him, thrashing and whimpering.

"It's me, Shaun. It's okay. You're safe."

The words must have penetrated the haze of her subconscious, because she stopped fighting and collapsed against him, sobbing.

He brushed his hand over her hair, stunned. He'd never seen her like this. So completely vulnerable, so obviously terrorized.

"Jesus, Arden. You're shaking." He rubbed his hands briskly over her bare arms, trying to warm her.

"I'm okay," she said. "Just a little cold."

"You're not okay."

"It's not the first time I've had this nightmare," she admitted, her voice not quite steady. "And I'm sure it won't be the last."

"Tell me about it," he said.

"I don't want to talk about it. I don't want to relive it again."

"Not talking about it hasn't helped you forget."

She shook her head. "It's just a nightmare. I know that, but I can't stop it. It keeps happening, over and over."

"What is it?"

She closed her eyes but finally responded. "It's the night Denise and Brian Hemingway were killed."

He continued to hold her, but he didn't ask any more questions. He just waited for her to talk.

"She first came to see me just a couple of months before that," Arden told him. "Her sister had taken her to the shelter, after she was released from the hospital. Her husband had beaten her up pretty badly. She had a couple of cracked ribs, a dislocated shoulder, multiple cuts and bruises. And he'd knocked Brian down the stairs, when the little boy tried to stop him from kicking his mother.

"She didn't want the restraining order," she admitted. "He would be angry enough that she'd left and taken his son with her, and a piece of paper forbidding contact would only make him angrier. But he'd hurt her and he'd threatened their child, and she was scared enough to let me talk her into it."

She swallowed, swiped at the tears that coursed down her cheeks. "I should have listened to her."

"What happened?" he asked, gently brushing her hair away from her face.

"He got served with the order, and he went ballistic." She shook her head. "Denise called me, the night they were killed. He was at the house, banging on the door, yelling and swearing at her. She called me—not the police—*me*. I don't know what she thought I could do. I'm just a lawyer, for Christ's sake. But she trusted me, because I'd told her that a damn piece of paper could protect her and her child. And I was wrong."

She grabbed a tissue to wipe her nose. "Brian must have unlocked the door while she was still on the phone with me. Because the next thing I heard was a gunshot." She squeezed her eyes shut, and he knew she was reliving it again. "Then I heard Brian crying, and another gunshot. Then another. Then silence.

"He killed them," Arden said. "He shot his wife and his child, then he turned the gun on himself."

"It wasn't your fault," Shaun said.

"Wasn't it?"

"Of course not. How can you take this upon yourself?"

"Somebody has to be held responsible for what happened."

"How about the man who pulled the trigger?" he suggested.

She shrugged, and he knew that no matter what he said, she would always carry the guilt with her. He couldn't imagine the horror of what she'd gone through, listening to the sound of gunshots over the phone while some psycho executed his wife and child. Unable to do anything to help.

No wonder she'd fallen apart the day of the funeral. He couldn't believe she'd managed to hold it together as long as she had, and that she'd recovered as well as she had. He wished he could have been there for her, was determined to be there for her now.

"There was nothing you could have done," he said gently.

She nodded. "That doesn't make it any easier to accept."

He knew she was right, and he didn't know what else he could say or do to ease her mind. So he kissed her softly.

"Make love to me, Shaun. Help me to forget for a little while."

He couldn't refuse her request. He didn't want to.

He knew she wanted to lose herself in passion, that she was looking for an outlet for her frustration. He was determined to give her that, and so much more. He was going to make her forget the nightmares, and he was going to make her realize that she could count on him.

Always.

When three weeks passed without another letter, Arden began to allow herself to hope that her anonymous pen pal had given up. She knew that Lieutenant Creighton believed there was a connection between the fire in her apartment and the letters, but the police had no evidence to support his theory and no suspects in either case. If it was the letter writer who had torched her building, maybe that destruction had satisfied his thirst for vengeance. She still didn't know why he was seeking revenge, but she was willing to believe that his personal vendetta may have been satisfied.

When Marcy paged Arden at the courthouse just before the start of a trial Wednesday morning, she was convinced otherwise.

"A bomb?" she repeated Marcy's words into the phone, certain she must have misunderstood.

"I came in early and found the alarm had been disconnected. I called the police right away," Marcy explained. "They found the bomb."

Arden slumped against the wall and closed her eyes, wondering what was the purpose in having an alarm system if it could be so easily circumvented. "What kind of a bomb?"

"A homemade explosive device on a timer. It was in a box on your desk."

"Are the police still there?"

"Yeah. They brought the dogs in to sniff around, to make sure they haven't missed anything. And Lieutenant Creighton wants to see you."

"Now?" She glanced at her watch. Court was scheduled to start in ten minutes.

"Now," Marcy confirmed.

Arden hung up the phone and went to adjourn her trial.

As she walked back to the office, she thought that her day couldn't possibly get any worse. She should have known better.

By the time she arrived on the scene, the local media were there. She cursed under her breath. If this incident made the news, she'd have no choice but to tell Nikki about the threats.

"Ms. Doherty," a reporter shoved a microphone in Arden's face as she tried to sidestep the cameras. "Is it true hat this is the second attempt on your life within the past wo weeks?"

"I hardly think this could be considered an attempt on ny life when I wasn't even here," Arden said evenly.

"Are you denying that there have been threats made against you?"

"No comment." She forced a smile and pushed her way hrough the throng of people and into her office.

Arden called Nikki as soon as she was finished with Lieutenant Creighton. After she'd spent the better part of half an hour trying to alleviate her cousin's fears, she phoned Shaun's office. She knew he'd be annoyed if he heard the news from anyone else. But he wasn't in his office, and he hadn't returned her call by the time she was ready to leave for the day.

"I saw you on the news," Shaun said when he got home from work later.

"My two minutes of fame," Arden said dryly, as she continued sprinkling breadcrumbs over the top of something hat looked like a casserole. It was, he remembered, her night to cook, but that usually meant some kind of takeout. She shoved the casserole pan into the oven, then turned to face him. "They have a suspect in custody."

He knew that, too. "Simon Granger. An out-of-towner with a criminal record for two previous arsons and a reputation as a torch for hire. Do you know him?"

Arden shook her head. "The police don't believe he's responsible for the letters. It's more likely he was hired by whoever is, and they're hoping they can get that information from him."

"I don't think they'll get very far."

"Why do you say that?"

"Because he started shouting for his lawyer as soon as hey arrested him."

Arden shrugged. "That doesn't surprise me."

"Yeah, well, this might," he warned.

"What?" she asked warily.

"When they asked who his lawyer was, he named me."

"What...why?"

"I don't know."

She backed away from him, her eyes clouded with confusion. "He asked for you by name?"

"Yes."

"How does he know you?"

"He doesn't." Shaun raked his hands through his hair. "I think he was given my name by whoever hired him, to cast suspicion in my direction."

Arden didn't respond. She only continued to stare at him, wide-eyed and wary.

"And it worked, didn't it?"

"I don't know."

It was an effort to remain calm. He shouldn't blame her for being suspicious of everyone and everything after all that had happened over the past several weeks, but he couldn't help feeling disappointed that she didn't trust him.

"What possible reason would I have for tormenting you like this?"

"I don't know," she said again. "I can't think of a reason for anyone to be doing this."

"But you believe I could be responsible?"

"No." She looked away again, shrugged. "Maybe."

Her lack of faith in him, in their relationship, combined with his own frustration at the situation, were too much. "Dammit, Arden." He slammed his fist down on the counter.

She flinched as if he'd struck her, and all trace of color drained from her cheeks.

Her reaction only infuriated him more. He grabbed her by the shoulders, his fingers digging into her flesh. "Don't look at me like you think I'm capable of something like this."

"I've seen too much of what I didn't want to believe someone was capable of," she told him, her voice trembling lightly.

"You know me, Arden."

"All I know is that someone started a fire in my apartment, and you're the only person besides myself who had a key."

He dropped his hands. "I never asked for the damn key."

"But you took it."

"Because I wanted to get your bookshelves done and you were never there."

She shrugged.

"Don't you know I'd die before I'd hurt you, Arden?" He softened his tone, pleading with her for faith and understanding.

"I don't know anything anymore," she said miserably.

Arden slept alone that night.

She hadn't really expected that he'd join her in the bed they'd shared every night for the past couple of weeks. After their confrontation in the kitchen, he seemed intent on avoiding her for the rest of the evening. Not that she could blame him. She'd been wrong to doubt him, and her mistrust had hurt him.

Lying alone in the big empty bed, she realized that she'd baited him. She'd practically dared him to fight back, to lash out at her. But he hadn't. He'd been upset and hurt and angry, but he hadn't taken his frustration out on her. He hadn't hit her.

She hadn't consciously been testing him; it was more that she'd been testing herself. She knew only too well how the cycle of violence perpetuated itself, and she'd been so afraid that she wouldn't break free from that cycle. Her stepfather had had a quick temper, quicker fists. Shaun might be quick to anger, but he wouldn't hurt her. She knew that now.

Relief washed over her, followed quickly by a wave of

guilt. She'd pushed him, provoked him, then turned away from him. She was surprised he hadn't walked out on her. She certainly wouldn't have blamed him if he had.

Had she wanted him to walk out? Had she hoped he'd abandon her—as her father had done, as Brad had done? It would have proven she had reason to distrust him. It would have justified her desire to maintain an emotional distance.

But he hadn't walked out; he hadn't abandoned her. And she realized that maybe he was different. Maybe she could trust him to stand by her.

She found him in his den the next morning, looking as miserable and exhausted as she felt.

"What do you want, Arden?"

She stepped farther into the room. "I wanted to—" she cleared her throat "—to apologize."

"For what?"

"The things I said last night."

He shrugged as if it didn't matter. But she knew that it did.

"I am sorry," she said. "I know you aren't responsible for any of what's happened."

He looked at her now, really looked at her for the first time since she'd stepped into the room. "Do you?"

"Yes."

He hesitated, then nodded. "Okay."

"Okay?" She chewed on her bottom lip, wondering why, if it was okay, he still hadn't made a move toward her.

Finally he pushed away from his desk and stood up. He held out his arms, and she went into them. She laid her head against his chest, took comfort in the strong and steady beat of his heart, in the warm strength of his arms around her.

"Why don't we go away for a while?" he suggested.

"Why?"

"To give the police a chance to find this guy."

She pulled out of his arms, wishing they could have had

more of a reprieve before the next round of battle. "I have obligations, Shaun. I can't just take off."

"You won't be any good to your clients if you're dead," he said bluntly.

She swallowed. "Are you trying to scare me?"

"You should be scared. Someone's trying to kill you."

"You don't know that for sure."

"Why else would someone plant a bomb in your office?"

"I don't know." And it was that not knowing that terrified her. "Maybe there's some kind of evidence in my office that they wanted to destroy."

"If he got into your office to plant the bomb, why not just take the evidence?"

She shook her head. "I don't know," she said again.

"You might be willing to take chances with your life, but I'm not."

"If I run away, I let him win."

Shaun sighed. "Did you know that they released Granger?"

She hadn't known, and the revelation hit her like a sucker punch to the gut. She took a deep breath, exhaled slowly. "You—" she swallowed "—you got him bail?"

"Christ, Arden. Do you really think I'd represent the man who's accused of planting a bomb in your office and who may be responsible for burning down your apartment?" He shook his head before she could respond. "Forget it. I don't want you to answer that. No, I didn't get him bail. Blake released him."

"Why?"

"The only evidence they had was that of an old man who saw the suspect vehicle parked outside your office at four o'clock in the morning. They wanted him to come in to pick Granger out of a lineup, but they can't find him."

"The witness?"

Shaun nodded grimly. "Without him, the prosecution's whole case falls apart. There are no prints on the box with the bomb, none in your office, none in the vehicle—whic was apparently stolen from somewhere in Arizona thre days earlier.''

Arizona. Arden shook off the feeling of unease. It cou only be a coincidence. Nothing more. She had enough prob lems in her present without worrying about ghosts from h past.

''Blake wouldn't tell me anything else,'' he continue ''but I spoke briefly to Creighton and he said that they' continuing to investigate. If they manage to find the witnes or any new evidence, they'll bring Granger back in an refile charges.''

In the meantime Arden somehow had to get through da after day never knowing when or where her stalker migl strike again. And he would strike again. She couldn't sa how she knew for sure, but she did. He was still out ther waiting for the right moment. She shuddered.

Shaun wrapped his arms around her, dropped a kiss o the top of her forehead. ''I got a preliminary report fro Logan yesterday.''

''A report on what?''

''Blake.''

''Warren?''

''Yes, Warren.''

She pulled out of his arms, stunned. ''You had an assi tant district attorney investigated?''

Shaun shrugged. ''I simply asked Logan to look into hi background.''

''Why?''

''Because I don't trust him.''

''You don't like him,'' Arden corrected.

''That, too,'' he agreed. ''But I wouldn't have had hir checked out without reason.''

''And your reason is?''

''Did he ever tell you that he was married?'' Shaun asked Arden frowned. ''No.''

"It seems he hasn't told anyone about his ill-fated marriage."

"It's not a crime to be divorced," Arden said.

"He's not divorced. He's widowed."

"Is that why you had him investigated?" This wasn't making any sense to her.

"Greg Madison," Shaun named his law partner, "was at Blake's wedding about six years ago."

Arden waited, with what she thought of as infinite patience, for Shaun to get to the point.

"He married a woman by the name of Angela Edwards, right here in Fairweather.

"Greg and Angela had been good friends in high school, and they kept in touch after graduation. Even when Angela moved out to California to study art at Berkeley."

"What happened to her?" Arden asked.

"She was killed in a motor vehicle accident a couple of years ago."

"Maybe Warren doesn't talk about it because he's still mourning her."

"It's not just that he never mentioned having been married, but that he never mentioned any connection to Fairweather. That's something that should have come up in conversation.

"And," Shaun continued, "Greg told me that Angela contacted him just a few months before she died, wanting a recommendation for a divorce attorney in California."

Arden rubbed at her temple. "What are you suggesting now—that Blake had his wife killed?"

"It might have been an unfortunate accident," Shaun agreed. "But the affidavit she filed with the court when she petitioned to end her marriage included allegations of abuse."

"*Allegations,*" she repeated.

"Come on, Arden. You've dedicated your life to working

with abused women. Have you ever had a client who lie
about being battered?''

"No," she admitted. "But that doesn't mean it couldn
happen."

"Why are you defending him?"

"I'm not defending him. But even if he abused his wife—
and that's still just an 'if'—I still don't understand why yo
felt it necessary to dig into his background."

"I think Blake could be connected to the threats you'v
been getting."

"That's ridiculous."

"Why are you so unwilling to consider the possibilit
that he might be responsible for the letters when last nigh
you practically accused me of being your stalker?"

"I apologized for last night," she reminded him. "'
wasn't thinking clearly."

"But you're thinking clearly now," Shaun countered
"and you need to consider all possibilities."

"What possible motive could he have for wanting t
harm me?"

"You're a powerful voice for abused women. A threat t
the men who hurt them."

"Warren Blake lived in California until a few month
ago. Even if his wife grew up in Pennsylvania, *I* never me
her."

But she could tell by the determined expression o
Shaun's face that he wasn't prepared to let go of his theory

"You're grasping at straws," she said gently.

He sighed. "Maybe I am. Because at this point it's al
we've got."

She shook her head, frustrated that he was right, terrifie
to think of what other straws he might find to grasp at. "'
want you to call off the investigation. Please. Let the polic
handle it."

"I can't." He was adamant.

She was frantic. "Why not?"

"Because I love you."

Chapter 15

It wasn't the way Shaun had planned to tell her. When he finally got around to saying the words he'd carried for so long in his heart, he'd thought there would be candlelight and soft music. He hadn't expected to blurt them out in a moment of frustration. But he had, and now Arden just stared at him, pale and stunned.

"Okay," he said, trying to lighten the moment, hoping to ease the tight band around his heart. "I guess you weren't quite ready to hear that, but it's true. It's how I feel, Arden."

"We—" she cleared her throat, wrapped her arms around herself "—we haven't even been dating two months."

"I didn't realize there was a term requirement on falling in love," he said dryly.

"It just seems kind of fast."

"I started to fall in love with you that first day in the park."

"That's *really* too fast."

"Obviously you don't feel the same way."

"I'm not sure how I feel," she admitted. "I care about

you, more than I've ever cared for anyone else. But love
I'm not sure I'm even capable of love.''

"He must have hurt you very badly."

She started to shake her head, then stopped. "I can't..
don't know if I can talk to you about it. Not yet."

"I wish you would tell me. Not because I need to kno
all the secrets of your past, but because I want you to tru
me enough to want to talk about it."

"I've never told anyone about it."

"I'm not just anyone," he said.

"No." She managed a smile. "You're not."

"I can wait."

"I might never be ready to talk about it. To...to lov
you."

"I'll wait as long as I need to." It was true. It was th
one thing he was certain of. He couldn't imagine his lif
without Arden; he wouldn't consider a future that didn
have her in it.

"I can't ask that of you. You deserve so much more tha
I can give you."

"I want *you*, Arden. But I'm not going to push for some
thing you're not ready for. Let's just take things one day
a time and see what happens."

"Are you sure that's okay?"

"Yeah, I'm sure."

"Okay," she agreed hesitantly.

"Good. Now for more immediate matters."

"Such as?"

"Thanksgiving."

"What about it?"

"It's next week, and I thought it might be nice to coo
a turkey here. Invite Colin and Nikki and Carly, do a famil
sort of thing." Ease her into the idea of being part of hi
family. Show her how wonderful it would be if she staye
with him forever.

"That sounds like a nice idea."

He smiled, pleased by her agreement. "Have you ever cooked a turkey?"

"No."

"Me, neither."

"Someone needs to write a basic cookbook," Arden said, scanning the contents of the thick volume on the counter. *"Thanksgiving Dinner for Dummies.* This one has a recipe for sage dressing and candied yams, but nowhere does it say how long the turkey's supposed to cook."

"Until it's done."

"You're a big help," Arden muttered.

"I think there were cooking instructions on the wrapper."

"The wrapper that you put out in the garbage?"

He winced. "Yeah, that one."

"Great."

"Why don't you just call Nikki?"

"No." She hated to admit that she was so inept in the kitchen that she couldn't even cook a turkey. But she could call Rebecca. Her secretary was well aware of her lack of culinary expertise, and she wasn't likely to make too much fun of the woman who signed her paychecks.

"How long does it have to cook?" Shaun asked when she hung up the phone.

"Until the little button in the turkey pops out," Arden said.

Shaun looked at the bird. "What button?"

"The button that's in the kind of turkey that Rebecca buys so that she knows when it's cooked."

"I guess we didn't get one with a button."

"You guessed right."

He pulled her into his arms, kissed her long and hard. "To hell with the turkey," Shaun said. "Let's order Chinese."

"We can't have Chinese for Thanksgiving," Arden protested. "It's very un-American."

"Says who?" Shaun countered. "There are millions of Chinese Americans, and I bet at least some of them are having Chinese for dinner."

"Probably sweet-and-sour turkey balls."

"If I can find out how long this bird needs to cook, will you marry me?"

She dropped the can of cranberry she'd taken out of the cupboard. She knew he was teasing, but something tightened inside her. It wasn't an entirely uncomfortable feeling, almost a longing. Whatever it was, she pushed it aside. "If you find out how to cook it, I'll do the dishes," she countered.

"Deal."

It took him less than five minutes on the computer to download the necessary instructions from the Internet.

"I never realized you were so resourceful," she commented when he handed her the printed page. She knew she'd been conned, but she was so relieved to have the information she didn't care. And she knew he'd help with the cleanup, anyway.

"You'd be amazed what kind of information you can get from the Internet," Shaun told her, slipping his arms around her waist and nuzzling the back of her neck.

Arden felt her blood heat, her body ache. "Such as?"

"The entire Kama Sutra. With pictures." He turned her to face him, lowered his head to nibble on her lips.

"Really?"

"Mmm-hmm." He was too busy raining kisses over her jaw to give a more audible response.

"We'll save that lesson for another time," she said. "Right now we have to get this bird in the oven."

"Or we could order Chinese and use our time more...creatively," he suggested.

Arden laughed and pushed him away. "This Thanksgiving dinner was your idea."

He sighed but gamely rolled up his sleeves. "I'll peel the potatoes."

As much as Arden had stressed about preparing her first Thanksgiving meal, she enjoyed puttering around the kitchen with Shaun. In the few weeks that they'd been living together, they'd established an easy camaraderie. It was almost too easy, she thought sometimes.

That worried her. Even though they'd agreed to take things one step at a time, and he'd promised not to push her, she was worried. They'd been pretty much inseparable for the past few weeks, but that was normal at the beginning of a relationship. Wasn't it?

She didn't really know. She hadn't had a relationship like this since...well, never. The last semi-serious relationship she'd had was back in law school, and her experience with Brad had taught her to protect herself, to guard her heart.

And she'd done so. Until now.

Her relationship with Shaun was anything but casual. Somehow he'd disabled her defenses, gotten closer to her than anyone else ever had. And what worried her most, she was forced to admit, were her own feelings. She liked going to sleep beside him every night, waking up with him in the morning. She liked not being alone.

Was it possible that this could work out? Or was it only a matter of time until she would be alone again?

Shaun was just taking the turkey out of the oven when the doorbell rang. Arden was mashing the potatoes, so he set the turkey on top of the stove and went to open the door for their guests.

It was cold outside, especially compared to the heat in the kitchen, and Carly's cheeks were rosy with it. "Happy Thanksgiving, Uncle Shaun."

"Happy Thanksgiving, yourself," he said. "Come on in."

She skipped into the house, already stripping off her coat

and gloves. Nikki came next, kissing his cheek as she passed, and carrying the pumpkin pie she'd promised to bring. Colin was behind her, a large cardboard box in his arms.

"Arden's in the kitchen," Shaun told them. "Just finishing up a few things."

"I found this in the back of the closet in your old room," Nikki said to Arden, gesturing to the cardboard box in Colin's arms.

"What is it?" Arden seemed more interested in the pumpkin pie Nikki was carrying. She took it from her cousin's hands; Shaun took the box from his brother.

"It's yours," Nikki said. "Mostly old photo albums. Pictures of you when you were a baby."

Arden's face paled and she turned away quickly to put the pie on the counter.

It was interesting, Shaun mused wryly, that it wasn't only a declaration of love that caused such a reaction. He stood holding the box, uncertain what to do with it in light of Arden's response. She busied herself at the counter, refused to look at him or the box he held.

"Baby pictures," he teased. "That's something I'd love to see."

"I don't want them," Arden said.

Nikki frowned. "But there are pictures of your dad in there. You and your mom and dad."

"Is that—" she swallowed "—is that all?"

"Yeah."

Arden hesitated a moment longer, eyeing the box cautiously, then she took it from his hands and dropped it into a corner.

He tried to forget about it: the box and Arden's reaction to it. It wasn't so hard while Colin and Nikki and Carly were there. Conversation over dinner was light and casual. Dinner turned out well, for a first attempt. The turkey was a little overcooked, the carrots a little undercooked, the gravy slightly lumpy. But there weren't many leftovers, so he figured the meal was a success. More gratifying to Shaun was the atmosphere. The easy camaraderie of family. The presence of the woman he loved.

It was just after seven when Colin rounded up his family for the trip home. Shaun stood beside Arden at the window to wave goodbye as the first flakes began to fall, swirling carelessly, unhurriedly, in the dark sky.

"Look," he said. "It's starting to snow."

She smiled. "I've always loved the first snow of the season."

"Let's take a walk," he said impulsively.

"Now?"

"Why not? We need to work off some of that turkey and pumpkin pie."

"But it's snowing."

"It's romantic," he told her.

"Since when are you such an expert on romance?" she countered.

"Since you came into my life."

She smiled, almost reluctantly. "Let's go for a walk."

It was a beautiful night. Despite the falling snow, the sky was mostly clear, the stars sparkling against the dark blanket of the sky like so many diamonds on velvet. The neighborhood was quiet, the streets empty, and it seemed as if there was no one in the world except the two of them. It was magic.

"It was a good day, wasn't it?" Arden asked as they walked hand in hand down the street.

"Wonderful," he agreed.

"The turkey wasn't too overcooked?"

"It was delicious."

"I'm glad we did this," she said. "I really miss Nikki and Colin and Carly sometimes."

"They're so happy together," Shaun commented. "And now there's another baby on the way."

"They deserve to be happy. They've been through a lot."

"Do you think happiness is something that has to be earned?"

"No." She shrugged. "I don't know."

"Don't you deserve to be happy? Don't *we* deserve to be happy?"

"I *am* happy," Arden told him.

"Are you?"

"Yes." And she meant it. Maybe she was worried about her psycho pen pal, maybe she was afraid her relationship with Shaun wouldn't—couldn't—last, but right now she was happy. She didn't dare look any further than that.

"It's been a while since you've got a letter," Shaun said.

She nodded.

"Maybe he's given up."

"Maybe."

"But you don't think so?"

"I don't know. I want to believe he has, but I can't help thinking that he's just lulling me into a false sense of security."

"You're safe here, Arden. I won't let anything happen to you."

"I know."

They walked to the end of the street, where the playground equipment stood silent, empty.

"This park has been here forever," Shaun told her. "Colin and I used to come here as kids, to play on the swings, climb the jungle gym, throw a baseball around."

"Did you have a happy childhood?"

"For the most part," he agreed. "My mom was terrific. She spent a lot of time with us."

"What about your dad?"

"He was always too busy to pay much attention to us.

He spent a lot of time at the courthouse, and when he was home, we had to tiptoe around so as not to disturb him."

"But you were close to him?"

"I respected him," Shaun said. "We were always told how important he was, and I wanted to grow up to be like him someday. Until I got older. Then I realized I only wanted to be a lawyer...I didn't want to be like my father."

"He was a good judge."

"He was a lousy father."

She nodded. "Do you ever wonder if..."

"If what?" Shaun prompted.

"If you could be a good father, despite the example he set."

"I used to have doubts," he admitted. "But Colin had the same father I did, and he's adjusted to fatherhood with little difficulty. I think the only thing that matters is wanting to be a good parent. If you do, you can make it work."

She nodded.

"Is that what bothers you? Did losing your parents leave that much of a void in your life?"

She shook her head, feeling a twinge of guilt for not correcting his misconception about her family. "No. After—when I came to live with Aunt Tess, it was a big adjustment. But she showed me what a family should be like. She was so much more of a mother to me than mine ever was." She rubbed her hands briskly over her arms, wondering why she'd volunteered that piece of information. "It's getting cold. Let's walk some more."

He curved his arm around her shoulders. "Can you still feel your toes?"

"Barely."

"Good."

She raised an eyebrow.

"I did have an ulterior motive in suggesting this little outing."

"Which was?"

"You're going to need some help warming up when we get back to the house."

"Hot chocolate and a crackling fire would be great."

He grinned. "Among other things."

Arden was smiling as she followed the scent of fresh coffee down the stairs the following morning. There were definite advantages to this living arrangement, and having her morning coffee made for her was the least of them.

Her smile faded when she caught a glimpse of Shaun in the dining room. She stopped in the doorway, her quest for caffeine forgotten. The box Nikki and Colin had delivered the previous day was on the table, the top opened. Shaun held a framed photograph in his hands.

"What are you doing?"

He glanced up at her, the quick flash of guilt replaced by an easy smile. "I'm unpacking this for you."

"I don't want it unpacked."

"Why not?"

"I just don't."

He wiped the dust off the glass with his fingers. "This must be your mom," Shaun said. "She looks like she could be your twin."

"Yeah." Arden took the picture from him, shoved it back into the box. The resemblance between her and her mother thirty years ago was uncanny and disconcerting. She couldn't help but think that a resemblance so strong, so deep, was indicative of other similarities. The last thing she'd ever wanted was to be like her mother.

"She was beautiful."

Arden ignored the comment and folded the flaps on the top of the box.

"Is this your dad?" Shaun asked, holding another frame he'd set aside.

Arden sighed, wishing he would just leave it alone. But obviously Shaun had other ideas. She glanced at the picture in his hands, at the handsome couple all smiles and joy. The man was tall and dark-haired and holding a baby in his arms. The slender woman beside him was a mirror image of herself, her hand over her husband's, on top of the baby's tummy.

"Yes, that's my father," she told him. She hated that her memories of him were so faded. That the memories of everything that happened after his death were so painfully clear.

"How old were you when he died?"

"Five."

"That must have been hard on you."

She shrugged and moved away, not wanting to dig any deeper into the painful memories. "It's never easy to lose someone you love."

He nodded, and she knew he was thinking about his own parents. "No, it's not," he agreed. Then, "They looked happy together."

"Can we please not do this right now?"

"I didn't mean to upset you by bringing it up," he said.

She shrugged off his concern. "I just don't like talking about them."

"But they're your family, Arden."

"I don't have any family anymore." It was better that way.

"Who's this?" he asked, holding up a small unframed photo that was crinkled around the edges.

She couldn't see the picture from where she was standing, but she didn't need to look at it to know that the edges were bent from years spent tucked in her pocket, the photo smudged by young fingers tracing the smiling faces. And she was helpless to prevent the tears that filled her eyes, stunned that the grief could come back so sharp, so strong, after so many years.

She blinked away the tears, cleared her throat. "That's me."

"Yeah, I kind of figured that," he said. "Who's the little girl with you?"

"My sister."

Chapter 16

Shaun felt his mouth drop open, snapped it shut again. "Your...sister?"

Arden nodded and took the picture from his hand. He could see the sheen of tears in her eyes as she lovingly traced the smiling face of the younger child, could feel the heartache she carried inside her.

"Her name's Rheanne," she told him. A single tear trembled for a moment on the edge of her lashes before slipping slowly down the curve of her cheek.

She set the picture on the table and turned toward the kitchen. Her hands weren't quite steady, he noted, as she took a mug from the cupboard and filled it from the carafe. He suspected that she wanted something to do more than she wanted the coffee.

She came back into the dining room and sat down at the table, her hands cradled around the mug. "The last time I saw her, she wasn't even two years old."

The questions swirled through Shaun's mind, but he waited silently for her to continue.

"My mother remarried less than a year after my father died, then we moved with her new husband to North Carolina, then Oregon, then Arizona. As far as I know, she's still in Arizona."

Shaun frowned, wondering why Arden had grown up with Nikki's family in Fairweather if her mother was in Arizona and why Arden never talked about her mother.

"Everything was okay at first," Arden continued. "After my mom and Gavin got married. At least, I think it was. I don't remember that much of the first couple of years. And then my mom got pregnant, and they started to argue. A lot. I don't know what they fought about. I only remember that they always seemed to be fighting.

"Then Rheanne was born." She smiled a little at the memory. "She was so tiny, so beautiful. The fighting got even worse after that and Gavin—" she swallowed "—my stepfather, liked to drink. And when he drank, he got abusive. Just verbally, at first. Then he started to knock my mom around.

"Sometimes he'd hit me, too, although usually he just ignored me. And I tried to keep Rheanne quiet, so he wouldn't have a reason to yell. So he wouldn't hurt her, too.

"It became harder to hide from him as I got older. What worried me more than the yelling and hitting, though, was when—" she took a sip of coffee, continued to stare into the cup "—when he started paying attention to me. He'd look at me and he'd smile at me, and I'm not sure I understood why it scared me, but it did. There was something about the look in his eyes that didn't seem right.

"Sometimes he'd come into the bathroom while I was in the tub, or into my bedroom while I was changing. And he'd watch me. If I locked the door, he'd hit me. Then he started touching me."

Somehow he'd known this revelation was coming, yet he couldn't prevent the churning in the pit of his stomach, or the burning rage and helplessness.

"He never—" she swallowed "—he never raped me. But what he did was bad enough."

Shaun didn't know what to say or do. He was appalled that this man, a man she should have been able to rely on and look up to, had abused her trust and destroyed her innocence. Shaun wanted to tell her that she had no reason to be ashamed, but he knew words would be inadequate. He wanted to hold her, but he was afraid to touch her, afraid she'd shy away from him.

"Did you tell…anyone? Your mother?"

She nodded. "I tried to, anyway. I didn't know how to explain what he was doing, and she didn't want to hear it. She said only little girls with naughty secrets locked their doors. And when I told her I didn't like the way he touched me, she said he was only showing me that he loved me and…" Her voice faltered, but she drew a deep breath and forged ahead. "She told me I should be grateful that he was able to love me as if I was his own daughter."

"Jesus." Shaun couldn't hold back his anger any longer. "How could she not have known?"

"She didn't want to know." Arden tried to shrug, but the movement was stiff. "Then Aunt Tess brought Nikki out for a visit, for my tenth birthday. I don't think she was there two days before she figured out the situation. Gavin had bought me a new dress for my birthday, and he insisted on helping me try it on. Aunt Tess came into my room while I was undressed and found him there.

"She tried to talk to my mother about it. I overheard them arguing. My mother called her a liar and a troublemaker and told her to get out of her house.

"The next morning Aunt Tess came back and threatened to file for legal custody of me and Rheanne. My mother consented to her taking me. I think she was starting to believe that there was something unnatural in my relationship with my stepfather, but it was obviously my fault.

"She fought to keep Rheanne, though. After all, she was

Gavin's daughter, and she was still in love with Gavin.
was terrified that Rheanne would have to stay in that house
and that he'd do to her what he'd done to me.''

"What happened to her?"

"I don't know. Aunt Tess contacted Family Services to
take Rheanne into protective custody until Tess could be
approved as a foster mother. But when she followed up with
the agency, Rheanne was already gone." Arden blinked
away the tears that filled her eyes. "She'd been adopted."

"Do you know where she is now?"

Arden looked away. "No."

"What happened to Gavin? Did he go to jail?"

"No, I...he was never charged. The prosecutor who in-
terviewed me didn't think I'd make a...a credible witness."

"Why not?" Shaun couldn't help but feel outraged on
her behalf.

"Because I didn't want to talk about what he'd done.
didn't think anyone would believe me. My own mother
didn't believe me."

"Is she still with your stepfather?"

"As far as I know. I haven't even heard from her in
years."

"At least you had your aunt Tess."

Arden nodded. "Yes. And she understood that the only
thing that really mattered to me at the time was getting out
of that house so he couldn't hurt me anymore."

"And that's when she brought you back to Fairweather."

She nodded again. "For all intents and purposes, that's
when my life began. I try not to think about anything that
happened before I came to live with her and Nikki. But
know I won't ever forget."

"I'm sorry," Shaun said. "Not just about everything that
happened, but for making you talk about it."

Her shrug was a little more natural this time. "I've
wanted to tell you. I know you deserved to know the truth
but I was afraid."

"Why?"

She took a deep breath. "The first time I ever had sex…I was seventeen years old and determined to take back control of my body. And my life. It was a disaster. I don't imagine any 'first' sexual experience is ideal, especially when you're seventeen," she admitted. "But after that I was convinced I wouldn't be missing anything if I never had sex again.

"And it wasn't until law school that I did. It was a little better, but I know I was still uncomfortable. It was an effort to remember that the hands touching me weren't my step-father's, that I wanted them on me—or was supposed to, anyway.

"Brad didn't seem to mind that I wasn't very enthusiastic in the bedroom. He just thought I was inexperienced. He even talked about us getting married, so I thought I should tell him about my…past."

She got up to pour more coffee.

"When I told him, he didn't want me anymore. I was, to use his words, 'damaged goods.' He preferred to think I was frigid than to know what had been done to me."

The rage simmering inside Shaun started to boil, threatened to spill over. He clamped a lid on his emotions, knowing that Arden didn't need to deal with those on top of everything else she'd been through.

"I haven't been with anyone else since then," she told him. "I hadn't wanted to. Until you."

He swallowed. He'd been her first lover in six years? No wonder she'd seemed hesitant in the beginning, surprised by the intensity of her own responses. It awed him, that she'd given him the gift of herself, and it terrified him to think that his touch might bring back unpleasant memories for her.

He cleared his throat, afraid to ask but needing to know. "Is it…uh…okay…when we…make love?"

Arden glanced away again, soft color rising in her cheeks. "It's more than okay. When I'm with you, I don't have to

make a conscious effort to shut out the bad memories. Jus
being with you does that for me.''

It boggled his mind to think about everything she'd bee
through, and how she'd managed to use her experience t
become a stronger and better person. ''That's why you d
what you do, isn't it?'' he asked. ''You want to help th
women and children who can't help themselves.'' Wome
like her mother; children like she had been.

She nodded again. ''It matters to me to be able to mak
a difference for someone. And that,'' she added, with force
casualness, ''is the sordid story of my life.''

''Is that what you thought would change the way I fee
about you?''

''Doesn't it?'' she asked.

''No. Yes.''

She almost smiled. Her lips started to curve, then trem
bled, and he saw the sheen of moisture in her eyes.

''What you told me only reinforces what I already
knew—that you're an incredible woman. You survived
hell that no child should ever have to endure, and you mad
yourself into a woman that anyone would be proud of.''

''I can't forget,'' she said softly. ''I try so hard to bloc
it all out sometimes, and then I feel guilty for forgetting th
good parts.'' She picked up the photograph again.

''I love you, Arden. I love everything about you.''

She did manage to smile this time. ''You keep telling m
that, I might start to believe it.''

''I'm counting on it,'' he told her. And he was countin
on her realizing that love was a positive emotion, and tha
he would never use his love to hurt her.

''I still need time, Shaun.''

''I know,'' he admitted. ''And I'm trying to be patient.'

''What if I'm never ready for this?''

''You will be,'' he said. The fact that she'd opened up t
him about her past proved that she was beginning to trus

to him, and he knew their relationship could only grow stronger. "And I can be patient a little while longer."

"What will happen when your patience runs out?"

"Then we'll get married."

"What?"

He grinned. "You're the woman I'm going to spend the rest of my life with," he told her. "And I want to have a family with you. Since I tend to be a traditionalist in certain matters, I'll want you to marry me first."

"Anything else you want?" she asked dryly.

"Maybe a dog, but that's negotiable."

Saturday, when Arden opened the morning newspaper, a letter fell onto the kitchen table.

Shaun, thankfully, was in the shower, and she just stood there—she didn't know for how long—staring blankly at the white envelope with her name inscribed on the front in blood-red ink.

She didn't want to touch the envelope. If she picked it up, if she held it in her hand, it would have to be real. She didn't want it to be. She didn't want to deal with this anymore.

Tears of anger and frustration filled her eyes, tightened her throat, immobilized her. She felt the scream build inside, tearing its way to her throat, clawing for release. She fought it back, battered it down. She couldn't lose control. She couldn't fall apart. She couldn't let Shaun know.

After their discussion the previous day, Arden had let herself believe that she and Shaun might have a future together. His acceptance of her past had helped her see through the fog of painful memories and focus on what mattered—the present.

This letter changed everything.

She heard the water shut off and knew Shaun would be downstairs in a few minutes. She grabbed the envelope and stuffed it into the pocket of her robe. Then she sat down because she wasn't sure her legs would continue to support her.

Somehow she made it through the day without revealing her inner turmoil. Shaun knew she was distracted, edgy, but he probably figured she was still upset that he'd opened the box of photos. It was easier to let him believe that than to admit the truth.

She was more than scared now. She was terrified. Whoever was sending the letters knew that she was staying with Shaun, which meant that he might be in danger. She couldn't bear to think that he might get caught in the crossfire.

And that was when she knew she had to leave.

She couldn't go back to Nikki and Colin's. No way would she put her cousin's family at risk, either. The only choice she had was to deal with this threat on her own.

She knew he wouldn't accept her decision easily, but she was determined to make her intentions clear. And if she had to hurt him to do so, well, she'd rather have him hate her than have him end up dead.

She came down to the kitchen with her briefcase in hand, the ominous letter tucked safely away inside.

"Where are you going?" Shaun asked.

"To the office," she said, as if it was perfectly normal for her to go to work early on a Saturday morning. A few weeks ago it had been. Shaun had changed everything for her.

"I didn't think you had any appointments today." He poured a mug of coffee, added a splash of milk, and handed it to her.

She hesitated for a second before accepting the offering. "I have things to do, and I need some space."

"Space?" he echoed, uncomprehending. "You can work in the den if you need space."

"I need some personal space. I'm starting to feel crowded here."

* * *

Personal space? Crowded? What was she talking about? Then suddenly he knew. She was trying to brush him off. What he didn't know was—why?

"What's going on, Arden?"

She shrugged, set her untouched mug of coffee aside. "I can't do this anymore, McIver."

"Do what?" He knew what she was trying to say, but he wasn't going to make it easy for her. If she was planning to walk, she'd better damned well explain why.

"This. Us."

"What's the problem?"

"It's getting too intense."

"Too intense?" he echoed, wondering at the emptiness in his heart. He'd told her that he loved her, and she was backing away because his feelings were too intense? "I never figured you'd be the type of person to walk away from something just because it wasn't easy."

"This isn't what I wanted. I told you that right from the beginning."

"Well, this is what you got."

"I'm going to look at an apartment this afternoon."

"Do you think I'm just going to let you move out? Walk away as if none of this matters?"

"It's not your decision to make," she said coolly.

"Like hell it isn't." He practically snarled the words at her, but he didn't care. He wasn't in a mood to handle this diplomatically.

"Save the macho routine for someone who might appreciate it."

"You're not going to brush me off that easily."

"I'm not going to fight with you about this," Arden said. "I'm just telling you the way it is."

"And I'm telling you that this isn't finished."

"It is for me."

That hurt, so much more than he was willing to admit. "Well then, we'll just say I'm not done with you."

"Back off, McIver."

"I don't think so." Anger and frustration propelled him toward her. She backed away, her eyes reflecting wariness...and desire. Yeah, she might say it was over. She might want it to *be* over. But it wasn't over between them. Not by a long shot.

She continued to match every step of his advance with one in retreat, until her back was against the wall. Then she lifted her chin, her eyes flashing. Before she could speak, before she could say anything else that he knew would only piss him off even more, he cupped the back of her head with his hand and captured her mouth with his.

He wasn't a man who acted on impulse. He was a thinker, a planner. But dammit if Arden didn't go straight to his blood. She struggled against the kiss. He'd expected no less. But he was relentless, demanding, and suddenly she wasn't fighting any longer. She was kissing him back.

Bodies crushed together, breaths mingled, tongues tangled. He wasn't proud of his own behavior, but he was satisfied with the results.

It was finished for her? Like hell, it was.

She pulled away from him, her breath coming in harsh and ragged gasps. "I don't appreciate being manhandled."

"You still want me as much as I want you."

"One kiss doesn't prove anything." But her icy reserve had melted, and she looked shaken, scared.

"Don't go, Arden. Please." He hated that he was begging, but he'd get down on his hands and knees if it would make her change her mind. He still didn't understand what had precipitated this sudden decision, but he knew he couldn't accept it. If she walked out of his life, she'd take his heart with her.

"I have to."

Was it his imagination, or did she actually sound regretful?

"Why?"

She shook her head. "It's over. It has to be."

Then she walked out, and he just stood there staring at the door she closed behind her.

Arden made it to the end of the block before she had to pull her car over to the side of the road. She was trembling inside and blinded by the tears that burned behind her eyes. Her fingers gripped the steering wheel. She took a deep breath, tried to convince herself that it had gone well. At least she'd managed to make it out of the house before she'd fallen to pieces.

But she'd hurt him. She'd broken his heart, and she'd done it deliberately and with premeditation. It didn't matter that she'd done what she needed to do, that she'd done it to protect him. The only thing that mattered was that she'd trampled all over his emotions.

It was no consolation that she felt equally raw and battered inside. She brushed the tears from her cheeks and pulled away from the curb.

After she'd handed the letter over to Lieutenant Creighton, she did go to the office. She had nowhere else to go. But she was restless, uneasy. She couldn't sit at her desk without remembering that someone had set a bomb in the middle of it. She couldn't stop the message in the latest letter from swimming in front of her eyes.

"THE TIME IS NEAR."

It wasn't the most blatant of the threats she'd received, but in light of what had already happened, she knew it was true. He would come for her. Soon. And the only way she could be sure of protecting Shaun would be to stay away from him.

She stayed at a hotel that night. She had nothing but the clothes on her back, but she didn't risk returning to Shaun's house to get any of her things. Not when she knew he'd be there. Her resolve wasn't that strong.

She didn't get much sleep. She tossed and turned on the lumpy mattress, missing the sound of Shaun's breathing close by, the warmth of his body next to her. It bothered her that she'd so quickly become accustomed to sharing his home, his bed. It bothered her more to know that her stalker was still out there and that he knew she'd been staying in Shaun's home. She couldn't bear it if something happened to him. She wouldn't let anything happen to him.

Did her determination to protect him mean that she loved him?

She didn't know. She didn't understand love; she didn't trust her emotions. She'd thought they could keep their relationship simple. Sex was, after all, a basic human drive. But somehow, over the past few weeks, the desires of her body had seemed to mesh with the needs of her heart. She still wanted him. She craved the fulfillment she'd only ever found in his arms. But it went so much deeper than the satisfaction of physical wants. When they came together, when their bodies joined as one, she felt a connection to him—a sense of completion she'd never before known.

Still, she didn't *want* to be in love with him. She couldn't afford to be irrational or irresponsible. She was the only person she had to rely on now.

Shaun tossed and turned in his empty bed. He should be used to sleeping alone, he'd done so for the better part of the past four years. But for the past four weeks, he'd gone to sleep every night with Arden tucked beside him. He'd woken with her in the morning. And he'd started to believe that it would be like that forever. Obviously, she had other ideas.

He didn't understand what had happened, although he'd come to know Arden well enough to know that she wasn't being completely honest with him. He'd called Logan as

oon as Arden left. He knew Arden wouldn't appreciate it
f she knew he'd sent his investigator to tail her, but until
he police caught the guy who was threatening her, he didn't
vant her to be alone.

Logan had checked in a couple of hours earlier from the
parking lot of the Coach House Hotel. He was camped out
n his car and promised that Arden wouldn't move from her
oom without him being aware of it. Shaun forced himself
o be satisfied with that, although what he really wanted was
o go down to the hotel himself and haul Arden back home.

He rolled onto his stomach, punched his pillow into
hape. Damn, the sheets even smelled like her. The subtle
nticing scent that was as much a part of her as those big
rown eyes. He threw his pillow against the wall.

His mood wasn't any better when he got up in the morn-
ng. Nor the morning after that. But at least it was Monday
hen, and he had an excuse to get out of the house that
eemed so empty without Arden.

He went through the motions of his day, the situation with
Arden in the forefront of his mind. Even his secretary no-
iced his preoccupation, and he practically bit her head off
or daring to comment on it.

By the time he left the office that night, his mood was
ven worse. He still hadn't decided how he was going to
leal with the situation, but he did know that he wasn't going
o accept that their relationship was over. Somehow, he
vould figure out what was going on, what had her so pan-
cked, and they'd deal with it. Together. He wasn't prepared
o consider any other option.

Shaun pulled into his driveway, not at all surprised to
ind that Arden's car wasn't there. No doubt she'd already
een here to pick up some of her things. He was surprised,
owever, when another vehicle pulled in behind him.

He recognized Lieutenant Creighton immediately.

"I'm looking for Arden Doherty," Creighton said. "Is
he still staying here?"

Shaun nodded. Just because she hadn't slept there the pas two nights didn't mean she wasn't still living there. Not i he had anything to say about it. "She had a late conferenc today. I'm not sure when she'll be back."

He didn't have the slightest idea where Arden was, bu he guessed the lieutenant would have tried her office befor coming here. And he figured it would work to his advantag if Creighton thought he was fully apprised of the situation

"I'll catch up with her some other time, then."

"Can I tell her why you stopped by?" Shaun prompted "Do you have any new information for her?"

"Not really," Creighton admitted. "I just wanted to le her know that we've already started canvassing the neigh borhood to see if anyone might have seen an unfamiliar fac or vehicle around here Saturday morning."

Here. That meant that Arden had received another letter delivered to *his* house, and she'd never bothered to tell hin about it. "We appreciate your quick response on this,' Shaun said.

Creighton nodded and started toward his car. He hesi tated, then turned back to Shaun. "Maybe you could te me where you were Saturday morning, Mr. McIver."

"What time?"

"Sometime before 8:30 a.m., when Ms. Doherty founc the letter tucked inside the newspaper."

He tried to think, but he couldn't seem to get his minc around the fact that Arden had received another letter. A his house. And that she hadn't told him about it. "Do you really think I could be sending her these letters?"

Creighton shrugged. "I'm just exploring all possibilities And since you live here, it would be easy enough to plan a letter in your own newspaper."

"I didn't," Shaun said.

"Then you won't mind telling me where you were."

"I was with Ms. Doherty, all night. I'm sure she car verify my whereabouts."

"I'm sure you understand that the question had to be asked. I appreciate your cooperation."

"The only reason you're getting it is that I'm as anxious s you are to find whoever is sending these letters to Arden. want her to feel safe."

Creighton nodded again. "I'll be in touch."

Arden had to go back to Shaun's house. She'd stopped y earlier in the day, when she was sure he'd be at the ffice, to pick up a few things she needed. But she'd for-otten a file of case law she'd put together, and she needed for an upcoming mediation. She'd tried to think of a way round it, but there was none. She needed the file.

By the time she pulled into his driveway, her stomach as tied in knots so tight Houdini wouldn't have managed o undo them. She wasn't up to going another round with haun about their relationship. She'd never wanted to hurt im, and she knew that she had. She also knew that she'd o it again if she had to. She'd do whatever was necessary o protect him.

He was in the living room, his feet propped up on the offee table, watching the news on television. She expected im to ask why she was there. He didn't.

"You just missed Lieutenant Creighton," he said instead.

Arden stiffened. "Did he need to see me?"

"He said he'd catch up with you at your office tomorrow. omething about the letter you got Saturday."

Arden just nodded.

"You didn't tell me you got another letter."

"It didn't say anything new."

"No, but it's the first one that was delivered here, wasn't ?"

She hesitated briefly. "Yes."

"Is that why you decided to move out?"

"I decided to move out because I've imposed on you long nough. I needed to find a place of my own again."

"I didn't think you minded staying here."

"It was fun for a while," she said flippantly. "But li
I said, it's time to move on."

"You got that letter, and you were scared that he mig
come after you here."

"I wouldn't want to be responsible for your house bur
ing down."

"Is that all it was?"

"Isn't that enough?"

"I want you to be honest with me, Arden. I want to kno
why you suddenly decided, the same day you got a lett
from your wacko pen pal, that you needed to move out, th
our relationship was over."

"I told you I wasn't good with relationships. It was on
a matter of time before things fell apart."

"But things didn't fall apart."

"Obviously we have different opinions."

"Do we?"

"Look, I have a lot of work to do tonight, so if you don
mind—"

"I do mind," he cut in. "I want some answers."

"I've given you all the answers I'm going to."

She started toward the stairs to retrieve the file sh
needed.

"I love you, Arden."

His words halted her in her tracks. A long, tense momer
passed before she turned to face him again. "I'll get the las
of my things out of here so I won't have to bother yo
again."

"You're running scared."

"So what if I am? There's some psycho sending m
threatening letters—to my office, my home, and now here
The cops are pretty sure he's responsible for torching m
apartment and placing a bomb on my desk, maybe eve
shooting out my windows, but they don't have a single clu

as to who it might be, and he's still coming after me. I think I'm entitled to feel scared.''

"You should be afraid of him," Shaun said calmly. "But you're more afraid of what's happening between us. Of the feelings you have for me."

"You're delusional."

"Am I?"

"Yes."

"Then why are you so determined to leave? Why now?"

"I told you—this isn't working out, and I thought it would be easier for both of us if I found somewhere else to stay."

He shrugged. "I have three spare bedrooms."

"Don't you think it would be a little awkward?"

"Not at all."

She knew his nonchalance was intended to annoy her, to make her lose her cool. She refused to give him the satisfaction. "Well, I do. I can't stay here anymore."

"You're safe here, Arden. I have a security system. I'll hire a twenty-four-hour guard if it will make you feel better. In any event, you're safer here than anywhere else."

"Goodbye, Shaun."

He made no move to stop her as she went upstairs to pack. But a few minutes later he came into the bedroom with a suitcase of his own and began stuffing his clothes into it.

She watched him for a moment, frowning.

"What are you doing?" she demanded at last.

"Packing."

"Why?"

"Because I'm going with you."

Chapter 17

"Where?" Arden sounded genuinely baffled.

"Wherever you're going," Shaun told her.

"No."

"Creighton thinks whoever has been writing the letters i getting more desperate."

"That's why I have to go."

His eyes narrowed. "You're afraid he'll come here, aren' you?"

"I need to deal with this on my own."

"Dammit, Arden. Why are you so determined to shut m out? Don't you know that whatever happens affects me too?"

"That's the point. I don't *want* this to affect you."

"It does. And it will, whether you're living here or no At least if you're here, you're not alone."

"Please let me go, Shaun."

"I can't. I need you, Arden."

"That's not fair."

"It's true." And he knew it carried more weight than hi

ove for her. That just plain terrified her. He hated that she
didn't trust his feelings, wouldn't trust her own. But he did
love her, and the love he felt gave him patience he ordinarily
wouldn't have. He'd give her time, as much time as she
needed. But he wouldn't give her up.

So he kissed her. It was supposed to be a simple kiss, a
silent pledge of his feelings. But both of their emotions were
running high, and their passions quickly escalated out of
control.

They made love wildly, desperately. His hands streaked
over her body, relentless, demanding. She responded to his
demands, countered with her own. They rolled across the
bed, on top of the covers, a tangle of limbs and needs. When
he plunged into the wet heat between her thighs, she
screamed out with her release. He tried to hold back, to
catch his breath, but she wrapped her legs around him and
pulled him deeper inside.

Lust took over, pushed everything else aside. He drove
into her, again and again, the slap of damp flesh against
damp flesh interspersed with their primitive grunts and
moans. It was unlike anything he'd ever experienced before.
Everything he felt was stronger, sharper, deeper, and the
intensity of his orgasm shook him to the very core.

Finally he collapsed on top of her, their bodies, slick with
sweat, still joined together. He wasn't sure whether he
should thank her or apologize, but he knew they'd both
needed the release they'd shared. And he needed to tell her
what was in his heart.

"I love you, Arden."

He felt her go completely still beneath him, her eyes
wide. It wasn't the first time he'd said the words to her, but
it was the first time he'd ever spoken them when their bodies
were joined together, warm and sated from lovemaking.
When she couldn't turn away.

"Shaun, please, you promised—"

He knew that if she hadn't been pinned beneath the

weight of his body on the bed she would have bolted. Sh
wanted to. He sensed that in her, fought the annoyance he
response elicited.

"I promised not to push you," he reminded her. "An
I'm not. I'm not asking for anything. But I need you t
know how I feel about you. I want you to get used to hear
ing it."

"I don't think I ever will," she admitted. "I don't un
derstand why you think you feel this way."

"Because you're the most incredible woman I've eve
known. You challenge me. You inspire me. You make m
a better person. And I want to spend the rest of my lif
loving you."

Later, in the warm comfort of Shaun's arms, she slep
deeply, contentedly. That simple fact proved to her wha
she'd been fighting for so long: she needed him. She wasn'
sure how or when it had happened, but he'd become a
integral part of her life, and she was no longer willing t
walk away from what they shared together. Not that h
would let her. And she was torn between relief and frustra
tion that he was so determined to stand by her.

She was also increasingly apprehensive. Two days ha
passed since she'd received the letter that promised the tim
was near. Soon this nightmare would be over.

She didn't expect it to be as soon as the next day.

It was just after five o'clock when he came in to he
office. Rebecca had gone for the day and Marcy was out a
a settlement conference. Arden was alone.

"Where is she?" his harsh gravelly voice demanded.

Arden's heart leaped into her throat, choking her. Sh
hadn't wanted to believe that it could be him. Not now. No
after so much time had passed.

She looked up from the file on her desk and cringed a
her eyes met his. His were glassy and bloodshot, his fac
haggard from too much drink over too many years, his hai

more gray than brown now. It had been twenty years since she'd seen Gavin Elliott, her stepfather, and the years had not been kind. But there was no doubt that it was him.

She clenched her hands into fists in her lap, tried to curb the rising panic. She couldn't help feeling like the frightened eight-year-old girl who wasn't sure what she'd done to displease him, only knowing that she'd get walloped for it. The terror rose inside her, because she knew him, and she knew what he was capable of.

Reminding herself that she was an adult and that he no longer had the power to hurt her, she straightened her shoulders and faced him. "If you're referring to my mother, I have no idea where she is. But since you're asking the question, I'll assume she finally walked out on you, and I can't tell you how happy that makes me."

He crossed over to the desk, not quite steady on his feet. But the backhanded slap was sharp enough to send her head reeling back, bring tears to her eyes. She forced her gaze to meet his evenly, but she couldn't disguise the quaver in her voice when she spoke again. "Get out of my office."

"I'm not going anywhere until you tell me where your mother is."

"I don't know where she is," Arden told him. "But even if I did, I wouldn't tell you."

"Don't tell me you don't know, you lying slut. You've been sending her stuff in the mail, women's lib propaganda."

Arden shook her head. Years ago she'd sent information to her mother, trying to make her understand that there were places she could go, people who would help. Her mother had told her not to interfere, and eventually Arden had given up. She didn't want to know what had finally compelled her mother to leave the man she'd always defended so staunchly.

"Get out of my office *now*," she said, rising to her feet, praying that her knees would support her weight. "Or I'll call the police."

Gavin grabbed the phone on top of the desk with bot
hands and heaved it across the room. The trickle of pani
that had surfaced when she'd seen him standing in the doo
way of her office gave way to full-fledged terror.

"I have a right to know where she is," he snarled. "She'
my *wife*."

"You have no right to—"

The words lodged in her throat as he wrapped his finge
in her hair, pulling her head back so hard and fast she sa
stars behind her eyes. This wasn't supposed to be happer
ing. Everything she'd read about abusive parents indicate
that they gave up when the kids fought back. But he wa
here, and she was scared.

"If I can't have her, maybe I'll settle for you." His lip
curled into something that might have been a smile.

Her stomach churned. His breath was hot and reeked o
whiskey.

"You've grown up real nice, Arden. You look just lik
your mother did when we first got married." One hand wa
still fisted in her hair, but he closed the other one over he
breast, squeezed.

Nausea rose in her throat. Desperation fueled her re
sponse. She brought her knee up hard and caught him be
tween the legs. Primitive, but effective. He released hi
grasp to clutch at himself as he fell to his knees. Arden ra
through the door and locked herself in Marcy's office. Sh
grabbed the phone, her hand trembling, her heart poundin

Her first instinct was to call Shaun. She desperatel
wanted to feel his arms around her, to have him tell her tha
everything was going to be okay. But the pounding o
Marcy's office door reminded her that everything wasn'
okay, and she knew there was nothing Shaun could do. Sh
wouldn't let all the old doubts and insecurities control he
actions. She had to be strong.

She dialed the police station.

* * *

Arden sat in a hard plastic chair, a cup of now-cold coffee clutched in her hands, calmly reciting the events for Lieutenant Creighton. The earlier debilitating terror had subsided, or had at least been shoved aside, as she went through the motions of doing what needed to be done. She wouldn't fall apart. She wouldn't be intimidated. She wouldn't be a victim anymore.

She'd thought her past was behind her. But if tonight had proven anything, it was that she wouldn't ever forget what had happened. The best she could hope for was to learn to live with it, and she knew that admitting what had happened so many years ago was the first step toward doing so.

Creighton believed that Gavin Elliott was the man who'd been tormenting her for the past few months. According to the information he'd obtained from Arden's stepfather, his wife had left him several months earlier, just a few weeks before Arden received the first letter.

She couldn't deny that the timing was suspicious, but the whole plan—the letters, the shooting, the fire, the bomb—had been too careful, too deliberate, to have been orchestrated by Gavin. Although he was a college professor, his appearance at her office tonight had seemed spontaneous, a desperate attack by a desperate man. She'd never got the impression that her pen pal was desperate. He seemed more calculating. More dangerous.

But there was also evidence that Simon Granger had spent time in Arizona, and while there was no hard evidence linking him to Gavin Elliott, it was another coincidence she couldn't ignore.

Still, she would have felt a lot better if Gavin would just confess. So far he hadn't done so. In fact, he continued to deny any knowledge of the threats. Of course, he'd also denied ever having hurt her in the past, so she knew his claims of innocence didn't count for much.

Arden hoped that Creighton was right. She wanted to p
this all behind her. She didn't want to be afraid anymore

"Ms. Doherty?"

She glanced up. "Sorry."

"Are you okay? Do you want to go to the hospital?"

"No." She shook her head firmly, then winced as t
motion sent pain radiating through her skull. "I'm fine.
just want to go home."

Creighton nodded. "I'll have a uniform take you as so
as we get your statement signed."

She started to protest, to say that her car was still in t
parking lot behind her office. But common sense prevaile
As much as she wanted to pretend everything was okay, s
was still too shaky to drive. So she nodded slowly, mindf
of the pounding in her head. "Thank you."

But when he came back, it wasn't a uniformed offic
who was with him.

It was Shaun.

He stood in the doorway, watching her. She looked
small and alone, huddled under a threadbare blanket, h
eyes focused straight ahead. Her face was alarmingly pa
except for the dark red welt across one cheek. Ang
churned furiously inside him. Anger at the man who'd do
this to her. Anger at himself for letting it happen. For n
asking Joel Logan to continue to tail Arden. He should ha
been there for her. He should have protected her.

As if sensing his presence, Arden glanced over. "Wh
are you doing here?"

Shaun ignored her question to ask his own. "Why did
you call me?"

She shrugged, then winced.

He crossed the room in two quick strides and hunker
down in front of her. "Why didn't you call me?" he ask
again.

"It was my problem," she said. "And I dealt with it."

"It doesn't work that way, Arden. Not anymore."

"Just because I'm sleeping with you doesn't give you the ght to know every little detail of my life."

He ignored the sharp pain her words caused. He knew 1e was lashing out because she was hurting inside. So he ok a deep breath and tried another tack. "Have you had 1at looked at?" He indicated her swollen cheek.

"No. It's fine."

It wasn't fine. Her cheek was already starting to discolor, ut he wasn't going to debate with her about it.

"Come on." He pried the untouched cup of coffee loose om her fingers and set it aside on the desk. "Let's get you ome and put some ice on that."

He expected her to argue some more, knew it was a sign f how upset she was that she didn't do so. He helped her her feet, and the blanket slid off her shoulder. Her blouse as torn, gaping open at the front. As much as he appre-iated Creighton calling him, he wished the lieutenant would ave gone a step further and given him five minutes alone ith the man who'd done this to Arden. It was little con-olation to know that her stalker was behind bars. Not when .rden was still trembling visibly.

He picked up the blanket to cover her again.

"I need Ms. Doherty to sign her statement," Creighton aid.

"Tomorrow." Shaun's tone brooked no argument. Right now I'm taking her home."

So Shaun took her home, and he put ice on her swollen heek. He heard her quick indrawn breath as the cold towel ontacted her flesh, but she didn't pull away.

"I don't need you to take care of me," she told him.

"I know. But I want to take care of you." He kissed her oftly. "Let me take care of you." He brushed his lips over er cheek. "Please."

He felt her body yield slightly, heard her soft sigh.

"Just for tonight," he said.

"I don't want to need you," she told him.

"Do you?"

She closed her eyes, her response little more than a wh per. "Yes."

That single word filled him with unspeakable pleasure. was hardly a declaration of undying love, but he knew was a big step for Arden. And it gave him confidence th they might finally be able to move forward together.

Chapter 18

For the first time in her life, Arden called in sick the next day. She didn't have any court scheduled, and Marcy assured her that she could handle the afternoon office appointments. Still, Arden was uneasy about neglecting her professional responsibilities to deal with a personal crisis.

When Shaun suggested that he stay home with her, she put her foot down. She wasn't going to fall apart, and if he respected her needs, he'd leave her alone for a while. So he'd gone to his office, although she knew he'd done so reluctantly.

She did need some time alone, to think about everything that had happened and to reevaluate. There had been several occasions in their short relationship when Arden had thought Shaun would walk away, more than a few when she'd expected him to. But he'd stood by her. Not always quietly, not without question, but he'd always been there for her. She knew he always would be.

He'd changed her life, just by being a part of it. By loving

her. She wasn't sure what kind of miracle had allowed th
to happen, but she was grateful. And still a little bit afrai

Every time she'd let herself believe someone loved he
they'd hurt her. Her father had loved her, then he'd di
and left her. Her mother had claimed to love her, but she
signed over custody without so much as a backward glan
Every time Gavin had touched her, he'd told her how mu
he loved her. And Brad had said the same words befo
he'd bolted from her life.

But she knew that Shaun was different, and even as sl
decided that maybe she could open up her heart and tru
him to love her, she knew that she already had. And th
she loved him, too. And she resolved that she would final
tell him so. Tonight.

Her lips curved as she heard the slam of a car door. (
maybe she'd tell him sooner.

She pulled back the curtains, expecting to see Shaun's c
in the driveway. Instead there was a glossy black BM
parked there, and Warren Blake was striding up the wa
toward the front door.

She fought back the disappointment as she went to op
the door. "Warren, hi."

He smiled, but there was something in his eyes that ma
her uneasy. Or maybe she was just a little paranoid aft
everything that had happened over the past several week
But that was behind her now, and Gavin was behind bar

"Hello, Arden. Can I come in for a minute?"

She hesitated only a fraction of a second, certain th
Shaun wouldn't approve of her entertaining the man in h
home, but she couldn't be rude to a professional acquai
tance. She stepped away from the door. "I just made a p
of coffee," she said. "Would you like some?"

"No, thanks."

"Is this a social call?"

He shrugged. "I guess you could say that. I understa

ou had a little trouble at your office yesterday. Are you
kay?''

She touched a hand to the bruise on the side of her face.
he swelling had gone down considerably, but she knew it
dn't look pretty. ''I'm fine, thanks.''

''I wanted to let you know that we found the witness who
w Granger outside your office the day the bomb was
und.''

''Oh.'' Her stepfather's arrest had put everything else out
her mind. But Granger had still committed a crime, and
should be held responsible for what he'd done even if
e man who'd hired him was already behind bars. ''I guess
ou'll be bringing Granger back in for questioning, then.''

''No,'' Warren said shortly. ''The witness is dead.''

''Oh.''

''He was murdered.''

Arden swallowed, closed her eyes. ''Please tell me it had
othing to do with what he saw.'' She couldn't bear to think
at someone had been killed for trying to help her. So many
nocent people had lost so much already.

''The police are working on the assumption that your pen
al wanted to ensure there were no loose ends connected
ck to him.''

''But I don't believe—I can't imagine—Gavin wouldn't
ll someone in cold blood.'' He'd done a lot of horrible
ings, but she couldn't believe he was capable of murder.

''I think anyone's capable of almost anything, given the
ght set of circumstances,'' Warren said.

She shook her head. She still couldn't believe it.

''Take you, for example,'' he continued. ''No one who
ows you would ever think you were suicidal.''

Arden frowned. ''What?''

''And yet you've been so distracted lately. Depressed. It's
ot inconceivable that the events of the past few months
ould have taken their toll, driven you to take your own
fe.''

Arden backed away from him. "I'm not suicidal."

"Of course you are. And you're going to write the n〈
that proves it."

Shaun hadn't finished his first cup of tea when Cla〈
buzzed through to him. He frowned. He'd canceled all 〈
his appointments for the day, knowing he'd be too bu〈
thinking and worrying about Arden to concentrate on le〈
strategy. He hadn't wanted to leave her alone, and 〈
wouldn't have done so if she hadn't insisted.

Still, he wasn't comfortable being away from her. She〈
been through so much lately. Maybe she didn't need him 〈
take care of her, but he needed to take care of her. 〈
needed to be with her. He *wanted* to be with her. And 〈
soon as he spoke to Claire, he would gather up some wo〈
and head home.

"Joel Logan's here," Claire told him.

"Send him in." Shaun didn't expect that the investiga〈
would have any information for him, but he'd thank him 〈
his time and pay him for the work he'd done.

Logan didn't waste any time. He tossed a folder on 〈
Shaun's desk. "You were right about Blake."

Shaun felt the bottom drop out of his stomach. "Right
how?"

"I found a connection between him and Simon Granger〈

"What kind of connection?" Shaun demanded.

"Blake used to do some criminal defense work when 〈
was in California. Turns out he was counsel of record 〈
Granger on his last charge. Arson."

"Christ." Shaun grabbed his car keys and pushed aw〈
from the desk. He had to get home to Arden. Now.

"There's more," Logan said.

"That's all I need to know right now," Shaun said.

It was more than enough to convince him that Arden w〈
in danger.

* * *

"I don't understand what's going on here," Arden said. But she knew enough to know that her nightmare wasn't over.

"And I always thought you were such a bright woman." He shook his head and handed her a folded sheet of paper. "Maybe this will clarify a few things."

Her blood was roaring in her ears, her limbs were weak, but somehow she managed to reach out and take it from him. She unfolded it, the bold red letters screaming at her from the stark whiteness of the page.

"NOW."

"It was you."

He smiled proudly. "Yes, it was me."

She swallowed the bile that had risen into her throat, struggled to remain calm, to think. "Why?"

"You really don't know?"

She shook her head, winced at the pain.

"Does the name Angela Blake ring a bell?"

"No."

"She was my wife."

"I thought—I mean, I'd heard you were divorced."

"Widowed," he corrected her. "But Angela had contacted a lawyer about a divorce, after attending a seminar you gave in Philadelphia. She'd come back for a visit, for her mother's birthday, and they went to a women's symposium."

"You think it's my fault that she left you?"

"It is," Blake said. "You filled her head with all kinds of nonsense."

"I don't even remember talking to her," Arden said, almost desperately.

"You did. I found one of your business cards in her purse. You not only talked to her, you turned her against me."

He was insane, she realized. Certifiable. But that was little consolation if he intended to kill her—it was hard to reason with a crazy person.

He pulled a legal pad and a pen out of his briefcase, pushed them across the table to her. "Write."

"I'm not going to write a suicide note," she said. "I'm not going to help you kill me."

He shrugged. "A note makes it easier, but it's not necessary."

She picked up the pen.

If he was determined to kill her, she was determined that he wouldn't get away with it. She tilted the pad of paper and began writing with the backhand slant she'd used as a child. Anyone who knew her would know it wasn't her usual handwriting.

The phone rang, and Arden instinctively started to rise from her chair to answer it. Warren put a restraining hand on her shoulder.

"Leave it," he instructed.

"It might be Shaun," she protested, half hoping and half fearing that it was. Surely he'd be suspicious if she didn't answer the phone.

"I can't risk you tipping him off," Warren said mildly.

"But he'll wonder why I'm not answering."

"More likely he'll assume you're in the bath, soaking away your troubles."

He was right, Arden realized dejectedly.

"Finish your note," Warren instructed.

She scribbled her name at the bottom, praying silently but fervently. She didn't want to die. She'd finally reached a point in her life when she was ready to move forward with the man she loved, and she didn't want to die before she ever had a chance to tell Shaun how she felt.

"Now we're going to go out to the garage," Warren said. "And you're going to get into your car."

"I'm not going anywhere with you."

"No, you're not going anywhere," he agreed pleasantly.

"In a few hours, when your lover comes home, he'll find you dead. Asphyxiated. It's the preferred method of suicide by women."

"Have you researched this?"

"Meticulously," he agreed. "Every tiny detail of this plan has been mapped out with the utmost care and attention."

"Do you really think you'll get away with this?"

"Yes, I will." He grabbed her by the arm, his fingers biting into her flesh, and dragged her toward the back door. "There will be an investigation, of course, and the conclusion will be suicide."

"No one who knows me would believe I'm suicidal."

"No one ever thinks someone they love would kill themselves. But then they'll look at the evidence—your stepfather's reappearance in your life—a painful reminder of the horrific childhood you endured. Your lingering guilt over the Hemingway incident. Your recent breakup with the boyfriend—"

"Shaun and I didn't break up," Arden interrupted.

"You've signed a lease on a new apartment."

She had signed a lease, and although she intended to cancel it, she hadn't yet done so. But how could Warren know? How had he learned the intimate details of her life? "You think you have it all figured out."

"I've been thinking about this for four long years," Warren admitted. "When I saw the posting for an ADA position in Fairweather, it was almost too easy. Since I got here, I've thought about several different ways to achieve the end result. I didn't want to move this soon, it seemed like so much more fun to string you along. But everything seems to have fallen into place right now. Especially considering your little injury—" He gestured to the bruise on the side of her head. "I expect I'll have to knock you unconscious, but no one will know that the injury wasn't sustained during yesterday's altercation with your daddy.

"If, for some reason, homicide is suspected, you know where they'll look." He smiled smugly. "After all, most of the women who are murdered in this country every year are killed by their partners or former partners."

"Killing me isn't going to bring your wife back," Arden told him, digging her heels into the ground outside the garage.

"Nothing will do that," he agreed. "This isn't about justice—it's about vengeance."

A sudden, sickening thought occurred to her. "Did you kill that man—the witness?"

"I had him killed," Warren said, as if that somehow lessened his responsibility for the death. "I don't like getting my hands dirty unnecessarily."

"But you have no qualms about killing me?"

"None at all," he agreed.

Then he smashed her head against the stone wall of the garage, and she slumped into unconsciousness.

Shaun tried calling Arden as he drove toward home, to warn her about Blake, but there was no response. Next he dialed the district attorney's office, and was advised that Blake was out of the office. Shaun pressed the accelerator to the floor.

He tried to contact Creighton at the police station, but had been forced to leave a frantic message on the lieutenant's voice mail. He knew he was jumping to conclusions. It was possible he'd get home and Arden would accuse him of overreacting…again. An old connection between Blake and Granger was hardly reason to suspect the ADA was capable of murder. But Shaun couldn't shake the feeling that his fears were warranted.

He recognized the BMW parked in his driveway as Blake's. The man was either overly confident or overly stupid to think he could just park in the driveway like an invited guest.

Shaun threw open the front door and called out for her. "Arden!"

There was no response.

He found the note on the kitchen table, frowned as he scanned the contents. His heart almost stopped.

A suicide note?

Then he realized it wasn't Arden's handwriting. It was her name on the bottom, but it wasn't her writing. He breathed a sigh of relief. She must have written it under duress, but she was obviously still thinking.

Good girl, he thought with more than a touch of pride. He knew she wouldn't let Blake take her down without a struggle.

But where was she?

Looking through the kitchen window, he could see that the side door of the garage was open and a light was on inside.

He didn't stop to think but ran through the back door to the garage. He almost plowed right into Blake, who was coming out the door as he was going in.

"Where is she, Blake?" His tone was lethal, his hands already clenched into fists. He was prepared, even eager, to fight. He would beat the man to a bloody pulp if he had to. He didn't think about the fierce protectiveness of his instincts. It was human nature to protect what belonged to you, and, whether or not Arden was ready to admit it, she belonged to him and he to her. He wasn't going to let Blake take their future away from them.

"You're too late," Blake said, his eyes cool, his lips curving in a self-satisfied smile.

"No!" He couldn't believe it, he wouldn't believe that he was too late. If Blake had already killed her, he wouldn't still be hanging around his garage. And Shaun would know, deep in his heart, that Arden was gone.

She was alive. She had to be.

"Don't worry," Blake said. "I'll be more than happy to

see that you join her.'' He took a step back and picked up an ax from the workbench. He waved it menacingly, the smug smile still on his face.

"You won't use that on me," Shaun said. "You're a bully and a coward. A coward who likes to beat women."

Blake's eyes narrowed, glittered dangerously, and Shaun was less confident that the man wouldn't use the weapon he'd grabbed hold of. If Blake was far enough gone to want to kill Arden, there was no telling what he would do.

"You don't know anything." Blake spat the words at him.

"I know you used to knock your wife around," Shaun said. "And that's why she left you."

"She loved me," Blake said, his voice trembling with suppressed fury.

"She left you because she was pregnant and she didn't want her child to grow up with you for a father."

Blake howled with outrage and swung wildly with the ax. Shaun ducked, and the lethal blade sank into the doorjamb less than a foot from his head. Before Blake could wrench the weapon free, Shaun pivoted and plowed his fist into his gut. As Blake doubled over, Shaun came up with his other fist and connected with his nose. He heard the crunch of bone, felt the spurt of blood.

Blake swore viciously, but he didn't hesitate to return the attack.

Arden blinked several times, tried to focus. Her head was pounding, her eyes were burning and her stomach was churning with nausea.

It was dark and something was digging into her ribs.

She eased back into a sitting position, winced as the pain in her head escalated, pressed a hand to her heaving stomach. She blinked again.

She was in her car.

In the garage.

And the motor was running.

Warren must have dumped her behind the steering wheel and put the key in the ignition.

She found the door handle and released the catch. She had to get out of the garage. She fell out of the car, smashed her knee against the concrete floor. The pain didn't register. She was aware of nothing but the throbbing agony in her head. Until she heard his voice.

Shaun.

Her heart fluttered with hope. He was home. He'd come for her.

She felt her way along the edge of the car, realized that his voice wasn't the only one she heard. Warren was still there. She could hear grunts and curses and the sound of fists connecting with flesh. Her eyes finally focused on the shadowy figures engaged in battle. Shaun's head snapped back as Warren landed a particularly harsh blow, and the force of the punch threw him off balance. Warren took advantage of the opportunity to lunge for the ax embedded in the doorjamb.

Arden's heart flipped over in her chest when she realized that Warren intended to kill Shaun, too. Shaun had the advantage of height, but Warren was stockier, and desperate. And Arden knew if she didn't do something soon, it would be too late.

Her fingers tightened around the smooth wooden handle of a garden shovel. It wasn't much of a weapon, but it was the best she could do.

Warren freed the ax.

Arden raised the shovel over her head and brought it down hard. Warren crumpled at her feet.

Lieutenant Creighton was on the scene almost immediately, with reinforcements arriving a few minutes later. It was at least an hour after that before Shaun and Arden were alone again.

Shaun's knuckles were raw and swollen, his lip bleeding. Arden wanted to throw herself into his arms, but she knew he was stiff and sore from his altercation with Warren.

"Are you okay?" she asked gently, moving to the sofa to sit beside him.

He tried to smile, grimaced when the action pulled open the cut on his lip again. She grabbed a tissue and dabbed at the drop of blood.

"I'm okay," he told her. "How about you?"

"I've had better days," she admitted, and folded her hands in her lap. "I'm sorry you got dragged into the middle of this."

"I'm not."

"Your garage is a crime scene because of me."

He shrugged. "I don't use it much, anyway."

She managed a small smile. "You're awfully cavalier about all of this."

"The only thing that matters to me is you, Arden. I'm just glad that this nightmare is finally over."

"It is, isn't it?"

"Yeah, it is." He lifted an arm to curve around her shoulders, pressed his lips gently against her temple. "Finally."

"I never would have suspected Warren." She shook her head.

"I can't say I ever liked the guy, but I didn't really think he was capable of something like this, either."

"He said he loved her. And that I took that away from him. That's why he did this."

"That isn't love, it's obsession," Shaun told her.

She nodded carefully so as not to amplify the throbbing in her head. She understood the difference now, and she knew that love was a gift, not a curse. Something to be embraced rather than feared. Something to share.

"I was afraid…I really thought I was going to die and…" her words faltered as she stifled a yawn. "There's something I need to tell you."

"You should get some rest," he said. "We can talk later."

"I don't want to wait. I was so afraid I wouldn't ever get chance…to tell you."

"Tell me what?"

Her heart was jumping crazily in her chest, but she took deep breath and braced herself to say the words she'd ever spoken to anyone before. She looked into his eyes, wanting to see his reaction when he first heard them, wanting him to see the truth of them in her own. "That I love you."

His eyes darkened perceptibly. "I love you, too, Arden."

She smiled. "I know."

Then he covered her lips in a kiss that was breathtakingly tender, agonizingly sweet, overflowing with love.

"It took me a long time to get to this point in my life, and I'm not sure that I'd be here now if it wasn't for you. I've dealt with the past and I'm ready to move on. With you."

"Does that mean you're going to cancel your lease on the new apartment?"

"That depends."

She could tell her equivocal response had surprised him. He frowned. "On what?"

"Whether or not you're willing to marry me."

He snapped his jaw shut, swallowed. "You want to get married?"

"Only to you."

"Really?" The beginnings of a smile curved his lips.

She shrugged. "I figured if I can handle this love thing, maybe the rest won't be so hard."

His tentative smile widened into a grin. "The rest? Marriage, kids, the whole deal?"

"The whole deal," she agreed. "You once told me that nothing that happened before matters, and you were right. My past has made me who I am, but it doesn't control me.

I'm ready to move on. And from this moment, I want to
with you.''

   "From this moment,'' he promised, and touched his li
to hers again. ''Forever.''

                    *   *   *   *   *

Anything. Anywhere. Anytime.

The crew of this C-17 squadron will leave you breathless!

WINGMEN WARRIORS

Catherine Mann's

edge-of-your-seat series continues in June with

PRIVATE MANEUVERS

First Lieutenant Darcy Renshaw flies headfirst into a dangerous undercover mission with handsome CIA agent Max Keegan, and the waters of Guam soon engulf them in a world of secrets, lies and undeniable attraction.

Don't miss this compelling installment available in June from

Silhouette®

INTIMATE MOMENTS™

Available at your favorite retail outlet.

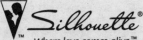

Silhouette®
Where love comes alive™

Silhouette®

COMING NEXT MONTH

INTIMATE MOMENTS®

SIMCNM05